DREAMSPINNER

Published by Merita King
Eastleigh
United Kingdom

This book is a work of fiction. Any resemblance between these fictional characters and actual persons, either living or dead, is purely coincidental.

ISBN 978-0-9928491-3-9

Cover design by Merita King copyright 2015

OTHER WORKS BY MERITA KING

The Lilean Chronicles: Book One ~ Redemption
The Lilean Chronicles: Book Two ~ The Sleeping
The Lilean Chronicles: Book Three ~ Changing Faces
The Lilean Chronicles: Book Four ~ Avalanche Effect
Floxham Island ~ Sinclair V-Log AZ267/M
Bygora Vandos ~ Sinclair V-Log LB734/A
The Trials of Nahda ~ Sinclair V-Log PA884/R
Fetish ~ Sinclair V-Log BY915/M
Acts of Life
A.W.O.L
Delectus Morbidium
Psychomanteum

ABOUT THE AUTHOR

Merita King describes herself as an eccentric, somewhat outspoken, autistic visionary. She lives in southern England with her two cats and a vivid imagination.

1

Consciousness drifted towards him and with it, the awareness of the pain in his back. Once acknowledged, it drove him the rest of the way to wakefulness and as the dark void receded, he realised that it was his only awareness. There was no immediate knowing of himself and his place in the universe, no flood of memories to bring smiles, tears, anguish, or joy. There was just the knowledge that he was awake and in pain, nothing more. In those first moments before his eyes opened, his mind was empty, an aching void of silence both tranquil and terrifying. As his eyes flickered open, thoughts flooded inside and his soul rang with questions, all but one of which he had no answers for.

"Where am I?" Hauling himself up into a sitting position, he looked around at his immediate surroundings, which loomed large from his vantage point on the floor. Not recognising where he was, this first question went unanswered. How he got there was the next mystery for which there was no explanation. Trying to think back in time, he searched for answers to these questions but with growing dismay, found himself strangely detached from the few memories and patchy grains of knowledge he did find. For one terrifying moment, his own name remained a mystery, but then it came and his anguished mind grabbed it as a child might grab at a favourite toy when frightened. "Lindo. I'm Tearan Lindo of Inter-Galactic Elite Command, Unit 389C4. That's who I am. So where the fuck am I and why am I here?"

He closed his eyes again momentarily, as much to calm his rising panic as with relief at remembering who he was. As he dragged himself to his feet, he frowned at the way his body seemed to drag, the way it took just a second too long to obey the commands of his troubled mind. "Have I been drugged or something?" he asked as he brushed himself off, then his eyes caught the name patch above the breast pocket of his grey and black jacket. "Lindo 389C4," embroidered in pale grey thread met his gaze. "Well at least I got that right," he muttered as he examined his pockets and found them all empty except for a single small flashlight. His sidearm was also missing and he cursed aloud, before turning his attention back to his immediate surroundings.

A long corridor ran away from him at forty-five degrees to his left, while another identical one ran off at forty-five degrees to his right. A flutter of menace tickled his empty mind as he gazed down each one. The emptiness spooked him, the innate knowledge of his aloneness felt sinister and he shuddered. He had woken up on the floor at the intersection of the two, the wall curving around behind him revealing two doors. The walls and floor felt metallic to his touch and his boot steps echoed as he approached them.

'Section 8b, Deck 4,' in cheerful yellow letters decorated the wall between the two.

"Okay. Deck 4. That means I'm on a ship of some kind. Ships have decks. Yeah, it's definitely a ship." The thoughts came quickly and were acknowledged by Tearan's consciousness as he struggled to make sense of what had happened. Forcing his mind back as far as it would go, he frowned when he realised he had no memory of boarding a ship. Shaking his head with frustration, he slapped the heel of his right hand to his temple. "Think dammit, think." No matter how hard he squeezed his eyes shut, there was no manufacturing any memories that told him where he was nor why he was there. The frustrated growl echoed down the corridor as he thumped the wall in anger.

"Gas. It must be gas of some kind. A drug maybe. Yeah a drug is more likely. Gas or drugs can cause temporary amnesia. My unit obviously got caught and they gassed us or drugged us." Such was the strength of this conviction that Tearan guessed he must have considerable past experience of similar situations. Whoever had done the gassing or drugging, whomever it was that constituted, 'they,' eluded him still. Pleased that he was starting to understand the situation, at least in part, he focussed his attention on the doors that faced him. Neither had anything that distinguished it from its neighbour, so he approached the one on the left and pressed an ear to it. The metallic surface was cold against his skin, but no sound emanated from within. The one on the right was the same so he decided to take the left first. Scanning the doorframe, he noticed the touch pad.

"A swisher," he whispered to himself. The nickname swisher refers to the noise these doors make when they open and close. "A swisher means this is a general access area open to all personnel. It's not engineering; there would be noise and vibration if it were. It might be storage or something though, mess room perhaps."

Flashlight in hand, Tearan approached the door and readied himself for defensive action. Slapping a hand to the touch pad, he was on full alert as the door swished open to reveal a storeroom. Shelved racks filled the small room, each one laden with boxes and cartons of what he quickly realised were electrical components, wire of all sizes and colours, technological bits and pieces of every size and shape imaginable. Examining the cartons and boxes, he was dismayed to find that none of it was stirring memories nor feelings of familiarity within his mind.

"So I guess I'm not an electrical engineer, he shrugged and was about to leave when a thought made him stop in his tracks. "This is obviously a storeroom used by the ship's electrical engineers. That means engineering must be close by. They wouldn't put an engineer's storeroom too far away from where he does his job, would they? This is Deck 4, so I guess I can assume the main engineering section is on this deck too."

The room next door also opened by means of a swisher, and Tearan entered to find two offices. A quick examination showed these two rooms to be some sort of administration centre. Lists, rotas, manifests, requisitions, all the usual admin stuff one would expect for a busy engineering section of a large ship, it was all there. Unfortunately, Tearan found nothing that identified the ship or its purpose and groaned with frustration as he went back out into the corridor and considered the two options that lay before him.

"Left or right?" he muttered and headed left after no more than a moment's hesitation. The echo of his boots on the hard metallic floor was strangely comforting. Those steps had purpose and direction. Indecision melted away as his boot steps tick-ticked confidently along and he focussed his mind on the sound to keep the fear away. The vast emptiness within his mind where he knew memories should be, filled him with dread. Not knowing much more than his own name and occupation was the most frightening thing he had ever known. He stopped mid stride and frowned. "How the fuck do I know that's the most frightening thing I've ever known? I can't remember anything other than my name and occupation, that I'm thirty three and from Arlenika Prime." Not finding an answer to this problem, he shook his head and continued down the corridor, his focus firmly fixed once again upon the comforting tick-ticking of his boot steps.

After negotiating several doglegs, the corridor ended at another intersection. This one offered one door and a single new corridor that went at right angles to the one he had just traversed. The large double door was yet another swisher and Tearan looked at the four-inch high bright yellow lettering that adorned it.

'Main Engineering – authorised personnel only.'

The hour Tearan spent in the engineering section proved two things beyond doubt. The first was confirmation that he knew nothing about engines. Nothing held any sense of familiarity nor sparked memories of any kind and he dared not even guess at the function of most of it. The second thing that was obvious even to him was that nothing was working. There were no flickering lights on any of the consoles, no beeps or buzzers assaulted his ears, no vibrations tickled up through the soles of his boots. The place was cold, dead. In one area, several panels had been removed and bundles of wires, tubing, and piles of components lay strewn around the floor. He guessed that something was broken, being upgraded perhaps, then wondered why no one was around working on it. Maybe it was lunchtime or something, he mused as he wandered around, but then realised that something as important as a ship's engine would be monitored constantly, not left alone. There would always be someone on duty, a rota system of some kind surely.

"I guess if it's broken down it doesn't matter if they leave it by itself," he said as he made his way towards the railing ahead. Peering over and down at the twenty-foot high bullet shaped structure, its immense size took his breath away. It was made of some clear material, the dirty green sludge contained within proving it to be dead. Shiny metallic tubes came out from around the sides of this huge canister, into the surrounding walls of the curved chamber. Tearan waited for several moments but as nothing flickered within the void inside his head, he shrugged and walked away.

Back in the corridor, he continued down the new section and came upon a large workshop.

'Section 8a, Deck 4,' adorned the wall next to the door. Inside he found obvious signs of small-scale manufacturing and tool making. On one wall hung a large poster of a half naked woman with a bald head and pointed ears. Examining the printing along the bottom, he learned that her name was Casira and that she was from Demuay 3. Tearan was unimpressed.

"That's another thing I've learned about myself," he muttered as he went back out into the corridor. "I don't fancy the women from Demuay 3." Another corridor revealed a room laid out like a meeting room or boardroom. Tearan surmised that whoever was in charge of the engineering section held their meetings here, discussed upgrade schedules, held staff interviews, brainstormed problems and all the things engineering people needed to do to keep a ship running smoothly. On one wall was a drinks dispenser so he wandered over. A stack of cups sat nearby, so he took one and held it under the nozzle as he stabbed at one of the buttons. For a second nothing happened and then he heard a hum as his cup filled with hot brown liquid. Lifting it to his face, he sniffed and then took a tentative taste. It had a tang of bitterness but it was not unpleasant and he drank it gratefully, unaware up to then how thirsty he was.

The drink revived him and he spent the few minutes trying to come up with something resembling a plan of action. He knew his first priority must be to discover the location of any crew. Then he hoped to find out what ship this was, why he was on it, and its location. He already knew the engine was not working, which meant the ship was becalmed and drifting, but he needed to know the precise location in order that he call for help. It seemed sensible to get to the bridge and find out if the navigation section could offer him anything useful. This thought stirred something within his mind and he stopped, the cup held midway between the table and his lips.

"How do I know that the navigation section will be on the bridge? I guess I know my way around a ship, even if I'm no engineer."

After draining his cup, Tearan set it down and went to walk away before once again stopping mid stride and turning back, eyes wide and mouth open as a surge of adrenaline coursed through his body. The second half drained cup almost went by unnoticed, and he now stared at it. The dregs in the bottom were cold but had not started to decompose. No mould decorated the surface of the liquid, and there was no smell coming from it, which told him that whoever had drunk the contents had done so within the past day.

"I'm not alone here," he whispered to the empty room.

Finding evidence that at least one other person inhabited the ship gave Tearan hope, but dismayed him at the same time. Were they friendly or hostile? Should he try to link up with them or remain hidden? He knew he was part of a unit of soldiers like himself, Unit 389C4. Common sense told him that his unit buddies should be here somewhere. Dead or alive, they should be aboard. Maybe one of them used this cup. Rummaging in a draw, he found a marker pen and wrote on the wall above the drinks dispenser.

'Tearan Lindo. Unit 389C4. Alive.' Whoever had drunk from the cup was alive less than a day ago, and even if they turn out to be strangers to him, they might have useful information. He needed to arm himself as soon as possible, just in case they turned out to be hostile. Knowing that the engineering section had been empty minutes ago, he returned to the workshop and armed himself with a stout metallic rod. It would do until he found a gun, or at least a knife with which to defend himself if necessary.

Feeling happier now that he had a means of defence, he headed back and continued down the corridor.

The next intersection offered Tearan an elevator, a set of stairs both up and down, and another corridor. The corridor took him back to where he had woken up and ,he realised that he had done a complete circuit of deck 4. He went back to the intersection and tried the elevator. It was dead, which did not surprise him given the state of the engine, so he headed towards the stairs. On the wall by the stairs was a map of the ship. A bird's eye view of deck 4 confirmed that he had seen all it had to offer, whilst a side view of the whole ship showed him that the vessel was comprised of eight decks. The bridge was at the top of the ship, on deck 1, so he started up the stairs. Six flights of stairs up, he puffed to get his breath as he stood outside the main door to the bridge. The door to the security headquarters lay to the right, and offered him a new sidearm with plenty of ammunition. Feeling much more secure now he was armed, he approached the door to the bridge and examined it. A pad on the left hand wall made him curse aloud.

"Fuck, it's a code lock." Knowing how long it might take to try every possible combination of numbers and letters to gain entry, this approach was not an option, so he went back into the security headquarters and rummaged in the arms locker. With a nod of determination, he picked up the small magnetic gadget and went back to the locked door. After securing the gadget to the keypad with its inbuilt magnetic grip, the unit sends out short pulses of multi-phase voksel waves, which confuses electrical and digital locks in such a way as to over stimulate the circuits. This over stimulation makes the governing system think it needs to shut it down to avoid an explosion, switching off the locking mechanism altogether. All that is then required is to pull the door to gain access. Tearan did not want to call attention to himself by firing his gun when there was an alternative; the element of surprise was always to be preserved if possible. Using the stout blade he had picked up in the security headquarters, he forced the door aside far enough to get his fingers in and push it all the way open. It slid aside and he entered the bridge.

A chill traced its way up Tearan's spine as he entered the large empty space and faced the huge viewing window. The stygian void raced forward to envelop him and he felt the breath leave his lungs as adrenaline flooded his system. The sheer size of the viewing window meant that by standing anywhere on the bridge and keeping your eyes fixed forwards, you could almost believe you were out there in space. Tearan felt the ship around him melt away as the vacuum of space embraced him, enfolded him, and carried him away. He floated through the void and felt a mixture of bone crushing fear, exhilaration, and awe. For more than a minute, he lost himself in the illusion, transfixed by the enormity of the universe before he found himself once again back in the eerily silent and abandoned bridge of the as yet unnamed ship.

"Where the fuck is everyone?" he hissed as a shudder of apprehension raised the tiny hairs on his arms. Seeing the bridge empty like that gave him a feeling of vulnerability that had him hugging his arms around himself. With no pilot at the helm, no captain in the large comfy chair, no flight crew steering the vessel safely, Tearan's mind filled with horrific images of the ship breaking up during an uncontrolled re-entry after being caught in the gravitational pull of a planet. For a moment, he was rooted to the spot with terror before shaking himself free.

"Shit."

Scouting around the various workstations, he realised that whatever he had done in life, it had not involved piloting a space ship for the controls meant nothing to him. Not once did he feel anything stirring deep within, no blip of recognition in his gut. All the consoles, dials, displays, and readouts were dead and much of it was alien to him. More than once Tearan was tempted to flip a switch, press a button, turn a dial, just to see what would happen. Fear stayed his hand though; he had no desire to send the ship into a horrifying suicidal dance. The thought of the ship breaking up around him was too terrifying to contemplate so he kept his hands to himself. One thing he did recognise was the navigation station. Star charts and system maps had something inside his mind leaping with joy and he smiled as he studied them.

"So I know how to read a star chart at least," he muttered as he reached out and flipped a switch that he knew should tell him the name of the nearest system to the ship's current position. Nothing happened and he swore as he flipped a few more, knowing that it was safe for him to fiddle this time. Deep inside his mind, his unconscious knew these dials and switches would not send the ship into a suicide nosedive, even if they did work. Not that it mattered as they were all dead and he banged his fist down onto the console in frustration. "What the fuck happened here? I can't fix this on my own." With a growl of irritation, he sat down and ran both hands through his hair. Primarily, he needed to understand the situation. There was no hope of fixing things until he knew what he was dealing with and the first step in reaching that understanding was a full search of the entire ship.

"Perimeter search and evaluate. Basic soldiering one oh one," he muttered as he got to his feet.

A separate elevator and stairs led down from one corner of the bridge to a suite of rooms for use by officers. A briefing room with much finer quality furnishings than the one he discovered on deck 4, a room that looked like the Captain's personal office, and another office. The only access to this suite of rooms was via the bridge so Tearan guessed they were for the sole use of the Captain and his most senior officers. Back on the bridge, he left and went down the main stairs to deck two and studied the map on the wall. This deck contained the Senior Officer's dining lounge and kitchen, Senior Officer's observation lounge, Senior Officer's quarters, computer lab, and science lab. The kitchen and dining rooms were empty, but he found the food preparation systems working perfectly. The observation lounge offered another breathtaking view but little else other than snack and drinks dispensers, which were also functioning properly.

"Well at least I won't starve to death."

All but one of the Senior Officer's quarters were empty and Tearan gaped as he entered to find clear signs of the room being inhabited. A pile of discarded clothes lay in a box in one corner, all made for a man of similar size to himself. He held a pair of pants up against himself. "I bet these would fit me perfectly. I know where to come if I need a change," he mused. The bathroom contained a man's washing necessities, the uncapped tube of toothpaste having been squeezed in the middle. This fact alone told him whoever occupied this room was neither a soldier nor an officer. It takes discipline and hard work to become a good soldier or officer and a man with a disciplined mind would never squeeze the toothpaste in the middle and then leave the cap off. Such a lack of care shows a certain attitude and Tearan decided that a man with such an attitude was not someone he could look up to. It is not a case of being obsessional, it is the kind of self discipline and attention to detail required of good soldiers and effective officers. A wasteful soldier will run out of something quicker, would have to go without sooner, and when roughing it on some shit hole of a planet for weeks at a time, those small comforts make the experience that bit more tolerable. An officer who showed such lack of care for the little things that might at first seem unimportant would be less likely to think of the little things that might save the ship in a battle situation. No, this room may have been designed to house an officer, but its current occupant was anything but.

Tearan quickly found he had an aptitude for neither computers or science, as neither of the labs brought forth any recognition or memories. The science lab was large and had sections for the various disciplines. Biophysics, chemistry, astrophysics, anthropology, and many others, all were represented and all abandoned. He brushed his fingers over the consoles, dials, and switches but felt nothing stir within his mind. "So I'm not a scientist either." As with everywhere he had been so far, the drinks dispenser worked perfectly, as did the lights, heating, food preparation, and water. He knew that he was on the brink of an important realisation but trying to force it forwards made it retreat even further into the empty void inside his mind. Not having any memories was frustrating as well as frightening and he was anxious to start filling that void as soon as possible. At each elevator and stairs, a map of the ship adorned the wall and Tearan studied the one on deck 3 as he reached the bottom of the stairs.

Deck three contained the main computer, gravity field generator and control, life support systems generators, main sensor array governor, ballistics and weapons control, security, and a large briefing room. Tearan found the computer array operational, the flickering lights, beeps and updating readouts told him that, but whatever it was operating was a mystery. The gravity field generator was working, which was no surprise as he had been able to walk around without floating into the air. As there were no signs of life, he left and went next door into Life Support and found the whole place alive with beeping, flickering lights, and readouts.

"So this explains why all the food and drinks dispensers are working, the swishers are still operating and there's heat. Anything connected with life support is functional, but nothing else is. The ship's engines are dead, as is navigation and the weapons probably are too. I can however, get food and drink, I can breathe, I can walk around normally, and I'm warm. I can stay alive but I can't find out where I am or go anywhere else. This is too weird."

Sure enough, next door in ballistics and weapons control, all was dead, but Tearan did find flickers of recognition stirring within as he touched the various dials and switches. "This is familiar too, just like in navigation. I know this." The security centre had him grinning from ear to ear when he discovered several arms lockers that offered him all manner of arms both large and small. "Hello baby," he grinned as he took down a Cortik 4 laser pistol and caressed its smooth lines. Familiarity flooded into his mind and he almost cried with relief as he registered the knowledge that he had handled this weapon before. After pocketing half a dozen spare cells, he found a door that led to a firing range and spent a little time putting it through its paces before restocking with cells and continuing his search. The security centre had its own small kitchen and dining area, vidicom movie screen, gaming table and several cots for on duty personnel to catch some rack time. A small area at one end was kitted out as a gymnasium and martial arts practice area and more flutters registered in Tearan's mind as he did a tour of the rooms. The place felt comfortable and catered for all his needs, so he decided to use this as his base until further notice. One cabinet yielded a whole lot of key cards for the various lockable rooms on board, and with the aid of a well thumbed manual he found in a drawer, he was able to reconfigure the lock on the main door. This generous space afforded him food and drink, arms, exercise, a place to sleep and even some entertainment. Most importantly, it gave him a feeling of safety, somewhere to call home and defend.

After locking the door behind him, Tearan reached up with the marker pen he had pocketed from the deck four engineering briefing room.

'Inter-Galactic Elite Command, Unit 389C4 Headquarters. T Lindo Commanding Officer.'

Satisfied, he headed for the stairs. Having already investigated deck four, he headed down to deck five. The map showed this deck to comprise of staff quarters, kitchen, dining area, and recreation rooms and like everywhere else, they were almost devoid of any signs of life. Two of the staff quarters showed similar signs of occupation as in the Senior Officer's quarters on deck two. In one room, he found a large selection of knives and blades hidden under the bed, which told him he was not the only one aboard interested in defending himself.

"Wow. Let's hope he's just a collector and not a user," he muttered to himself as he went to explore the kitchen and dining room. As before, all things related to the storage, preparation and cooking of food seemed to be in perfect working order, as was the water treatment system and waste disposal. The vidicom movie system was not working, but the gaming tables were. "So I can't watch a movie but I can play myself at Tapshots." After making plans to return and raid some of the staff quarters for bed linens and washing necessities, he made his way back to the stairs.

Deck six contained the medical bay, isolation ward, medical research lab, morgue, funeral room, and multi denominational temple. A blip of emotion coursed through his body as he entered the morgue and stayed with him as he examined the funeral room and temple. He was aware of the feeling inside him, a heavy weight on his heart that pricked at the corners of his eyes, but he was unable to explain it. Finding himself within the temple, he wondered if anyone would mourn him if he died. Was there a family somewhere worrying for him, a lover missing his presence, children perhaps? He had no idea but there was something about this area of the ship that moved him.

Deck seven comprised a shuttle bay and massive storage hangar. Tearan approached the shuttle bay and stopped, the flashing red sign above the door explaining why it would not be a good idea to enter.

'Danger – bay doors open – enter via airlock only.'

Peering through the round glass window, the open bay doors at the far end of the room revealed the infinite void of space beyond. Two shuttlecraft sat on pads within and several hover loaders stood idle along one wall. Around a corner, another door announced itself as shuttle bay preparation and airlock, so he entered. Racks of space suits and breather units hung along one long wall, magnetic soled boots standing sentinel beneath each one and Tearan felt a vague sense of familiarity as he gazed at each in turn.

"I've worn a suit before," he said to himself as he approached the first and reached out a hand to touch the fabric. "I know how to do this." Glancing over the breather unit, he felt recognition within and knew that he could enter the shuttle bay safely. Deciding to return at the earliest opportunity and check out the shuttle bay itself, he left the room and went in search of the storage hangar. The space was huge, and contained cartons and crates of everything imaginable. There were food supplies to last years if he was careful with it, as well as clothing, cleaning supplies, and medical supplies. Another section of shelving held all manner of stuff that he guessed belonged to the engineering section, digital components, and all manner of things he was unable to identify. Several hover carts stood around the edges of the room and he decided his first task must be to stock his new home base with food and essentials.

Deck eight contained a single room that announced itself as a hazardous storage bay. A notice pinned to the door told him that under no circumstances was he to touch anything without first donning appropriate safety clothing; that if he had not been trained and certificated in handling hazardous materials to grade three or higher, he was not to enter without the supervision of someone who had.

"Well fuck you," he retorted as he pushed open the door and entered. A large space spread out before him, containing twenty-seven drums strapped to racks that were themselves bolted to the floor. Each one sported a digital display that beeped quietly, a readout giving the temperature and status of the contents. Apart from a small room containing cartons of safety clothing and a bin for clothing to be cleaned, there was nothing of interest. Having searched the whole ship and found signs of life that told him there must be four others aboard, but no actual people to account for those signs, Tearan was more than a little confused. He knew he had not searched thoroughly; he knew it would be easy for someone to avoid him by backtracking, but why would they do so? Why were they avoiding being found? Did that mean they were hostile or afraid that he might be? He had no way of knowing but he was tired and hungry, so he made his way back to security and his new safe base for a meal and some down time. His priority now was to secure his own position and safety first before thinking about the larger situation. He would make more of an effort to find the others later, he decided.

2

The pain in his head drove him to wakefulness from an empty and dreamless void. Opening his eyes slowly so as not to exacerbate the pain that throbbed in his temples, Mykus found himself on a bed within what appeared to be a cheap hotel room. The frown that furrowed his brow deepened as he realised he had no knowledge of where he was nor how he got there. With one swift movement, he swung his legs to the floor and sat on the edge of the bed as he tried to focus his mind. There were no memories of how he might have arrived at this room, so he thought back to the day before and was horrified to find no memories of anything at all.

"I can't remember anything? What the fuck is going on?" he said as he grasped his head in his hands and squeezed his eyes shut. "I'm Mykus Romin. I'm twenty-eight and I'm from Arlenika Prime. I'm a mechanical engineer and I, I umm, that is I." He let out a shriek when he found nothing more within his mind, a shriek more of fear than anger. Fear swept into his empty mind, grasped his senses and sent him panicking into a crouch on the floor, his back to the bed. Trying to make himself as small as possible, he shivered and cried under the weight of vulnerability. After several minutes allowing panic to direct his inaction, Mykus wiped his nose on his sleeve, dried his eyes and stood. No one had come to accost him so far, so he risked indulging his curiosity and went to investigate his immediate surroundings.

The room was basic but comfortable and offered him a bed, closet, nightstand, desk, and chair. Through a partition wall, he found a toilet, basin, and shower. His fingers caressed the washcloth that hung over the side of the basin, he lifted the tube of toothpaste and examined the label but nothing stirred within his mind. Although the items he found within the bathroom were more than adequate for his needs, he felt no familiarity with any of them. He did not know whether those particular brands of soap and toothpaste were his favourites or not. They were there, as was he, so he assumed they were for his use. The face that gazed back at him made him jump. For a fraction of a second, the face was that of a stranger, but then a finger of recognition stirred and he knew it was his own. The sense of it belonging to him was tenuous but he did not doubt its truth. As he stared at himself, he felt he were meeting a friend he had not seen in many years and examined the reflection in detail so as to fix the image within his mind once again.

Slipping the key card he found hanging from the door handle into his pocket, he opened the door and peered out. The number eighty-eight was painted on the door, and he slipped it into his memory alongside the image of his own face as he looked both ways down the corridor he found outside. His boots tapped on the metallic floor as he walked to his left, past more numbered doors which he chose to assume led to similar rooms to the one in which he had woken up. He knew immediately that he was not within a building built on solid ground. There was something about his surroundings that told him he was on board a ship of some kind, but he did not know what gave him that conviction. Maybe it was the lack of windows, or perhaps it was the metallic floor and walls, he was not sure but he knew without a doubt that he would not find himself opening a door and stepping out into a sunny afternoon. The large kitchen and dining area he found were deserted, despite his calling out and he thought it strange that a space ship large enough to warrant such a large dining room would have no staff busy in the kitchen preparing for the next meal.

"Perhaps it's the middle of the night," he muttered as he wandered along the corridor and found a recreation room that was also empty of life. When he eventually found himself back outside door number eighty-eight, he retraced his steps to the elevator and stairs he had passed. It was here he learned that he was indeed aboard a space ship as the map on the wall confirmed. Studying the map closely, he learned he was on deck five, and that everything to do with engineering was one deck above. "There's always someone on duty in engineering," he mused as he punched the button for the elevator. More than a minute passed by, during which Mykus stabbed at the elevator call button several times, before he gave up and took the stairs two at a time.

'Main engineering – authorised personnel only,' the notice on the door announced. Mykus hesitated for no more than a second before opening the door and peering through. Expecting to be refused entry, he was dismayed to find no one in the immediate vicinity, so he entered and called out.

"Hello? Can someone help me? Hello?" His call echoed around the large space but no reply was forthcoming. After calling out again, he made his way into the engineering section and soon found the entire place deserted. Not only was he alone in the section, but nothing seemed to be working. He recognised all of the consoles and workstations but why was nothing operational? When he reached the mezzanine overlooking the engine bay and peered down at the huge bullet shaped object, he had no problem identifying it but was dismayed by its condition. The green sludge within the clear casing told him the unit had been switched off at least three months ago, for he knew that was how long it took for this particular type of engine system to revert to this state of non-operation. The two liquid gases that power the engine are normally kept in a state of constant motion much like a food processor mixing ingredients. The two liquid gases are not able to mix while in this state of motion, and it is this dynamic flow that produces the energy to drive the ship. When such an engine is switched off, it takes three months for both liquid gases to cool and then combine into a green sludge.

Three hours later, he sat down and ran a hand through his hair. His investigation had revealed nothing that might explain why the engine was non-operational. There was no obvious damage to any of the systems that he found and everything seemed to be in perfect working order. Once he had replaced the last of the panels, he realised he had been alone in Main Engineering for hours and had accessed all systems without being accosted by security. This should not have happened. A stranger would never be allowed to wander freely in the engineering section of a space ship and fiddle around as he had done.

"I have to go and find someone," he said aloud and left the room. By the time he found himself back outside Main Engineering, he had found the engineering storeroom, two offices, a workshop, and a meeting room, none of which had yielded any personnel or explanation for his situation. In one corner of the briefing room was a drinks dispenser with two used cups nearby. Their contents was cold but Mykus knew it meant he was not alone. Written on the wall above was something that made his heart leap in his breast.

'Tearan Lindo. Unit 389C4. Alive.'

He read and re-read the message several times, not knowing how to process it in his mind. The first thing he felt sure of was that the message was not a normal part of the room's decor. It was scrawled in what appeared to be marker pen, which told him whoever wrote it did so in a hurry. That word at the end gave him a feeling of fear. *'Alive.'* A person would only write that if they wanted others to know they had survived something. That message conveyed the unspoken truth, *'I survived something'*. Mykus knew it meant that some sort of danger was present that needed to be survived, or not. That message was written by someone who felt it necessary to convey it, that others might want to know. More importantly to Mykus, it meant the possibility that whoever this Tearan Lindo was, he might still be alive. Racing back to the two engineering offices, he rummaged in a desk and grabbed a marker pen. He stood facing the message and for a moment was unsure how he should reply. His instinct was to scrawl a long message expressing his relief, introducing himself and asking to meet, but he decided to err on the side of caution and reply in a similar manner to the message Tearan Lindo had written.

'Mykus Romin. Engineer. Alive.' He stood back and regarded his reply. Tearan Lindo had kept his own message short and to the point and might appreciate a reply made in a similar manner. At the same time as relief flooded through him, Mykus registered a flutter of apprehension deep

inside. The fact that Tearan Lindo had not made it clear where he was, nor had made his presence known in any other fashion, made him think about his situation in a new way. It was entirely possible that Tearan Lindo would know how this situation came about, why the ship should be so short of personnel and what form any danger took. There was also the possibility that he was the cause of whatever it was that brought Mykus here to this moment, afraid and unable to remember anything about himself other than a few basic facts. Mykus had not investigated the entire ship, the fact that the main engineering section was deserted told him something was very wrong, but now he questioned his decision to go on a ship wide search. Maybe Tearan Lindo knew something he did not; maybe that was why he was keeping his head down. Perhaps something awful had taken place, something that was still a danger.

Mykus allowed his mind to dwell on the possibility that violence had taken place and that more violence would be needed to ensure his survival. The thought horrified him and told him that whatever he had done with his life so far, he had not been the aggressive type. Lifting his arms, he flexed his muscles and dipped at the knees to get the feel of his own physical condition. He nodded appreciatively.

"I obviously work out regularly," he muttered as he pushed up his shirt sleeve and examined his upper arm muscles. An exclamation of surprise and appreciation followed when he lifted his shirt to reveal a six-pack. "Wow." This told him he no doubt had the ability to defend himself if need be, but deep within the void of his mind, something fluttered to life. This something was the inescapable conviction that he was not a fighter and if he were to put money on it, he would bet that violence scared him. Having changed his mind about searching the ship, he decided to return to deck five and make something to eat in the kitchen.

The silent corridor seemed somehow menacing now that Mykus knew someone else was aboard; the thought he might have been alone was frightening but in a different way. Now he had good reason to believe he was not the only person aboard, but he had no way of knowing if this

Tearan Lindo would meet him with aggression or the open hand of friendship. If there was anything worse than being totally alone on a becalmed spaceship, it was sharing one with a violent maniac and of these two awful scenarios, Mykus preferred the thought of the former rather than the latter. Fear momentarily froze his feet to the floor as he left the main engineering section and entered the corridor down which he knew he had to travel in order to reach the stairs. After a moment's hesitation, he cursed under his breath. "Oh for fuck's sake I can't stand here forever, I have to move. If I meet this Tearan Lindo, or anyone else, I'll try to be friendly and smile a lot. I'm not armed so I'm obviously not a threat to anyone." He strode down the corridor whistling a tune in an attempt at nonchalance, skipped down the stairs and headed for the kitchen.

The meat was pale in colour and delicately flavoured, and Mykus found he knew instinctively which of the herbs to use from the large selection in order to enhance the subtle taste of the meat. Other meats were available; the kitchen was very well stocked but he seemed to know the darker, richer meats would not please his palette. As he ate, he briefly wondered how many aspects of a man were so ingrained that they would survive amnesia. Had he always preferred the lighter flavoured meats to the richer ones, or was this something new now that his memory had been wiped and his palette was able to experience things afresh? The questions were put to the back of his mind. He was an engineer, his existence was concerned with things that can be measured and quantified. It was the solidly real and physical things he understood best, parameters that demanded exacting standards with no margins for error. He was a man of the physical, measurable world not the abstract. Philosophical things confused him, so he avoided them.

Once he finished eating, he sat down with a hot drink and contemplated on what he had discovered during his time in the engineering section and what it meant for his current situation. Although his investigation of the engine systems had not been thorough, he had so far found nothing obviously wrong to explain why the ship was becalmed.

Many questions ran through his head as he thought about possible causes. Some were dismissed right away, others were unlikely but not impossible and still others were more likely. In the absence of anything else to do, he would put his engineering knowledge and skills to good use, try to discover why the ship's engine was not working and if possible, fix it. Tearan Lindo could occupy himself with working out the cause of this weirdness, he thought.

Back in engineering, Mykus approached the wall and scratched his chin. Raising the marker pen he still kept in his pocket, he wrote down everything that might cause the engine to cease operating. The list was written in order of priority, with the most likely and probable causes higher than the more outlandish ones. After ten minutes of chin scratching, scrawling on the wall, rubbing out and rewriting, he stood back, satisfied. He was in his element and was pleased that he now had a plan of action he felt comfortable with and was confident of achieving. He would work his way down this first list from top to bottom and hope to find in which of the ship's systems was the problem. Top of the list was to examine the body of the engine housing itself. Any tiny cracks or imperfections could prevent the gases within from behaving in the proper manner. Mykus knew this was the most likely cause, but he also knew that if this were the problem, he would be unable to fix it. There was no way the engine housing was repairable; such a problem always necessitated an entire engine replacement, which also meant a new gas system was needed. The green sludge that now lay within the current engine housing could not be used within a brand new one, even if one were available. To add to these problems was the fact that Mykus would be unable to replace the engine housing and gas supply alone. The twenty-foot high engine housing weighed several tons, and the procedure for attaching it was a delicate operation that demanded pinpoint accuracy. Make a microscopic mistake and the whole ship might blow apart.

A search of the engineering storeroom yielded the tools and safety equipment necessary for the job, and Mykus hummed as he stepped into the harness and tightened the straps. This job would normally be achieved with the aid of special computerised programmes and robotic apparatus, but since he had been unable to make any of the computer systems function beyond the ones that governed the life support systems, he would have to do the job manually. This meant an inch by inch examination of the engine housing using the special goggles, and he estimated the job would take three days to complete. Having such a long an engrossing task to complete meant that he would not have time to dwell on the strangeness of his situation, which would lessen the anxiety. While concentrating on the job, he would be unable to let his imagination run away with him. If anyone should turn up and question him, his delight at not being alone would allay any fear of discipline. With renewed determination, he climbed into the engine bay.

An hour and a half later, his concentration was interrupted by the distinct sound of gunfire from somewhere above. Having been so engrossed in his work, the sudden explosion of noise made him leap from the side of the engine housing and end up swinging from his harness in mid air. Gasping in fright, his arms and legs flailed as he scrabbled to grasp the engine housing. With both arms wrapped around one of the stanchions that fixed the housing into the engine bay, Mykus closed his eyes and listened to his heart thumping in his breast. For long moments, he did not know what to do, so he did nothing but hang onto the engine housing, his eyes darting around the room in fright. Another burst of gunfire almost made him fall from the housing again and he was grateful for the harness that prevented him from falling to his death. The silence in between the bursts of gunfire throbbed with menace and he found himself tensing as he waited for the next volley.

"Shit. Fuck," he gasped in between the painful thuds in his chest as his heart hammered against his ribcage. Panic rippled through his empty mind and filled the aching void where memories and self knowledge should be with horrific imaginings. "What the fuck do I do? Oh shit, there's a gun toting maniac after me. Oh help me, someone please." Tears of panic sprang from his eyes, desperate sobs of terror wracked his body as he clung to the stanchion too terrified to move. The initial wave of panic was over quickly and in its wake came a moment of deadness in which he felt nothing but the cold knowledge that he must move. Wiping his eyes on his sleeve, he sniffed and took a moment to enjoy the afterglow left behind after blind panic.

Realising that whilst hanging by his harness from the engine housing, neither hiding nor investigating was possible, he forced himself to act and climbed down to floor level. After discarding the harness, he tip toed to the main door and pressed his ear to its surface. When the next volley came, he knew it was coming from above, so he opened the door enough to put his head out and look both ways down the corridor. Seeing no one, he wondered whether to go back down to deck five and hide in his room or venture upstairs and find out what was going on. With his initial panic now under some control, he was able to concentrate enough to notice that the gunfire came in volleys a minute or so apart. There was nothing haphazard about it, as one might expect in a gunfight. These shots came at regularly spaced intervals and they sounded like they all came from the same gun. Mykus had no memories of guns to call upon, but he knew somewhere deep within that guns all sound different. These sounded the same though and without warning, the thought leapt to the front of his mind.

"That's not a gunfight, it's one person firing off a gun. Like on a firing range or something. Maybe it's a security guy practising his sharpshooting." That sound might indicate someone in a position of authority with an explanation for the dead engine and lack of crew. Mykus leapt up the stairs to deck three with hope pounding afresh in his heart. Following the sound, he made his way down the corridor and stopped outside a door marked 'Security.' He knew the gunfire was coming from within, but did not know whether to walk in unannounced or knock. Deciding that it was probably sensible to be cautious, especially as he was unarmed, he waited until the current volley ended and knocked loudly. After what he estimated to be around half a minute and with no more gunfire evident from behind the closed door, Mykus knocked again.

"Hello. Hello, is someone there? Can you help me? Hello?" His calls went unanswered and he suddenly felt unsure about what he should do. Whoever was inside must have heard him calling, so why refuse to answer the door? He could tell him to get lost if necessary, but to deliberately not acknowledge him was strange and made Mykus think it was probably because whoever it was with the gun, was not someone he felt comfortable trusting. Suddenly regretting having announced his presence to someone who may very well be either aggressive or crazy or both, Mykus decided that no good ever came from trying to hide when another action is available. A crazy man with a gun in the relatively confined environment of a space ship was not something he could easily avoid anyway. A slot to the side of the door waited for a key card and he hesitated for no more than a moment. Fishing in his pocket, he found the key card for room eighty-eight in which he had woken up and slid it into the slot. To his complete surprise, he heard a click that told him the door had accepted the card and was now unlocked.

"Hello? Is someone there? I knocked but you didn't hear me," he called in his most friendly voice as he gently pushed the door open, his heart thumping in his chest. No answer came, so he pushed the door open and stepped through. He found himself in a reception area with a desk by the door, behind which were several large lockers that ran the whole length of one wall. Despite calling out several times, he got no reply and eventually plucked up the courage to investigate further. He found a small kitchen and dining area, several basic beds, gaming table, vidicom screen and through another door, a firing range. Fully expecting to find Tearan Lindo, he went in but the place was as deserted as everywhere else he had been so far. This was getting weirder by the second. He distinctly heard gunfire up until he was right outside the door and yet there was no one there. He yelled at the top of his voice, irritation over riding his fear and the silence that greeted him annoyed him.

"But there should be someone here, I heard the gunfire." With a frown, he scratched his head and did another tour of the whole security complex but found no one. He opened all the closets and lockers, even knocked on the walls for hidden doors but found nothing. In a last ditch effort to find an explanation, he moved seating and tables in case they hid secret panels and examined the ceiling and floor for escape hatches. There was no way for anyone to get out without using the main door. Back in the firing range, he searched for traces of gunfire having taken place, but realising his knowledge of guns was either non existent or still well hidden within the fog of his amnesia, he was not sure what to look for. There was nothing that immediately announced recent gunfire having taken place, but he did not discount the possibility that whatever weapon had been used was one that left no obvious trace.

Nothing further was to be gained by remaining within security, so he retraced his steps and went back out into the corridor, having decided that while he was here he might as well investigate what else deck three had to offer. As he shut the door behind him, he glanced up at it.

'Inter-Galactic Elite Command, Unit 389C4 Headquarters. T Lindo Commanding Officer.'

Registering the same name as in the message in the engineering briefing room, his frown deepened as he muttered to himself. "The Lindo guy again. Inter-Galactic Elite Command. That sounds official I guess. Maybe he's the security around here and not a crazy after all."

Next door was a briefing room, its drink and snack dispensers working perfectly, as were the ones down in Engineering and on deck five. Wandering on down the corridor, he came to another door.

'Ballistics and Weapons Control – Authorised Personnel Only – passes must be shown.'

Inside the large room, Mykus found the computerised control centre for the ship's weapons systems, the enormous power pack for the laser torpedoes stood silent, its darkened display panel telling him it was non-operational.

"I hope we don't get set upon by pirates. With no weapons we haven't a prayer."

Next door was the main sensor array and he noticed that the ship had an impressive sensor system. Looking at it closely, he scratched his chin and frowned. The sensor system employed on this ship was of the type used by top-secret military reconnaissance ships, which meant this was not a low budget passenger liner he had woken up on. With a shrug of resignation, he left and continued down the corridor.

'Life Support Control Centre.'

"I bet a hundred this is working," he said aloud as he slapped the touchpad and entered, no longer caring about whether anyone was around to object to his trespassing. The room contained one long panel of dials, switches, display screens, keypads, and data chip slots. On the wall above were maps of the various life support networks, the heating, water, air filtration, power, and lighting. The panel rang with beeps, buzzes, flickering lights, digital readouts, and displays. "I knew it. Everything necessary for life support is working, but the ship won't move, we've no sensors, and no weapons. I'll bet there's no navigation or communications either." Shaking his head in frustration, he left the room.

The last two rooms contained the gravity field generator and control, which was operational and seemed to be working perfectly and the main ship's computer. This was partially working; registering all the life support systems but nothing else. Mykus stared at the banks of consoles and shook his head. This situation was getting more and more weird and each new piece of information just made it stranger than ever. Shaking his head to dispel the growing feeling of dread, he returned to Engineering and continued his inspection of the engine housing. He figured that until he knew for certain that there was not a problem with the engine or power system, he could not speculate on what might have happened to the ship. Another reason for wanting to get the ship's main computer up and running was the hope that some of the crew had recorded logs of what was happening around them, which might explain their absence. Besides, it would give him something positive to do with his time. Keeping busy would help prevent him from dwelling on the fact that he had woken up alone on a strange spaceship with no memories other than his name, age, race, and occupation.

Four hours later, Mykus stepped out of the safety harness and pulled off the goggles. With his hands on his hips, he stretched his back and legs before walking over to a large expanse of wall with the marker pen.

'Day 1 – sections 1-70 – no visible damage.'

With almost two hundred separate sections of engine housing to view through the special goggles, Mykus knew he would not be finished within another two days. If he worked three four-hour shifts each day, with an hour between each for a meal and a break, he would know definitively if the engine housing was faulty. If so, repair was out of the question. If not, then he would continue on to something else. His engineer's mind was in full control now and he would methodically examine each section until he found the problem. When he did find it, he would know whether it was repairable or not. Right now, he needed a shower and a drink, so he returned to his room on deck five. A change of clothes would be nice too, he decided.

As the hot water cascaded down over his body, Mykus allowed his mind to dwell on more abstract thoughts. What would he do if he could neither find nor fix the engine? What if he found himself stuck here forever? He decided there was no harm in doing an inventory of food supplies so he would know how to ration himself to make the fullest use of what he had. The thought of remaining aboard this becalmed ship, possibly for years into the future, scared him. Then he remembered the message left by Tearan Lindo. At least with a companion around he would not go crazy with loneliness, at least not as quickly as he would alone.

"What if the guy's a psycho murderer?" he mused aloud as he soaped himself. Not knowing which was worse, being totally alone or having to avoid a crazy psycho all the time, he decided to assume this T Lindo was trustworthy until he found out otherwise. He did not need the anxiety of worrying about it yet so he pushed it from his mind. Once showered and with a fresh set of clothes on, he wandered along to the kitchen and made himself a snack and a hot drink. Finding the vidicom screen not working, he turned his attention to one of the gaming tables and spent an hour shooting down pirates in a fighter ship simulator. When the yawns became noticeably frequent, he went back to his room, cleaned his teeth and went to bed.

"Maybe I'll wake up and find this has all been a horrible dream."

3

He awoke with a start, almost falling from the bed and rubbed his eyes. Light shined down from somewhere above, right into his eyes and he raised a hand to shield them from the glare. Raising up onto one elbow, he recognised his surroundings as a medical facility of some kind. Frowning, he searched his memory for an explanation as to how he got there but was terrified to find almost nothing within his mind at all. Swinging his legs to the floor, he sat on the edge of the bed and tried to make his mind think. He failed, so after running a hand through his hair and yawning, he stood and reached for the white coat that hung limp over a gurney to his left.

'Dr Soval Arma.' His eyes swept over the name badge sewn to the breast pocket; he did not want to wear someone else's coat and confuse any patients. Besides, it was one of the few things he knew to be true. His almost empty mind knew for certain that his knowledge of medicine was substantial, but that was all he knew apart from his name, his age, and that he came from Arlenika Prime.

"I seem to have amnesia," he said aloud, putting a hand to his temple and massaging gently. Searching his medical knowledge for all the possible causes of memory loss, he went over to a mirror that hung on one wall. After careful examination of his face and head, he decided a head injury was not apparently to blame. There was no blood, no bruising, and no pain when he carefully pressed with his fingertips. An injury capable of causing amnesia to this degree would leave visible clues and their absence told him this was not the cause. The next obvious thing to check for was drug use so he wandered over to the blood filtration unit and switched it on. This machine takes a sample of blood and analyses it for any substances contained within it. They are standard issue in even the most basic medical facilities and he knew instinctively that he was completely familiar with its use. Ten minutes later, he knew that he had not taken any drugs capable of causing amnesia within the last sixty days. There were traces of recent sedatives and the presence of a high nutritional compound told him he must have been kept sedated for quite a long time.

Knowing that various degenerative brain diseases can cause amnesia, he went over to the body scanner on the far side of the room and punched buttons on the console. Taking the mobile controller, he lay down and placed the neural helmet on his head. Twenty minutes later, he punched keys on the console and waited for the display of his brain function to appear. A few more key punches later, the readout confirmed there was no discernible degeneration of his brain that might cause amnesia. The only other possible cause for his lack of memory was some kind of psychological trauma and this was something he was unable to test for.

"But if I had some deeply damaging psychological trauma, either in childhood or more recently, why did it not erase my medical knowledge?" he asked himself aloud. "It is essentially possible I suppose that my medical knowledge is so deeply ingrained that it survived the trauma. My troubled mind probably sought refuge in the order and discipline of that knowledge in an effort to survive whatever happened. Unless I can find my own medical file, I will never know until either someone tells me or my memory returns."

Assuming that he was a patient in this medical facility, despite being a doctor himself, he wandered around and called out for a doctor or nurse. "Hello? Is there someone here? This is Doctor Soval Arma; I'm awake and relatively unharmed apart from almost total retrograde amnesia. Hello, anyone?" He searched the whole room and realised that he was in a medical research lab. A door opened into a corridor that curved gently away in both directions. Stepping out into the corridor, he looked at the door through which he had come.

'Medical Research, Lab and Scanning,' was painted onto the door in bright yellow lettering. Smiling to himself, he wandered to his left.

'Medical Bay.' The same bright yellow lettering adorned the next door he came to and he frowned. "Medical Bay? That means this is a ship. I'm

aboard a space ship?" He shook his head slightly in shock but did not know why he should react this way. Without bothering to knock, he entered and approached the reception desk. It took him less than a minute to search the medical bay and find it devoid of life. The examination cubicles, recovery ward, operating theatre, duty nurse's bunks, and visitors waiting area, all were silent. Soval found it disquieting being the only person around in a place that should be busy with people and he shivered.

Next door, he found an isolation ward with three more duty nurse's bunks and not a single person anywhere. Further on down the corridor was the morgue, which gave him his second mystery. Not only was the morgue empty but the refrigeration unit was not working. Opening the large heavy door, he found twenty refrigerated pods but all were as warm as the other rooms he had been in. Not only were there no bodies in storage but whoever was in charge had obviously chosen not to be ready should any arrive. However small the chances of having a deceased casualty arrive in a medical facility, Soval knew that the facility for handling them should always be ready, just in case. For this refrigeration unit to be non-functioning was extremely odd and against standard medical practice.

'Non-Denominational Place of Worship. This place of peace and tranquility is open to all who wish to use it for contemplation, meditation, and prayer. If you require assistance, the religious and cultural affairs team are available at any time day or night and can be found in the booth inside.'

Soval read the notice. This was standard wording on space ship places of worship, where people from all different planets, cultures, and belief systems might very well be found. The wording was carefully constructed to extend a welcome to people of all religious beliefs who might wish to use the space. These rooms were simply furnished, deliberately devoid of any religious iconography that might visually tie in to any one particular religion above another. This was so as not to cause offence to those belief systems that might feel under represented. Paintings of peaceful landscapes, forests, mountains, waterfalls and lakes gazed down at him from the walls. Colourful birds flew in the skies and here and there, painted columns gave the room a more pleasing appearance. Fabric drapes hung between some of the painted columns and comfortable seating was plentiful. Soval delighted in the peace he felt rippling through his heart before leaving the room.

Continuing down the corridor, he found himself back at the medical research lab. He had noticed an elevator and staircase by the main medical bay door, so he continued on. After pressing the button for the elevator, he assumed it was faulty and approached the map on the wall by the stairs.

"So this is deck six," he said to himself as he studied the map and noticed that the deck above contained the main kitchen and dining area, as well as proper staff quarters. Deciding that his first priority must be to try to find other people, he decided to search until he found someone. There was no way a ship's medical facility should be empty of staff and with the morgue also being non-functioning, the weirdness level was way off the scale. Another person would make him feel more secure, even if they did not understand what had happened any more than he did. At least being with someone would lessen his anxiety.

He found no one aboard, and only twice was there any evidence of other people. On deck four he found himself in the main engineering section and noticed several panels removed from machinery, revealing wires, tubes, conduits, and digital components. Tools lay on the floor, together with various bits of wire, lengths of conduit, and a box of blue metallic components. Someone was working on one of the machines, that was obvious, which meant a chance that whoever it was might still be around somewhere. Further along the same corridor, he found a meeting room, which he surmised was used by the engineering personnel and noticed drinks and snack dispensers in one corner. On the small table beside the drinks dispenser were two used and unwashed cups.

'Tearan Lindo. Unit 389C4. Alive' was written on the wall, and below it, *'Mykus Romin. Engineer. Alive.'* Perhaps it was an inventory of people left after some kind of terrible tragedy. Patting himself all over, he discovered a pen and a standard medical issue hand held recording device in his trouser pocket. Perhaps it would be sensible to add his own name to the list, he

thought. It would not hurt anyway and the other two people might be relieved to know that a trained doctor was alive among them. Lifting the recording device to his lips, he recorded his own greeting.

'Hi there. I'm Dr Soval Arma. I'm a medical practitioner and I'm also alive. Anyone have any idea what has happened here?'

After putting the device down on top of the drinks dispenser, he drew an arrow pointing down, underneath the two names. They would be able to convey much more information by speaking than writing, he thought to himself. There was also the possibility that by asking a direct question, he might find himself with some welcome company before long. Being the only person on board was not an idea he felt comfortable with and now it was evident that at least two people were around somewhere, he felt happier. There was always the possibility that they might work together to discover the cause of their current predicament, and maybe even find a solution. With this new mood of positivity trickling through his being, he allowed hope to course through the void that was his empty mind. The engineer was most likely to be the cause of the open panels and tools in the main engineering section.

"A skilled engineer is always a useful member of any team," he muttered, before turning his attention to the other name. He had noticed that same name written on the door of the security room on deck three, but had no clue exactly what the Inter-Galactic Elite Command might be. "It sounds military, so he's probably a trigger happy grunt with the intelligence of a Cavindole Worm. No matter, we can put him to work lifting and carrying things. Failing that, he can prepare food. Military types are all taught to provide food for themselves, so he should be capable in a well stocked kitchen such as the one on deck five."

Now he knew that there were potentially just three people alive on the entire ship, he realised that there would probably not be too high a demand for his skills as a doctor. Suddenly at a loss to know how he would fill his time, he decided to spend some time doing a thorough inventory of the medical bay supplies and then draw up a cleaning schedule. It was not entirely necessary, but it would keep him occupied. Now that he had something resembling a plan of action, he headed to the stairs and prepared to descend. His foot halted in mid air and his heart leapt in shock as the sound of gunfire exploded from somewhere above. The open space of the stairwell acted to help amplify and carry the sound, which echoed as it drifted down to him. Freezing in terror, his doctor's sense for details noticed something that he found interesting. The gunfire terrified him.

"So I'm scared of guns eh?" he muttered in the brief respite between explosive volleys. "That's not a surprise. I'm a doctor. My job is to preserve life, not endanger it further." Another loud volley erupted, sending him into a huddled crouch on the floor, his hands over his ears in terror. Without warning, his mind suddenly filled with the conviction that whoever was firing the gun was out to kill him. Horror stricken, he leapt to his feet and spun around, certain someone was right behind him with a gun. Crying out in terror, he backed to the wall and found himself facing the door to the main engineering section. Fresh terror swept over him as images filled his mind unbidden. He was falling through the air, the cable that had held him safe now cut and sending him to his death.

Crying out in fear, he watched the ground come up to meet him, heard the crunch as his bones broke and felt the wetness of blood as his skull cracked before the images changed and new horrors assaulted his mind. The woman's eyes were wide with horror before him, her mouth open to cry out for mercy. Light glinted off the blade that sliced across her throat, cutting through her vocal chords and silencing her cries. Soval reared back in alarm, attempting to physically distance himself from this new horror that invaded his mind but the images stayed with him. Deeper and deeper the blade sliced until it came to a stop against her spine, the blood that sprayed from the wound soaking his face and entering his mouth. The metallic tang swept over his tongue and he spat involuntarily. Frantic hands swiped at his mouth and he spat. He spat and cried out in disgust and horror as the woman crumpled to the floor, her dead eyes staring up at him.

As quickly as they began, the images stopped and Soval found himself still at the top of the stairs, his tears wet upon his cheeks as his shaking hands still wiped at his mouth. Examining his hands, he was relieved but mystified to find them clear of blood. His lab coat was white and pristine, not red and sodden as he expected and his frown deepened. Gasping to calm himself, he squeezed his eyes shut and sat down on the top step. "Hallucinations. That's what it was, a hallucination that's all. It's not real. It's just my mind trying to find itself again through the amnesia. It's bound to happen and might continue for some time. I must be prepared for it." Wiping both hands across his brow and through his hair, he waited for his heart to calm. "It was so real though, so real. Oh, what is happening to me? Someone help me please."

Soval decided to go down to deck five and make himself something to eat in the kitchen. He thought that by occupying himself with a task so ordinary and run of the mill his mind might recover quicker. Taking the large joint of meat he found in the meat stasis unit, he smiled. A few slices would make a very acceptable sandwich, he thought and reached up to a rack of knives. The blade sank effortlessly into the dark brown meat, but Soval was dismayed to see blood seeping from the cut and dripping onto the work surface. As his knife sank deeper, the trickle of blood became a strong flow that ran down the blade and dripped onto the work surface, forming a red puddle beneath the dish. Unable to tear his gaze away, he remained transfixed as the dark brown colour of the cooked meat paled until it was raw and red, the white skin that now covered it marked with his own bloody fingerprints.

Leaping away in terror, he noticed a dismembered leg and recognised the rounded nub of bone where it had been ripped from the socket at the hip. As he stepped back in horror, his foot banged against something, which sent him sprawling backwards. He braced himself for an impact and ended up face to face with the same dead eyes that regarded him at the top of the stairs a few minutes previously. With a cry of horror, he scrabbled inelegantly away from the woman's corpse and covered his eyes with his hands. She still regarded him with dead eyes and he hoped the image was within his mind and not real.

"Go away," he screamed. "It's not real, go away." Forcing his mind to calm, he started counting backwards in sixes, then sevens, then eights. By giving his mind something concrete to do that would necessitate considerable focus, he hoped to prevent it from seeing the horrific hallucinations. Having lost his appetite, he decided to return to the medical bay and record his experience. In a closet in the research lab, he found another digital recorder like the one he left in the briefing room on deck four and sat down to record his experience. His record was concise and included not only the events as he experienced them, but his diagnosis as to their cause and how long they might continue. After searching the drugs locker for a sedative with which to calm himself, he found several substances that he might use should a patient present with similar symptoms and administered an injection of one of them into a vein in his left arm.

Soval knew that he would feel a little drowsy within a few minutes, so he went into the medical bay, lay down on one of the beds in the recovery ward and closed his eyes. Pulling the blanket up to his chin, he tried to get comfortable. As he turned over, he felt something bump into his arm and opened his eyes. A shriek of horror echoed around the medical bay as he leapt away and fell from the bed, landing in a heap on the floor. Still screaming, he scrambled to his feet and backed away, bumping into the edge of the next bed along. The severed head lay on his pillow and he knew for certain it had not been there moments before. There was no way he would have failed to notice it no matter how tired he was. Still shaking with horror, he tried to force his mind under control but his nerves were shot and he sobbed in fear.

With a huge effort of will, he forced his Doctor's sense to the forefront of his mind, swallowed hard, and examined the head. It was clearly a female child and bore similar features to the image of the woman whose throat he had been forced to witness being cut. Curious now, he leaned nearer to the head and realised that both it and the image of the woman were of the same race as his own. They were obviously from Arlenika Prime. The pale skin and white hair, the large round blue eyes of such an intense hue that other races find them mesmerising, they were very recognisable Arlenikan attributes.

"Well it's not surprising that I should hallucinate images of people from my own race. It's what is most familiar to me, so it stands to reason that my troubled mind would use images it is familiar with. Of course, since I'm a doctor, it's not too much of a stretch to believe that my mind would show me images of bodies cut up and dismembered. I've done countless operations and have cut into lots of bodies whilst operating on them. Yes, it's my mind trying to make sense of the memories it has temporarily lost. This is a good sign. It shows my memories are still there and trying to come back. I must expect this to continue for a while."

Once the image of the child's head faded, Soval sat back down on the bed and cradled his head in his hands. Despite knowing he was hallucinating and the probable cause of it, his heart clamoured in his chest and throbbed in his temples. The images were very real and terrifying and he was alone. Waves of loneliness washed over him unbidden and tears threatened at the corners of his eyes. As if hit by a bullet, his body arched back as a fresh wave of hallucinations took hold of his mind. This time he heard shouts, angry voices that threatened violence. When the images began, he found himself running through long grass that whipped at his legs and tried to trip him, his feet catching in the matted tussocks. Men were in pursuit, their angry shouts getting closer by the second and he quickly realised he had no hope of outrunning them. With a loud cry of anguish, Soval's head cleared and he found himself sitting on the floor of the medical bay clutching at the bed sheet that dangled from the side of the bed. Dropping his head into his hands, he sobbed loudly.

Groaning in pain, Soval awoke and took a few moments to realise where he was. Having fallen asleep on the floor beneath the bed in the medical bay, his hip was painful and his back, stiff. Wincing, he dragged himself to his feet and climbed into the bed, drawing the sheet right up to his chin as a child might clutch at a favourite blanket. He was about to close his eyes when the door burst open and he leapt to a sitting position in fright. The bed had gone. In its place was a soiled mattress on the stone floor of a cell that stank of urine. A group of angry faced men grabbed at his arms and dragged him from the stinking mattress to his feet, ignoring his screams. Suddenly the room went dark as many arms grabbed and flailed towards him, a hundred or more it seemed. He recoiled in horror but still they pawed and clawed at him as they growled and spat in anger, their words incomprehensible to his anguished senses.

The light exploded in his eyes, revealing the bodies before him. The same woman and a female child with the head he recognised from earlier. An infant boy completed the grisly trio and Soval gazed at them, horrified but transfixed at the carnage. All had been dismembered in a most inexpert fashion, he noticed and the woman's legs appeared to have been half hacked and half torn from the body. The female child's head was detached but lay almost in the right position above the neck, the gap making her neck seem oddly long. Some kind of wadded material was visible inside the infant boy's mouth and his arms were obviously broken, the white ends of bone that stuck through the bloody rents in the skin, testament to the most horrific torture imaginable.

"Please stop," he sobbed aloud. "I know why it's happening but I can't take this much longer. Please."

Without warning, it stopped and Soval found himself back in bed in the medical bay, the sheet clutched to his throat in a defensive gesture. Holding his breath, he waited for the next onslaught that would surely send him mad, but nothing happened. His forehead dripped with sweat and he wiped the sheet across it as he moaned long and slow, closing his eyes in a bid to calm himself.

"I don't know how much more of this I can take," he muttered as he climbed out of the bed and wandered over to the drinks dispenser. "Maybe if I write it all down it would help. It might act like therapy and help my mind to make sense of it. Yes, that's what I'll do." He went to the medical records computer, switched it on and spent the next hour outlining his hallucinations in meticulous detail. Once this was completed, he then read it aloud taking the role of therapist and asking questions which he would then answer as himself. This went on for a couple of hours until he was tired and hungry, so he made his way back up to deck five and returned to the kitchen where he successfully made himself a meal without incident.

With a full stomach, Soval felt much better and decided that what his mind needed was order. A strict schedule would occupy his mind as it struggled to retrieve the lost memories, allowing them to slip back into their proper place without his troubled consciousness fighting the process. Hoping this might lessen the hallucinations, he decided to draw up a cleaning schedule for the medical bay. The whole place needed to be tidied and scrubbed, all the instruments sterilised, the drugs locker inventoried, he would even change and wash the bed linens. Anything to occupy himself while his mind was struggling. Happy that he now had a positive plan of action, he returned to deck six and began immediately.

The isolation ward was first on his hit list and he had the beds stripped within ten minutes, the empty beds wiped with anti-bactericide and remade with fresh linen within another hour. With a bucket of chemical wash, he cleaned all the surfaces and washed the floor, before heading to the morgue. It was while doing an inventory of body bags that he had another couple of hallucinations. As he reached for another bag, he noticed the tell-tale shape of a body within, and backed away as the now familiar flush of fear coursed through him.

"No, I must not give in to it," he admonished himself. "It is just a hallucination." He strode forwards, grabbed the body bag and flung the top aside, expecting to find it empty as the hallucination faded under his assertive stance. The woman's impassive gaze regarded him accusingly and he backed away in horror, his hand going to his mouth instinctively.

"Why did you do it, Daddy?"

Soval swung around, startled out of his wits by the sudden voice behind him. The female child, very much alive with her head attached firmly to her body stood gazing at him, the infant boy on her hip. "What?" he said, before realising the stupidity of the remark.

"Why did you do it?"

Soval turned a full circle, expecting to meet whomever the child was referring to as Daddy, but there was no one else and the child's eyes were firmly fixed on his own. "Me? Oh, you've made a mistake. I'm not your Daddy. I'm a doctor. I can help you if you want me to."

"Daddy. Why, Daddy?" the girl begged as her image faded slightly, giving Soval a glimpse of the empty gurney behind her. The image regained solidity but only for a moment and she continued to fade and solidify repeatedly as he looked on in horror. For a moment, he wondered if the whole experience had not been a hallucination after all, but a haunting. The spectres of these two children appeared exactly like all the ghosts he had ever heard about. Although he had never contemplated whether he believed in such things or not, this was actually happening and he pondered the question now. Try as he might, he was unable to pretend they were not there. He tried several times, closing his eyes, counting to ten, then opening them again but they were still there. He tried counting to twenty before opening his eyes, then thirty but still they remained and asked the same question to which he had no answer.

"Did I do something bad, Daddy?" she asked as a tear formed at the corner of her left eye. "I'm sorry. Please don't be cross with us anymore. Please don't hurt Mummy again." She came towards him, her arms open wide to hug him and he backed away in terror. The thought of making physical contact with the spectre horrified him and although aware of the incongruity of that feeling, he was unable to change it. She was a little girl, whether dead, alive, or a figment of his troubled mind and was no threat to him. With this thought came a memory of her severed head as it lay on the pillow in his bed and he backed away, shaking his head.

"No. You were dead. I saw your head. You can't be standing here now all put back together again. Are you a ghost? Are you wandering in some spiritual way station unable to pass on due to having endured a violent death? Have I been witness to wicked hallucinations due to my amnesia, or am I haunted? Do you haunt this empty vessel? You must've been passengers on board and when whatever happened, happened, you were unable to pass on for some reason and now you're haunting the ship. Yes, that must be it. You're spectres of lives cut tragically short, but I am not your father and I cannot explain the reason for your awful predicament. I am sorry for you, child, but I am not who you mistake me for and I will not hug you. Please do not feel bad of me but I am as much a victim in this as you are. I am stuck here alone with no one except the spectre of a child who haunts me. Forgive me for my inability to give you aid. I will give thanks for your lives in the temple down the corridor if that will ease your spirits."

A noise caught Soval's attention and he turned from the spectres before him. The dead woman now stood behind him, naked and beautiful despite the multiple stab wounds that covered her abdomen and torso. Her breasts swayed slightly as she took a step towards him and he was horrified to feel his groin react.

"Why?" she demanded, her brow creasing into a frown. "Why?" She took another step towards him and he took another back.

"Daddy?" The voice from behind caught him by surprise and he spun around to find the spectre of the child, the infant still on her hip, walking towards him, her free arm outstretched. With the spectre of the child coming towards him and the reanimated corpse of who he presumed to be their mother advancing from his rear, he was unable to escape in the narrow confines between the two gurneys and he cried out in horror as his heart leapt in his breast. His last conscious thought before his mind ceased its panic and stilled for good, was the titillating way the woman's breasts swayed as she moved.

4

Tearan Lindo grunted his way through another hundred crunches before allowing himself the luxury of a shower and breakfast. He had awoken after a night of vivid dreams, after which a few precious memories filtered back and slotted into place. The fork paused halfway between his plate and his mouth as images exploded inside his mind. Instantly he was fifteen years old and standing in a long line of other boys his age, his parents standing amongst a crowd of others nearby. The line shuffled forwards as each boy reached the front, held out his wrist for his identity chip to be scanned, received a parcel containing pants, tunic and boots, and went to stand in a new line at the other side of the public square. Four similar lines of boys shuffled their way forwards, some faces smiling and excited, others frowning and fearful. At the end of their childhood, Arlenika Prime's most precious commodity did what they had done for countless generations; they gave their first seven years of manhood to the Arlenikan Security Force.

Arlenikan boys come of age at thirteen and join the military at fifteen, where they stay for seven years before returning to their families to make their way in life in whatever way they wish. They leave the loving safety of their parents' arms and join a new family, one that not only teaches them to become self sufficient and confident soldiers, but one that guides them through the emotional minefield that is the transition from boyhood to manhood. Joining the military is not the law for Arlenikan boys, but it is an accepted rite of passage that few wish to miss. Wide eyed boys leave their tearful parents and return seven years later 'grown men proud and true,' as the Arlenikan military song goes.

'Wipe your tears young man, fear not and cry no more.
Be brave my boy and save your tears for the dreadful hour of war.
Leave the weeping to your mother; it's seven long years for you.

When you return to her, you'll be a grown man proud and true.'

'Stand beside your brothers now, leave childhood things behind.
Stand straight and tall and find in each of them your peace of mind.
For each and every one of them is looking forward, as are you.
To coming home again one day a grown man proud and true.'

'These bright young eyes and steadfast feet, so eager to depart.
Although the pain of loss will dim the eyes, please son take heart.
You'll leave some brothers on the field; your heart will break in two.
Their spirits will return beside these grown men proud and true.'

'When you are far away from home, on field of war or peace.
Let not the memories of these seven long years of life decease.
But let the wisdom learned beside your brothers carry you
Every moment near and far, a grown man proud and true.'

Tearan's eyes welled up as he remembered and then sang the most famous Arlenikan military song of all. He was afraid that day when he stood in line and got his uniform alongside all the other boys. Together, all four hundred and seventeen of them stripped naked and donned the new pants, tunics and boots in front of the crowd of cheering fathers and sobbing mothers. After an inspiring speech by the man who would be their commanding officer and father figure for the entire seven years, they marched away leaving their piled clothes on the ground. The crowd of parents watched their children march away, not to meet them again for seven years, some never to see them alive again. The discarded clothes were left for the wind and weather to gradually wear away. When, after seven long years, the boys returned as grown men proud and true, they would go with their parents and collect what remained of their childhood garments. These would be saved in a special seven-year box that passed down the male line. The box gathered scraps of weathered fabric with each new generation of returning sons. Each male proudly placed his own scraps inside alongside those of his father, grandfather and many generations of the men who had endured the seven years before him.

Try as he might, he could not remember what had become of his seven-year box and hoped the memory would surface soon. Neither could he remember his parents' names, the images of their faces blurry and indistinct when he tried to force the memory forward. Growling with frustration, he reluctantly stopped pushing and relaxed. Maybe if he left it alone it would come back by itself like the memory of the day he joined the military did. Relieved that at last some memories were returning, he continued his breakfast and felt confident that before too long he would find his whole self again. He hoped that he might also remember what happened on board the ship, and was desperate for an explanation as to how he came to be there in the first place. As he finished his drink, a thought suddenly landed inside his mind and his eyes widened as he understood it.

"Of course. Shit, why didn't I think of that earlier?" He cursed aloud at not realising that a ship this size would have a full personnel manifest somewhere. Even if it were not possible to get the ship's main computers working, there might be personnel records in the medical bay. "People have allergies, illnesses, and some need regular drugs. The medical people are bound to have records of everyone aboard. Maybe there's a record of me there." Without further delay, he set off and took the stairs two at a time down to deck six. He decided to try the door marked, *'Medical Research and Scanning,'* first. It seemed the most likely place for medical records to be kept. As he checked the various machines, he realised something was off but did not understand what it was until he examined the body scanner and found several white hairs lying on the dark grey sheet.

"Someone's used this machine," he said as he peered at the hairs. "And that someone has hair like mine, which means there's another Arlenikan aboard." He then realised, as he searched the room with more focus, that things were a little different from when he had been there before. A chair moved here, a utensil moved there, hairs on the sheet and in a side cubicle, an unmade bed. It was a basic bed much like the one upstairs in the security room he now called his base, but the sheet was pulled aside and a hollow in the pillow gave testament to a head having lain there some time recently. There was no doubt he was not the only one aboard and he wondered if it might be the writer of the name on the wall in the engineering briefing room. "What was that name again? Mykus something I think. Maybe it's him."

Laying a hand on the butt of the gun at his hip, Tearan left and walked down the corridor.

'Medical Bay.' The bright yellow letters remained impassive and he frowned. If someone had set up home down here, he hoped they would prove to be friendly. He did not like the thought of remaining here alone forever, but he fancied the thought of having an armed psycho to avoid forever, even less. Taking the gun from its holster, he opened the door and marched in, kicking it so it flew back and hit the wall behind where anyone might be hiding ready to leap at him. More signs of habitation met his eyes. The door to a drug locker stood open. An injector lay on the floor beside it and Tearan noted the unpronounceable name on the drug phial attached to its top. Despite knowing he had no medical knowledge and would not know what the drug was for, he registered a feint flutter of recognition deep inside that was gone as quickly as it came. He frowned and wondered whether he had been given an injection recently or used this drug before. It was so maddening not being able to remember.

Laying the injector on a counter top, he wandered through a doorway into the operating theatre and stared in disbelief at the sight that greeted him.

"Holy shit," he cursed aloud at the writing scrawled over the walls. "This was definitely not here last time I was here." The words had obviously been written hurriedly, with little care taken to make them legible. Each line slanted down at one end and the words got smaller towards the end of each line. What was most surprising to Tearan was that it was written in Arlenikan. Despite this, the illegibility of the words made it difficult for him to read. From the little he made sense of, he gathered that someone was frightened of something that was only referred to as, 'them.' There was mention of bodies being cut up, a dead child and ghosts haunting relentlessly. "Whoa, what the hell was in that injector?" Another part talked about amnesia, and Tearan's eyebrows shot up in surprise. Someone was describing having no memories except knowing who and what he was. "Same here," he said aloud as he read on. Whoever it was seemed to be having a bad time with the amnesia, if all the stuff about ghosts and bodies was to be believed.

"If it's the engineer guy, he's not going to be much use to me with that level of paranoia going on." Tearan shook his head as he went through into the small ward. One of the beds had clearly been slept in, the sheet hung limp, half on the floor and the small bedside locker lay on its side, spilling its contents everywhere. "Ghosts I presume?" he muttered and left the room. The next room down the corridor was the morgue and he grasped the handle to let himself in and then hesitated. A sudden frisson of fear coursed through him and then was gone before he could try to understand it. Shaking his head, he pushed the door and entered to find it very much the same as he remembered from his previous visit. There was nothing that seemed out of the ordinary, so he left.

The isolation ward was not the same as he remembered. A huge cart labelled, 'bed linen – soiled,' stood by the door and he knew it had not been there during his last visit. Sniffing, he registered the strong chemical smell that hung in the air and wrinkled his nose. "I guess the psycho is a clean freak." Knowing the only remaining room on deck six was the non-denominational temple, he registered the same flutter of emotion as when he last visited it. The room was unchanged but he decided to linger for a few minutes to try to get a grip on this new feeling. The conviction that faith was somehow important to him again filled his heart and he thought back to the new memories of the day he left his family to join the military. There was no religious aspect to those memories but he would swear in any court anywhere in the galaxy at that moment, that he was a man with a strong faith. Growling in frustration, he shook his head and left, heading for the stairs back up to deck three and the safe confines of his new base.

At deck four, he hesitated before continuing up the stairs to deck three and looked down the corridor to his left. Although he had been here when he did his initial sweep of the whole ship, something nagged at him and he felt compelled to have another linger for a while. There was clear evidence of someone having spent a lot of time in the main engineering section. Tools, goggles, and some kind of harness lay on the mezzanine by the engine housing. Panels had been removed from various consoles and a carton of digital components lay on its side, spilling its contents onto the floor.

"Someone's been fiddling," he muttered. "Probably the engineer guy. Maybe he's fixing it so we can find out what's happened. Where the fuck is he though?" In the engineering briefing room, he got another surprise that gave him a partial answer at least to one question. Up on the wall by the drinks dispenser, underneath where he and Mykus Romin had written their names, an arrow was drawn. Following its direction, Tearan's eyes fell upon the digital recorder that lay on top of the drinks dispenser. Smiling, he snatched it up and switched it on.

"Hi there. I'm Dr Soval Arma. I'm a medical practitioner and I'm also alive. Anyone have any idea what has happened here?"

"Dr Soval Arma? That must be the psycho from the medical bay. So our only doctor is a crazy loon who's convinced he's haunted by cut up bodies. Just my luck." Clicking over to record, Tearan greeted the doctor.

"Hi there, Dr Arma, Tearan Lindo here. Sorry, I've no idea at all. I have started getting my memories back though. How about you guys, and where are you?"

It sounded like a friendly enough greeting, one that invited further interaction without being gushing or taking needless risks. He had not exactly hidden his own presence, having written as much on the entry door to the security room so he was not being anti-social. There was no more to do but wait until someone decided to answer, so he would check back a couple of times per day. Back at the stairs, he studied the map of the ship. Something made him frown every time he looked at it and so far, he could not understand why. All he knew was that something about the lowest two decks dismayed him. Something was off down there and as it had not gone away or lessened at all since he awoke, he decided to pay another visit. With a resigned shrug, he trudged down the stairs.

The red glow from the flashing warning above the shuttle bay door was visible from half way down the stairs and he was suddenly glad there was no accompanying alarm to drive him crazy. The space beyond the door was huge, it seemed a shame that it was going to waste and Tearan knew he must try to get those bay doors closed. The map of the ship showed the entire deck to be taken up with the shuttle bay, prep room, and cargo hangar, making him wonder if it had been a freighter or merchant vessel. The size of the shuttle bay seemed a little excessive for the size of the rest of the ship and this was the sort of incongruity that bothered him. Although the ship had eight decks, each was compact and he estimated the crew to be around fifty or so maximum.

Next door in the shuttle bay prep room, Tearan stripped down to his underwear and donned one of the suits that hung along the wall. It was all very familiar, his fingers knew what they were doing as they fastened clips, checked hose connectors and adjusted straps. He was again convinced that he had done this before but the memory remained elusive, the imagery lying just out of sight beyond the fog. Once fully installed within the suit, he clipped his hose to the breather unit outlet, then put on the helmet and switched on the visor display.

'WARNING – BREATHER UNIT MALFUNCTION – DO NOT USE.' The warning flashed up right in the centre of his vision, this time accompanied by a high pitched buzzer just in case he failed to notice the bright red flashing capital letters.

"Shit and fuck," he hissed as he switched off the visor display and began to extricate himself from the suit. He was sweating with the effort by the time he sat down in his underwear to catch his breath and had gone through his entire vocabulary of curses and swear words at least twice. The suit had been a little snug for him, which made getting in and out something of an effort. The next suit was slightly larger and far easier to get into but his heart sank when once again the warning flashed across his visor.

'WARNING – BREATHER UNIT MALFUNCTION – DO NOT USE.'

As each unit and suit were made in one piece, it meant getting out of the suit and putting on another each time. There was no way for him to find out if the unit was functioning until he had completely donned the suit. He did try putting on a helmet without the suit and swore when the visor display announced that he had failed to fool the system.

'WARNING – SUIT NOT PROPERLY SECURED – CALL FOR ASSISTANCE.'

There was no way to avoid having to put on each suit in turn before finding out if the breather unit worked or not and by the time he took off the last of the dozen suits, each one had failed. The problems ranged from breather unit malfunctions, helmets not securing properly, perished gaskets in glove/arm connectors, damaged hoses, and various other vague 'suit malfunction' problems.

"This is ridiculous," he yelled aloud and thumped a fist onto the wall. "There's a dozen suits here and not one of them is working? What kind of hayseed operation were they running here?" After screaming in frustration and thumping the wall several more times, he sat down and put his head in his hands. When he had calmed down, he dressed and thought about the problem as calmly as he could. "Okay so none of the suits are working. Maybe the crew took all the ones that worked as they left the ship. Ships always have more suits than crew in case of damage, so it's not unusual that there are a dozen here not working. Okay umm, think. C'mon think. None of them works but the reasons they don't work are all different. I know I can't repair any of them, even though I can feel recognition for wearing and operating a suit, I feel nothing at the thought of repairing one." Before he cursed with frustration, a thought occurred to him. "I can't, but maybe the engineer guy can. Mykus something or other, he might be able to repair one." With renewed hope, he went along the line of suits and grabbed one. "Perished gaskets at the wrist/arm connectors would seem to be the simplest to fix. We'll try this one first."

With the suit tucked under one arm, Tearan strode along to the cargo hangar and was again impressed by the size of it. Easily twice the size of the shuttle bay, the space was filled with carefully stacked cargo bins. He climbed into one of the hover carts and took a minute to familiarise himself with the controls. After ten minutes, he switched it off and climbed down, satisfied that he would have no difficulty in reaching even the highest of the cargo bins in the stacks. Hidden on the floor of one of the other hover carts was a digital cargo manifest, which he was delighted to find was fully functional. Sadly, there were no space suits amongst the cargo, but everything else he might ever need was there. He kept hold of the device and headed back to the stairs to check out deck eight.

Leaving the suit and digital manifest by the stairs, Tearan descended to deck eight, the map of deck seven catching his eye as he did so. His left foot stopped in mid air as his eyes widened in understanding.

"What the fuck?" he said aloud as he stepped back to the map and gave it his full focus. The plan of deck seven showed the cargo bay, the prep room and cargo hangar, but what he had not noticed before was the size of each of the spaces. Thinking back to when he had entered the cargo hangar a few minutes previously, he remembered thinking how it was around twice the size of the shuttle bay.

"The map is wrong," he muttered as he put a finger to it and traced the outline of the cargo bay. "It's bigger on the map than it is really. Much bigger actually, almost four times the size of the shuttle bay, at a guess. Holding out his middle finger, he measured the two rooms as they appeared on the map and sure enough, the cargo hangar was four times the size of the shuttle bay. Running down the corridor, he flung open the door to the cargo bay and entered, turning around a full circle to get as good a feel for the place as possible. He paced it out, then ran back to the shuttle bay and paced along the corridor. It was a very rough measurement, but he proved it to his own satisfaction. The cargo hangar was only twice the size of the shuttle bay, not four times as on the map.

"I wonder why that should be?" he mused as he sat down on the top step. Deck plans wouldn't be made with such glaring errors. I guess they decided to cordon off some of the available space and use it for something else, maybe whatever their emergency was made the decision necessary. Maybe the survivors are hiding in there." He leapt up and ran back to the cargo hangar and over to the far wall. If the crew had suffered some emergency and had time to construct a false wall behind which they were still hiding, then he wanted to know why they left him alone. Running the length of the wall, he yelled at the top of his voice.

"Hey in there. Hello, can anyone hear me? I know you're in there behind a false wall. You left me behind, assholes. Hey. Hello. Fucking answer me you morons." He ran up and down and yelled his lungs out as he tried to get a close up view of the wall. Shelving stacked with cargo bins ran the length of the entire room along the wall, preventing him from getting right up to it, but there were no obvious doorways or hatches visible. In order to examine the wall in detail, he would need to unload the whole length of shelving. "Okay. If that's what it takes, then that's what I'll do. It's not as if I don't have the time now is it? If I can get the engineer guy, Mykus, to fix the gaskets in that suit, I can throw stuff I won't need out through the bay doors and make space for the stuff on those shelves. There's loads of empty crew quarters and extra space in briefing rooms and along the corridors for all the other stuff too." With this new plan firmly set in his mind, Tearan approached the stairs and regarded the map. The ship was oval, with the power coils, exhaust and heat dump units stuck to the sides three quarters the way down to the rear end of the oval shape. Subsequently, decks four and five were the biggest, being situated around the widest point of the oval, and each subsequent deck both above and below was slightly smaller. Deck eight was the hazardous waste store and according to his estimation of the map, was approximately two-thirds the size of the cargo hangar.

After pacing out the hazardous waste store, he confirmed to himself that the room was approximately a quarter the size of the cargo hangar. This is something the engineer needs to see, he decided. One thing about the wall struck him immediately. If it had been constructed as a result of some emergency, then the builders were top class craftsmen. There was nothing that pointed to it having been put up in a hurry. What he could see of it looked as solid as the others and matched them in appearance. If it were not for the discrepancy on the map, he would never have noticed.

Glad that he had allowed his instincts to guide his actions, Tearan returned to the stairs and climbed to deck seven, collected the suit and digital manifest, then climbed to deck four. In the briefing room, he dumped the suit onto the table, went over to the wall and picked up the digital recorder.

"Mykus, it's Tearan Lindo here. Could you repair the wrist and arm connector gaskets on the suit please. I want to get the shuttle bay doors closed but none of the suits down there work. If you can't fix this one, there are others down there. I need one functioning suit so please help if you can. If we can get just one suit working, I can get in there and close those bay doors and we can then check out those shuttles. Maybe we could take off in one and rescue ourselves. I have made a discovery about the ship too and would appreciate your help. Can we meet up? Find me on deck three, in the security room. Thanks."

There was little more to do without the help of Mykus, so he picked up the digital manifest and headed back up to his base to make himself a meal. As he ate, he studied the manifest and thought about how to rearrange the stores. If he never gained access to the shuttle bay, he would need to find somewhere to store everything on that entire stack of shelves in the cargo hangar. From the manifest, all the food and items he would be using the most, were on the first two rows of shelving. He decided to move as much of the food as possible to the main kitchen, dining room, recreation room, and neighbouring crew quarters. He would do the same with cleaning materials, toiletries and anything he would use on a day to day basis. Anything to do with mechanics or ship repair and maintenance, he would take to engineering. Mykus could have input on that and anything that the two of them deemed unnecessary could be stored away in other areas of the ship. That would leave the first two shorter rows of shelving empty to receive everything from the much longer end wall shelving. He could then dismantle the racks and get close up to the wall. Even if it turned out to be a waste of time, it would give him something to do and it would be helpful having food and supplies a bit nearer to hand.

Two hours later, Tearan puffed as he ran up the stairs two at a time. The eight decks of the ship with their connecting staircases made an excellent running track that he took little time in making full use of. The ship had two staircases situated on opposite sides of the oval hull and Tearan used one to descend, the other to ascend. Three circuits of each deck before descending to the next, then the same on the way up made a very effective cardio vascular workout. After repeating the whole procedure five times, he returned to base to lift some weights in the small gymnasium set up in a corner of the main area. Realising that he felt at home here in the security room, he guessed that his role in the Inter-Galactic Elite Command was largely security based. He had discovered that not only was he totally at ease with guns but had an eye for detail, was a good strategist, was self disciplined, fit and strong. Not a bad set of qualities, he thought as he stepped into the shower and gave himself up to the pleasure of the hot water cascading down his body.

Pinpoints of light stared back at him as he gazed out through the viewing screen on the bridge. Having yielded to the temptation to revisit, he sat in the Captain's chair and stared out into the void. Feeling tiny in such a huge universe, vulnerability gripped him and pricked at his eyes as he allowed thoughts of what might happen to him if he never got off the ship, to linger at the forefront of his mind. He was well aware that all sorts of dangers lurk ready to catch even the most experienced space traveller.

Despite the mountains of food in storage, no matter the warmth or safety afforded him by the life support systems, a rogue comet or wandering asteroid means a horrible death at any time. Although the life support systems all appeared to be working now, any one of them could go wrong and he would have no idea how to fix it. If Mykus were unable to keep those of the ship's systems that appeared to be functioning, in working order, it would be a nasty end for them. Now that there was a doctor alive somewhere, they need not worry about minor injuries or illness, but if anything happened to him, neither he nor Mykus would be of use. The dangers were many but he knew almost nothing about how to overcome most of them, so he decided to keep his mind from dwelling on them. He would concentrate on more immediate needs and for the moment, that was rearranging the cargo hangar. Returning to the security room, he lay down and was asleep within twenty minutes.

5

Tovis Kerral awoke and realised within five seconds that something was wrong. Not the kind of wrong that brings a disquieting knowledge of something forgotten, but the kind that makes you sick to the stomach. This was the kind of wrong that keeps you awake at night listening to the sound of your own mind worrying. It was the sort of wrong that makes you wish you were five years old again so the grown ups will sort out the problem. His head throbbed but that was not what worried Tovis. Hangovers were no strangers to him and he endured them all, most of them without complaint knowing his own over indulgence was the cause. No, this head throbbing was the kind you get when you have been very ill and reminded him of the time he accidentally ate three Jurgmata fruits and almost died. The coma had lasted three weeks, or so he had been told by those responsible for his care at the time. When he finally awoke, his head throbbed night and day for another month; a constant drilling that drove right through his temples and almost drove him mad. He hoped this headache was not going to last that long. Reaching up with both hands, he closed his eyes and massaged his temples for over a minute before opening them again.

Without changing position, Tovis examined his immediate environment, which reminded him of a bedroom in a swanky hotel. It was definitely not the type of place in which he was used to spending the night, not in his line of work. Most of the time, he found himself having to sleep out in the open, in dirty alleyways surrounded by garbage and piss. Sometimes he bedded down in the rusting hulks of ancient discarded hover vehicles left to rot on vacant building lots. Once, he spent a night in a hole in the ground in a rocky valley on Serkulon 4. The open air was his usual bedding place, he was used to torrential rain, snow, howling gales, and burning sun. On several occasions, wild animals chased him, bugs ate him alive, and he once got soaked to the skin after spending three days and nights up to his waist in sewage. He long ago stopped counting the number of times various law enforcers, military guards, all sorts of personal bodyguards and hired muscle tried to chase him down. His chosen profession had made all of those things familiar and comfortable. Waking up in a high end hotel room was right out of his experience and put him immediately on his guard.

In one swift movement, Tovis sat up and swung his legs to the floor. His head swam sickeningly and he closed his eyes as he waited for the room to cease its swaying. Although unable to see the movement, he felt it inside his head and his stomach. When he felt brave enough, he opened his eyes and noticed a jug of water and a glass on the nightstand by the bed. He drank two full glasses straight down and felt immediately better. With his head clearing, he was able to think more about his immediate situation and instinct drove his hand to where he knew his gun should be. He was dressed in nothing but his underwear and panic rose up as he realised he was also unarmed. Leaping up, he frantically searched the bed, ripping the sheets from the mattress and tossing them aside in a vain attempt to locate the weapon that had become an extension of his own body. That gun was now ingrained into his personal body image, so much so that he felt lost and disorientated without it. For the past twenty-two years he had worked, carried, ate, and slept with at least one gun. To find himself suddenly without one was akin to having cut off a limb.

Thinking he was obviously in custody of some sort, he did a circuit of the room, taking in as much detail as possible. The bed was a quality piece of furniture, as was everything else. It was crafted rather than simply assembled. Running his fingers across the sheet, the texture told him it had been woven thread by thread, rather than extruded as a pulp and freeze dried as was usual with domestic linens. A person had made this item, not a robotic manufacturing plant. Tovis realised that whoever this room belonged to was seriously wealthy and powerful. Woven sheets cost not only money but someone's time, which itself requires influence on the part of the buyer. Someone with the influence to make a skilled craftsman take the time to weave bed linen by hand was someone with frightening power. People with that level of power are few and far between, and seldom needed the services of someone like Tovis Kerral. A man with that level of power did not need to pay a hired gun to sort out his problems.

Tovis thought back to everyone with whom he had come into contact during his career, but knew of no more than three men with that sort of money, power, and influence. One of them was definitely dead, the killing being witnessed by Tovis himself. Another was in Laksmay Penitentiary for fraud and conspiracy to commit mass murder, his trial having been broadcast over the media galaxy wide. The third was alleged to have died when the luxury inter-galactic liner he was holidaying aboard, crashed after a bomb ripped a hole in its belly. He then tried to think back to who he may have pissed off sufficiently to warrant imprisonment in such luxury and again hit the same problem. Although the list of people who might have cause to want him in custody was a long one, those that would have access to custody of this level of luxury were not only few, they were non existent.

Tovis wandered around the room, opened cupboards, pulled out draws and examined everything closely. The closets and drawers were filled with clothes that he guessed would fit him perfectly. After picking out pants, shirt and boots, he dressed and went through to the small bathroom. It was compact but the highest quality and offered him a shower, basin and toilet. Men's washing necessities were artfully arranged on a shelf and thick towels and robe hung from hooks on the wall. Zipping himself up after taking a pee, he wandered back through to the bedroom, angry that his search had yielded no weapons, and realised something important. There was no window. This was odd and he frowned.

"No window. That's weird. What kind of hotel room has no window?" His mind dwelt on the question and a few possible answers came. "An underground one won't have windows. A room they don't want me escaping from won't have them either. They might not want me to be able to identify where I am. Maybe it's built into a mountain like the homes on Driminos 7; they don't have any windows. Perhaps it's on a space ship. If this were a high end liner, it might explain the luxury in the room." Another door stood to his right and he approached it, looking for the locking mechanism. A touchpad was fixed to the left of the door, about half way up. On a small shelf by the door lay a key card on a cord and he stuffed it into his pocket. He stood for long moments, the furrows across his brow deepening as he tried to work out what was going on. With a shrug, he shook his head and approached the door. "I guess I'm expected to at least try and escape," he muttered as he slapped his hand to the pad.

With a swish, the door opened, taking Tovis by surprise and he stepped back in alarm. Expecting to be set upon by something with huge muscles and an angry sneer, he readied himself but nothing happened.

"What the fuck's going on, is this some kind of test or something?" he half whispered, half muttered aloud as he crept toward the still open door. The number ten was painted on the door in bright yellow letters, and corridors swept away in both directions, gently curving away out of sight and telling him that wherever he was, it was a curved structure. Deciding that his first priority was to know who was keeping him here and why, he called out and announced his presence.

"Hello, anybody here? I'm awake and hungry. Nice sheets by the way, classy pad. Hello?" He listened for over a minute before repeating the procedure, and after three minutes spent calling out and receiving no reply, he looked both ways and decided to go to the right. Thirty minutes later, his tour ended, having partially solved the mystery of his location. The view from the large observation lounge window gave him chills, but not because he was worried about being in space. It was the fact that he had not seen evidence of anyone else being aboard that worried him. The size of what he learned from the map on the wall was deck two, indicated a large crew, but he had neither met nor seen evidence of anyone. A full search of the ship was obviously his first job, so he headed back to the first set of stairs he came across and climbed to the top.

An hour later, Tovis sat down in the dining room on deck five and sipped his drink. A quick reconnoitre of the entire ship proved he was alone. He also discovered that apart from the life support systems, nothing on the ship was functioning. He could eat, drink, enjoy hot showers, and be warm but he was not allowed to watch a movie or start the ship's engine. Music was available, as were the gaming tables, and the medical bay, but he could not use the navigation station or call for help on the comms. Although seemingly trivial, the non-functioning vidicom screen intrigued him and he found his mind unable to let it go.

"Why can I listen to music but not watch a vidicom movie? Neither of them would help me escape, learn where I am, who has captured me, or why. Why are movies out of bounds but not music?" The more he thought about it, the more strange this point seemed but he knew deep in his gut that it was a relevant point. "It's not right. There's something about it that might be the key to all this." The vidicom screen hung suspended from the ceiling by a system of pneumatic cables. Press a button on the remote control and it descended. Press another button and it retracted again. A separate computerised unit held the movie library data, and was programmed to respond only to its dedicated screen and no other. Tovis wandered over and picked up the movie library console.

It took an hour and a half, with three trips to the engineering storeroom for tools, before Tovis sat back and scratched his head. Before him, carefully laid out on the table, were the constituent parts of the movie library console and in his hand, the tiny digital component with the broken wire that he knew prevented the unit from sending any signal to its dedicated screen. Peering through the high magnification goggles, he frowned. During his years as a gun for hire, there were times when part of his job entailed information gathering, and he had gleaned considerable electrical engineering skill. He had a natural skill for taking apart and cannibalising almost anything that was not purely mechanical and he was able to put it back together in a totally different way from its intended function. He grinned to himself as he remembered the time when he managed to make a working comms unit from a hover bike engine, a standard Unicom headset, and a stolen law enforcer's personal data recording device. He could cobble together anything from a pile of what most other people would call junk, and although it would not be pretty, it would function reasonably well. These skills had saved his own neck on several occasions and he was glad of them. The intense blue eyes gazed through the goggles at the component in his hands, and his experience made him frown.

"This wire's been cut," he muttered as he took off the goggles and rubbed his eyes. "But why?"

There was not a shred of doubt in his mind that the wire had been deliberately cut, his knowledge and skill was without question. Why would someone wish to prevent him from watching a few movies? Where was the harm? Shaking his head in frustration, he went back to the engineering storeroom for a replacement component. After two hours of rummaging through crates and boxes and a trip down to the main cargo hangar, he lost patience and ripped the engineering storeroom computer apart. Twenty minutes later he was watching ancient creatures wreak havoc after being accidentally released from a research facility and felt justly proud of his accomplishment. Two-thirds the way through the movie, the hero was caught with the beautiful heroine and needed to summon help from his band of brave cohorts. The comms on their shuttle was damaged so the hero was forced to scavenge for parts with which to repair it. Tovis sat bolt upright, the smile falling from his lips. "Of course, that's it. I can try repairing the ship's comms and call for help. Thanks, man," he grinned at the blue eyed muscle bound hero on the screen.

It took him seconds to rip the panelling from the side of the comms station on the bridge of the ship and he swallowed hard when he saw what lay behind. This was unlike anything he had encountered before; he had never attempted to fix a space ship's comms unit and he almost changed his mind. "All comms units work on the same principle. All I need to do is transmit a signal that can move through space and be picked up by a receiver. I need a transmitter with an antenna, that's all. It's not complicated. Keep it simple." Tovis always talked to himself when focussing on something important, he found it helped him concentrate in times of high stress. Now he hoped it would help him ignore the blinding array of wires and components that lay behind the panelling. Bit by bit, he slowly worked his way into the body of the comms station, taking it apart piece by piece and laying them aside carefully so he would be able to put it all back together again. Once he began to recognise components and make educated guesses as to their function, he could formulate ideas as to what the rest was for. After what seemed like the entire day buried head and shoulders into the body of the comms station, he finally found what he needed. Like a road map, now he knew exactly where he was in relation to where he needed to be, he could work out the best route to get there.

Now he knew where to begin, he extricated himself from the comms station and rolled his neck around. Having banged his head several times and now with a stiff neck and tight shoulders, he decided to have a rest and something to eat. On his way down to deck five and the kitchen, he stopped at deck three and remembered having discovered the security room, onto whose door a message had been scrawled in marker pen.

'Inter-Galactic Elite Command, Unit 389C4 Headquarters. T Lindo Commanding Officer.'

That message gave Tovis valuable information that told him something about this new and strange situation. Despite having once been the main security room on board, it had been taken over by someone called Lindo and used for his own purpose. The scrawling of names and designations onto a door was something he had seen done many times, but always by forces who had overthrown their current authority figures. If that room were designed to be used by Lindo, it would have been painted on in the same bright yellow lettering as the word, 'Security.' This Lindo was obviously not one of the original members of the crew and Tovis wondered if he was part of the cause of whatever had happened to the ship. Another thing his deck-by-deck inspection brought to light was that he was not the only person alive. Lindo was another, as was an Engineer called Mykus Romin and a Doctor named Soval Arma. These last two were possibly useful and Tovis decided to try to locate them before finding T Lindo, whom he was unsure of. He had seen the names scrawled onto the wall in the briefing room on deck four and listened to the messages on the recording device. Whatever it was T Lindo thought he had found out about the ship intrigued him.

He toyed with the idea of adding his own message, but hesitated. Experience taught him the benefit of remaining unseen for as long as possible, and he was not about to abandon what life taught him, at least until he was able to re-arm himself. Guessing that the security room now claimed by this T Lindo would contain arms, he wondered how to gain entry. The laser pipe connector felt comfortably heavy in his grasp as he hefted it and tested its weight. A jab to any exposed skin would be agonisingly painful and in close combat was a formidable weapon. Deciding to front it out and approach unarmed in the hope of engendering trust, he walked up to the security room door and knocked.

After several knocks and shouts received no reply, he wondered whether to go in uninvited. On a whim, he retrieved his own key card from his pocket and slammed it into the slot. The door opened with a swish and Tovis hefted the laser pipe connector, holding it in front of himself in a defensive gesture. Leaning forward, he peered through the open door before stepping through.

"Tearan Lindo? Hello, anyone home? I came to introduce myself to a fellow survivor. Hello?" After assuring himself that no one could possibly have failed to hear his calls, he lowered the pipe connecter a little and entered further into the room. Walking into each area of the security section, it was obvious that someone was using the rooms as a base and living quarters and Tovis assumed it was T Lindo as per the message on the outside of the door. He frowned as he thought of that message; he had never heard of the Inter-Galactic Elite Command before. If he did not know of them, they must be extremely secret. "Probably blacker than black ops," he muttered as he opened a locker and gazed upon an array of guns and ammunition. "Whoa, no wonder Lindo set up home in here. I'm sure he's not going to mind if I borrow a couple of these and if he does, tough break."

Once armed, Tovis felt much more secure and able to think straight. He wandered through a door and found himself in a firing range and was tempted to spend a few minutes with his new acquisitions, but did not want Lindo to come back and find him not only having helped himself but enjoying what he had stolen. That would not be a pleasant meeting, he decided so he left. As he walked to the door, something caught his attention in the corner of his eye. It was no more than a slight movement of shadow in the already gloomy room. With practiced ease, he swung around, drawing both guns and prepared to fire but found himself alone. Blood pulsed in his ears with the adrenaline that coursed through his body but Tovis remained in operation mode, years of experience and practice making him an expert in his field. Reminding himself that this was not yet a situation like the ones that earned him a good living over the years, he relaxed slightly.

"Who's there? Lindo, is that you?" he called again but got no reply. There was nowhere in the room for anyone to hide, so he headed towards the door back into the main security area. Twenty feet from the door, the sound of boot steps in the room beyond, a slight squeak of leather boot and tap of heel, together with two shadow feet that walked past the gap at the bottom of the door. His heart leapt in his breast and he had to acknowledge that he felt spooked at the weird way this person was evading him. It was almost as if he was being played with and that was annoying. Experience told him it was probably not a good idea to go through the door without announcing himself, especially as this was not his own territory, so he called out again before heading towards the door and stepping through boldly, a smile ready and waiting.

Two minutes later, another search of the security section revealed he was alone and he frowned. "There was someone here. There was a shadow under the door and I heard footsteps. So where the fuck are they?" The main door was shut and made an audible swishing noise when opening and closing, so he also knew whoever his mysterious prowler was did not leave the room that way. Deciding that there must be a secret panel or doorway somewhere, Tovis thought it would probably be best if he left. His pockets loaded down with spare cells for the pair of stolen guns, he left and headed back to the stairs.

Once he had managed to make himself an acceptable meal, he sat down and thought about his situation. What he needed were lists. Tovis loved lists, they helped him keep his priorities in order, helped him focus when things were dangerous, which was quite often when working as a hired gun. Some people called him an assassin, but he did not like that title. It was inaccurate for a start, for often there was no cause for him to kill anyone. Sometimes he only needed to rough someone up a bit, break a few bones here and there to get what he wanted. Most of his jobs entailed threatening someone with violence until they gave up information, money, or something else of that nature, but now and again he was hired to play the role of 'karma fairy' as he put it. Rich folks tend to hold grudges, he thought as he ate, which always means a good payday for him. People tend not to complain about the cost when passion is coursing through their veins.

People's need for vengeance afforded Tovis Kerral a good lifestyle. One such job usually paid five times as much as one of his 'information gathering with menaces' jobs ever did and it was just such a job that got him into the business. Back then, he was hired security for a gem mine owner on Lowembral 2. His boss paid well but often hinted to Tovis that he would like him to give services beyond his official job description. When the mine owner's daughter was raped, her father offered Tovis a huge sum to pay the guy back and he accepted. Once he had stepped over that line, it was impossible for him to return and although he had never wanted to end up doing that kind of work, he did try to stick to some sort of moral code.

A few jobs had been turned down flat and Tovis carried the scars to prove it. When you're a hired gun, the people who offer you jobs tend not to like it when you turn them down and there are always more guys with lower moral standards willing to take your place. Right back at the beginning of his shadowy career, he decided never to take a job that involved violence to anyone he considered a good guy, women, children, or anything that would result in innocent people suffering hardship. More times than he was happy with, Tovis had been approached by jilted husbands or lovers wanting him to kill the offending women, and one wanted their year old twins killed alongside her. Another, the owner of a water treatment equipment manufacturer who had been beaten to a huge contract by a rival firm, asked him to poison the water in a large reservoir that would mean thousands of people would have died, so the rival would get the blame. Tovis was shot for turning that job down and almost lost a leg. Six months later, after several operations and painful rehab, he enjoyed paying him back and later heard that his employees were very happy when their boss disappeared while out sailing one summer day.

Tovis knew there was a large price on his head and sometimes wished his life had gone in a different direction. There were a couple of occasions he had been tempted to hand himself in to the law enforcers, but he knew he would probably end up with the death penalty, which would not allow him to make any sort of amends. Secretly, he blamed his childhood for his later life going off the rails. Although born on Arlenika Prime to Arlenikan parents, they were young and ill equipped emotionally to care for a child and handed him over to the authorities to be cared for. Eventually, he ended up in Deep Space Orphanage 1740, where he remained until his fourteenth birthday, when they set him up with the statutory three years life skills training. Despite knowing why his parents had given him up and that it ensured he was well cared for, he still felt abandoned and angry and probably always would.

When he finished eating, he thought back to his last conscious memory before waking up alone in a strange room inside a strange and empty space ship. The last thing he remembered was waiting by the side of a night time street for his contact to show up with payment for the job he had completed. After successfully bribing the cute red head with a large amount of money to keep quiet about who the father of her child really was, he was waiting for the politician's personal assistant to arrive with the rest of the money he was owed. Tovis always insisted on half the money when he was hired, with the rest on completion and it always worked for him. He did not remember if the man ever turned up, for his memory became blank while he was waiting for him and his next awareness was waking up in the room on board the ship.

From out of nowhere, his reminiscences vanished as he became aware of the heavy presence of someone behind him. Time seemed to slow as Tovis registered the subtle feeling of someone's energy having entered his own body's energy field and reached for his guns. In one smooth movement, he rose from the chair, sending it flying to one side with a kick as he turned. He stood, both guns ready as he stared at the empty dining room and waited for his breathing to calm. After turning a full circle, he searched the kitchen and entire dining room area, but found himself as alone as ever.

"What the fuck is going on here?" he whispered aloud. His heart thudded in his breast and he took long slow breaths to calm it. "Either someone is fucking with me, or this ship is haunted." Not being a believer in the supernatural, he dismissed that option right off and chose to assume someone was playing with his nerves. "It's probably whoever brought me here trying to freak me out." Guessing that some rich businessman or influential politician was laughing his balls off watching the whole thing on hidden cameras, he raised one finger and turned another full circle to make sure wherever the hidden cameras were, the asshole got the message.

The hot water was pleasant to his stiff shoulders and neck, so he allowed himself extra time to enjoy the shower. Having decided to use the room he awoke in as his own quarters, he secured the door by taking the key card slot apart and disconnecting one of the wires. It would not open without him first reconnecting the wire, so no one would be able to gain entry and murder him as he slept. After a few hours' sleep, he would begin trying to fix the ship's comms system and hope to be able to send a message to get help. He had many contacts to call on for a favour, so he would be able to avoid having to call the authorities who might recognise him. Even if he were not able to get anyone to help him out, he would address the problem if and when it arose. For now, he needed some sleep.

6

Mykus frowned as he listened to the contents of the recording device he found on top of the drinks dispenser in the engineering briefing room. Three new messages had appeared.

"Hi there. I'm Dr Soval Arma. I'm a medical practitioner and I'm also alive. Anyone have any idea what has happened here?"

"Hi there, Dr Arma, Tearan Lindo here. Sorry, I've no idea at all. I have started getting my memories back though. How about you guys, and where are you?"

"Mykus, it's Tearan Lindo here. Could you repair the wrist and arm connector gaskets on the suit please. I want to get the shuttle bay doors closed but none of the suits down there work. If you can't fix this one, there are others down there. I need one functioning suit so please help if you can. If we can get just one suit working, I can get in there and close those bay doors and we can then check out those shuttles. Maybe we could take off in one and rescue ourselves. I have made a discovery about the ship too and would appreciate your help. Can we meet up? Find me on deck three, in the security room. Thanks."

A space suit sat on the briefing room table and Mykus went over to examine it. The wrist/arm connector gaskets Tearan said, so he took the connectors apart and examined them. They were fine as far as he could tell and he frowned. Taking off his pants, shirt, and boots, he donned the suit and switched on the visor display.

'WARNING – WRIST/ARM CONNECTOR GASKETS PERISHED – DO NOT USE.'

Sure enough, the suit claimed the gaskets were faulty. With a shrug, Mykus took off the suit, dressed, and wandered next door to the storeroom. Whoever had been responsible for overseeing the engineering storeroom should have been sacked, Mykus thought as he wandered around the untidy room and decided to rearrange everything when he had the time. After twenty minutes, he found a carton of gaskets and ripped it open, took two and walked back to the briefing room. Fitting them took no more than a couple of minutes and when he donned the suit once more to check them, deep furrows creased his brow.

'WARNING – FILTER VALVE 14 NON FUNCTIONAL – DO NOT USE.'

Without bothering to get dressed, Mykus marched back to the storeroom in his underwear, mumbling curses with the frustration. He remembered seeing a box of filter valve 14's during his search for the gaskets, so he was able to go right to them. This time, the fitting took almost a half hour, but he eventually climbed into the suit for a third time, fully expecting to get a green light and a beep to tell him it was ready for use.

'WARNING – SUIT BREECH – DO NOT USE.'

"What the actual fuck?" he snapped aloud, banging his gloved hand on the table. "Does nothing work in this bucket of bolts?" Fuelled by anger, Mykus strode down to deck seven in his underwear and dragged another suit from the rack, hauling it back up the stairs to the engineering briefing room on deck four. A couple of minutes later, after swapping the breather units over, he donned the new suit and switched on the visor display.

"WARNING – BREATHER UNIT MALFUNCTION – DO NOT USE.'

The scream of anger echoed around deck four and by the time he finished thumping his fists on the table, there were several dents in the dark stained wooden surface. "What the fuck is going on here? Why the fuck did someone bring me here? Get me the fuck off of this shit crate before I go mad," he screamed, his frustration pouring from him unchecked. Sitting down, he dropped his head into his hands. "And why the fuck can't I remember anything?" he whimpered and burst into tears. When his emotion was spent, Mykus dried his eyes and stood. Still wearing the suit, he left the room and trudged back down to deck seven, dragging the other suit behind him. There was something weird going on with the suits and his engineer's mind refused to let it go. He wanted to understand, to fix it and would spend as long as necessary trying.

The large expanse of the shuttle bay seemed benign as Mykus peered through the window in the door, the flashing warning quickly getting on his nerves. Two shuttlecraft lay within and he wished he could hop aboard and fly out through the bay doors and take his chance in open space. Someone might stumble upon him, a freighter or liner perhaps, but at least he would be doing something other than rotting on board this becalmed ghost ship. Although the two shuttles where less than a hundred yards from him, they might as well have been a light year away. Without a working suit, getting to them was impossible. Tearan's message said he wanted to get the bay doors shut and Mykus's next thought was about that.

"I wonder if there's another way to get them shut," he mused as he wandered through to the prep room and began working on the suits and breather units. For hours he worked, trudging up to the engineering storeroom on deck four several times, but his mind was occupied on alternative ways to get those bay doors shut. While taking a break to have a meal, he mused on the problem. By the time he dragged himself back upstairs for the eighteenth time, having determined that no combination of suit and breather would work, he thought he knew a possible answer.

After a shower, he wandered along to the briefing room and sat down with a drink. "There has to be a contingency plan to get the bay doors closed in an emergency," he thought aloud. "I can't believe a ship would not have an alternative method of getting them shut, or open come to that, if access to the shuttle bay control panel is not possible. I'll check in the main engineering section for an emergency control switch or something." When his cup was empty, Mykus decided to find Tearan Lindo and tell him about the suits, so he got up and wandered to the stairs.

'Inter-Galactic Elite Command, Unit 389C4 Headquarters. T Lindo Commanding Officer.'

"What the hell is the Inter-Galactic Elite Command anyway?" he muttered as he read Tearan's scrawled message. "Sounds military to me." After knocking three times and calling out, he returned to the briefing room and snatched up the digital recorder.

"Hi, Tearan, Mykus here. I spent all day checking all the suits and none of them will work no matter what I try. It's weird, they should work. I reckon whatever happened here fried their computer governing systems or something. I'm going to try to find another way to shut the bay doors, there has to be an emergency system somewhere. I came by and knocked on your door but got no reply. You can find me in room eighty-eight, deck five, if I'm not in the main engineering section. I'm interested in whatever it is you've found out about the ship by the way."

He put the recorder down and was about to leave when he realised he had not acknowledged the doctor, Soval Arma.

"Hi Doctor Arma. Do you have anything to help us get our memories back?"

Mykus went down to deck five and through to the recreation room, intending to spend an hour at one of the gaming tables before going to bed and noticed someone had been fiddling with the vidicom movie library digital console. The back had been ripped off and various components lay discarded on the table top. "Tearan didn't say he knew about electronics," he muttered as he tapped the screen to test it out. His eyebrows shot to the top of his forehead in surprise when the screen burst into life and he grinned as he flicked through the large library of movies.

Two hours later, he dragged himself to his room and fell into bed. His sleep was a dreamless void which neither refreshed nor relaxed him and he awoke heavy headed and lethargic. After a hot shower, which helped wake him a little, he went to the kitchen to make breakfast. Today's schedule was to investigate whether the shuttle bay doors could be operated from engineering, or anywhere else aboard other than the shuttle bay itself. There was little doubt in his mind that such a system would exist on board, but he was not confident it would be functioning when he found it. The futile hours spent fiddling with the suits had sapped his optimism and a blanket of depression hung around his shoulders. With a huge effort of will, he got up and headed to the main engineering section.

Finding the shuttle bay emergency back up control was not difficult. Mykus was standing by the panel flicking switches within fifteen minutes of entering the engineering section. His problem was that like everything else not connected with any of the life support systems, it did not work. The floor of the engineering section was not only hard on his buttocks, but cold too and he shuffled his backside to get comfortable. Leaning forward, he peered inside the body of the console, the discarded access panel lying by his side. A mass of wires, tubes, connections, and components seemed to mock him as he tried to find something he recognised with which to orientate himself. Once he found it, he was able to follow the wires and connections along and make sense of the whole thing.

It had taken Mykus an hour and a half to make enough sense of the mass of wires and connections so that he was able to confidently say what each bit was for and it all seemed to be in first rate condition. There was nothing obviously broken or missing, no burned circuits, no blown components, and no loose wires. The next two hours were spent carefully following each wire, connection, and cable along until it disappeared into the main engineering conduit behind the wall. As he sat and ate a light lunch, he knew the only thing to do next was to try to follow the connections along in the conduit until they disappeared through into the engineering crawlspace that he knew should lie behind the first of the three hulls that make up the body of the ship. Like nesting cups, Mykus knew the ship would have been constructed with three hulls, one inside the other. Between the first and second would be a narrow walkway for use by maintenance crews and engineers. The second and third hulls would be separated by a layer of gas to insulate the interior from the stygian cold of space. His next thought was to wonder how he knew all this.

"I seem to be getting something of a memory back." This was both a thrill and a relief and he grinned from ear to ear as he got up and stretched his back.

After his meal, Mykus went straight back to work, ripping the conduit access panels from the wall and tracing the path of each wire within. His keen eyes looked for breaks, splits in the protective sheathing, scorches that might indicate a burn out, even deliberate cuts but everything appeared to be in perfect condition. He traced the wires along through four conduit access panels before the whole thing turned through ninety degrees and headed towards the floor. After ripping up the floor level conduit access panels and examining the contents, relief washed through his heart. The floor conduit contained the bundles from all the engineering consoles and workstations, which joined the main conduit access tube at intervals, much like veins and arteries joining a spinal column. He was delighted that whoever built the ship had taken the trouble to ensure that the bundles were bunched and wired with different colours for each of the workstations and consoles. This would make the job of identifying which of the bundles originated from the shuttle bay emergency back up control, easy.

"At least someone did their job right," he muttered as he delved into the mass with careful fingers.

Mykus tore into the pile of hot vegetables, closing his eyes with appreciation as he chewed. After a long day, he had traced the wires all the way from the console to the access port that led through into the engineering crawlspace. Sure now that the problem did not lie within the main engineering section or the emergency shuttle bay back up control console itself, he pondered on his next move. He now had the unenviable task of continuing to trace the wire bundle along inside the engineering crawlspace, all the way to the shuttle bay itself if necessary. The task was a laborious one rather than difficult, involving creeping along the narrow walkway, climbing down between decks to deck seven, then around to the shuttle bay itself. The wire bundle would then disappear through another access port into the shuttle bay access conduit, which would only be accessible from inside the shuttle bay itself. If there were no obvious problems with any of the wires or connections along the way, he knew they were stuffed.

"By the end of the day tomorrow I'll know either way and can tell Tearan." When he finished his meal, he wandered back to the engineering briefing room intending to leave an update for him, There was a message waiting.

"Mykus, it's Tearan. Okay, that would seem obvious now you mention it. There must be some sort of back up in place for emergencies. I hope you have more success. I came to engineering but you weren't around. Never mind, you're busy anyway. There's something odd down on decks seven and eight too, a size discrepancy with the maps. Take a look next time you're down there, check the map against the actual size of the rooms. Is it just me that thinks there should be more room? Let me know what you think."

Mykus switched the device to record.

"Hi, Tearan. I can't find any problems with the shuttle bay emergency back up control between the console and the access port where the wires go through into the crawlspace. I'll check the rest of the journey through the crawlspace down to the shuttle bay tomorrow and will update you then. I'll also take a look at the maps of decks seven and eight too and see if I can see what you're on about. I will be inside the crawlspace for most of tomorrow, so I won't be around if you come down to engineering. By the way, thanks for fixing the vidicom screen in the Rec Room. I'm glad to have an electrical engineer around to help. Do you want to investigate the comms and see if it's fixable?"

He then noticed that the doctor had not replied to his last message, so he left another.

"Doctor Arma, are you still with us?"

When he thought about this new survivor who had done nothing other than introduce himself, Mykus felt a darkness flutter to life within his heart and then disappear as quickly as it came. There was suddenly no doubt in his mind that something awful had befallen the doctor and that he would not be replying to his message. If there was no reply within another day, he would mention it to Tearan, he decided. With a shrug, he went back down to deck five and wandered into the recreation room to watch a movie before going to bed.

The air inside the crawlspace was markedly colder than that inside the body of the spaceship and Mykus was glad he had put an extra layer of clothing on before stepping through the access panel. The job would entail him spending most of the day inside the narrow walkway and he intended to be as comfortable as possible. It was bad enough having to be in there at all and being cold as well would be too much to bear, he decided. As the hours wore on, he inched his way along and down each deck, his magnifying goggles making the task of examining the wires and connections, a little easier. He was beginning to despair by the time he reached the ceiling level of deck seven, when two things made his flagging energy and focus snap to attention. The first thing was that he found the problem. A four-inch section of one purple coloured wire was missing. An overload connection socket that would lie in the middle of the missing section was also gone and switching his goggles to full magnification, Mykus saw the wires at both ends of the missing section were cut cleanly.

"That's odd," he frowned and removed his goggles. "If I was the paranoid type I might think the system had been sabotaged. Tearan will be interested to know about this." As he turned around in the narrow confines of the walkway, the light on his goggles shone up ahead and illuminated where the whole mass of wires, tubes, and connections, disappeared through what was the ceiling level of deck seven. Holding the light above his head, Mykus shone the light ahead into the gloom. The furrows still evident upon his brow, deepened further as he realised that access down to the deck seven level was blocked off. The hole in the floor through which the ladder built into the wall descended was blocked and the walkway continued around deck six on the other side of what Mykus knew should be the access ladder. The ladder itself was there, built into the side of the middle hull. He shone his light up past the upper floors and their walkways, and knew the ladder should continue down to the lowest deck.

A return trip to engineering secured another length of the correct wire and the appropriate connector and Mykus had the missing section repaired within twenty minutes. Once he had repaired the break, he took the time to make an entire circuit of the walkway above deck seven, but found no access panels.

"This is ridiculous. There should be access to all decks within the walkway in case of emergencies. Why the fuck would they want to block access to the lower two decks?" Tearan's words came back to his mind and Mykus nodded. "I guess that answers Tearan's question about a discrepancy in the room sizes on the maps. I'll go and check it right now."

Squinting his eyes to focus properly, Mykus focussed on the maps and frowned. "I'd guess the storage hangar to be around four times the size of the shuttle bay." With a determined shrug, he marched along the corridor to the storage hangar and went inside. The size of the room in relation to the shuttle bay was immediately apparent. "No way is this four times bigger. Twice perhaps but four times? Never." Carefully, he paced it out, then paced along the corridor outside the shuttle bay and scratched his head. "Yep. Twice the size, approximately. So either their mapmaker had a really bad day when he did deck seven, or something is odd about this place. Something other than the walkway access being blocked off that is. Oh, and something other than nothing but the life support systems being functional."

Taking the stairs two at a time, Mykus went down to deck eight, checked the map and then paced out the hazardous waste store. Sure enough, the room was nowhere near as big as the map claimed. Taking the discrepancies on both decks together, he realised there was only one possible solution.

"There's a whole section of the ship sectioned off and not represented on the maps. Whoa, that tickles my paranoia circuits something chronic." Shaking his head, he climbed up to deck four and after trying the shuttle bay door emergency control, ran along to the briefing room. Snatching up the recorder, he listened to the message that waited for him.

"Mykus, Tearan here. I know we're all still suffering from amnesia, but one thing I can say with complete authority is that I'm no engineer. I'm glad the vidicom is working though, a movie does help the time to pass. I would advise that you don't ask me to fiddle with anything electrical or I'm likely to blow us all into oblivion. I do know about navigation though, the nav section on the bridge feels very familiar and comfortable, so if you can get this crate going, I will be able to direct us to the nearest system."

After listening a couple more times, Mykus allowed Tearan's words to sink in before trying to understand the ramifications of them. When he did, his eyes widened in shock."

"Tearan. I can assure you the vidicom has been fixed by someone. That means both you and I are both nuts, or there is someone else aboard with us. I feel sure it isn't Doctor Arma though, and I have a really bad feeling about him. I am willing to bet you a hundred that something horrible has happened to him. Call me crazy if you want, but I know what I'm feeling. Anyway, I followed the wiring along via the crawlspace right down to deck six and found a section of wire had been cut and removed. Cut, not broken by the way. Deliberately cut out. Four inches of it including an overload connection socket, cut out cleanly. Another thing too, the engineering crawlspace has been blocked off above deck seven. Access down there is impossible, I checked for access panels but there are none. This is very odd and against all the regulations in existence. I also agree about the size of the rooms on decks seven and eight. I paced it out and you're right, there's a large area of space sectioned off down there. Now for the bad news. Despite fixing the wire, the shuttle bay emergency back up control still will not work and I cannot get those bay doors shut. Sorry. I'm going to continue my inspection of the ship's systems. Come by when you have time and talk about it."

Mykus secured the harness and stepped over the railing into the engine bay, the massive bullet shaped engine towering above him. For the entire day, interrupted only by a break for lunch and two breaks to pee, he worked on the engine housing. With the special goggles secured to his eyes, he inched his way across and down and by the time he stopped for the day, he had checked two thirds of the engine housing and found no flaws to explain why the ship was becalmed. The following day saw the job finished and Mykus was pleased as he hauled himself back over the railing and discarded the safety harness.

There was now no doubt that the engine housing itself was not the cause of the lack of power. The housing was in perfect condition, the clear surface without a single flaw or minute crack that would adversely affect the mix of liquid gases within. Walking over to the wall and his list of possible causes for the ship's lack of power, he reached up and crossed off the first on the list. The next thing was to check the stanchions that held the housing in place within the curved engine bay. Along the top of two of these stout metal rods lay gas supply tubes, allowing the gases within the engine itself to be replenished as the production of power depleted them. Self-regulating valves at the end of each supply tube allowed the right amount of gases to enter the engine safely and at the right pressure to keep the whole thing working at optimum.

Mykus tossed and turned, his sleep no longer a dreamless void. The air, heavily humid after a recent rainstorm sapped his energy as he stood beneath the trees and listened to the wind. Leaves fell around him, dancing in the air as the wind caught them and tossed them along like the dancing bugs he used to watch as a boy. A sudden squeal from above rang through the howling wind and he craned his neck up. The large Fallowingall soared effortlessly despite the gale, its multi-coloured blue feathers the only bright spot in a grey and dismal day. Mykus knew that even if the sun were to shine and spring flowers to burst through the sodden ground on which he stood, the heaviness within his heart would still make the day grey and dismal.

The beautiful face filled his memory despite her name remaining a mystery and as is the way of dreams, he did not question why her name should be hidden from him. It did not matter anyway, her face was clear in his mind and he knew that he loved her more than life itself. That and the fact that she was dead. He knew that too and it was this fact that lay upon his heart like a stone. The woman was not his wife, of that he was as sure as he knew his own name. Neither were they lovers, although there might have been a connection long ago. So long ago. The feeling of his hands caressing the swell of her hips was as vague and fleeting as the touch of a blue green Fairy Fly. Those full pink lips had once kissed his own and although he could not bring the memories through into the dream, he was confident of their truth.

Bells chimed in the public square the day she married his best friend and he stood beside them, a fake smile hiding the rent in his heart that he knew would never be healed. Three years of marriage brought forth two children and Mykus gave them his blessings as they brought each infant home and became a proper family. Many times, he tried to draw away from the family, their obvious love like a knife within his heart, but always he would return the moment his friend called for him. There would always be questions and Mykus tried to evade them, feigning work responsibilities that needed his attention. It was too painful to be around them, watching her happy with another man who was unable to love her in the same way or to the same degree as he did. Eventually he moved to a non-existent job in a city far away and tried to get on with his life.

Mykus tossed and turned as the dream images flowed past ever quicker. Months passed, became years and his life moved on. Work took up much of his time and he poured himself into it, desiring to fill his mind and heart with anything other than the woman he loved but could not have. Friends came and he welcomed them warmly, for they claimed a few more of the empty lonely hours and occupied his mind. Five years after his best friend had brought his infant son home to join their year old daughter and proudly showed him to Mykus, his boss called him into the office and asked if he would oversee the setting up of an outpost in another city. There was no one else to do it and a substantial bonus would be the reward for a week of easy work. The boss pleaded and Mykus accepted.

It was not until he had accepted the job that he found out it was in the city he left behind, the city he vowed never to return to. Now it was too late to refuse without having to explain and he was stuck, he could not avoid it. Hoping to avoid coming into contact with the man who had been his lifelong friend and the woman who tormented his heart so, Mykus kept his head down and concentrated on the job. Everything was going well until the day before he was due to return and his sudden decision to stop in at a diner. If it were not for that decision, he would not be there standing under the trees listening to the plaintive cry of the Fallowingall after the rain.

Mykus cried out in his sleep, tossing the sheet aside as his anguished heart leapt in his breast, but did not awaken. The dreadful images kept him prisoner, forcing him to bear witness as he watched himself in the diner, eating the delicious food. The news broadcast was on the vidicom and someone shouted for the serving woman to turn the sound up. The clamour of voices fell silent as her eyes, the woman he had given his heart to all those years ago, found his own. The breath left his lungs as he listened to the reporter tell him how the woman's husband killed her and their two children, cut them up, then tried to pretend the wife killed the children and then herself. Leaving his food, he rushed outside and vomited.

The howling wind blew through the trees, sending a chilling shower of drops down onto Mykus' head as he stood under the grey sky. His best friend had been executed and Mykus had lost everyone he ever loved. The best friend, the woman, and the two children she bore. Months passed and he tried to get on with his life but found it impossible. While she lived, there was always a seed of hope that one day she might again be his, as she had been once, long ago. Now she was dead and he was forced to face the fact that he would never feel her lips on his nor her arms around his waist. Stepping out from the cover of the trees, Mykus felt the wind grab at his shirt and hair, chilling him through. Ignoring the sudden cold, he quickened his steps to a run and did not falter as he flung himself headlong from the cliff and waited to be dashed against the rocks four hundred feet below and, he allowed himself to hope, into the arms of his love in some other unknown existence.

7

He wondered why the alarm had not woken him and leapt to a sitting position, fearful of being late. Wincing with pain as his back complained, he found he had been asleep on the floor. Rubbing the face from his eyes, he yawned and examined his surroundings. When he felt fully awake, he got to his feet and found himself within a high spec science lab.

"What the fuck? How did I end up here, and exactly where is here anyway?" Thinking back, his next shock was when he found almost no memories within his mind. He knew he was Jole Smoy, a twenty year old botany student from Arlenika Prime. One of his few concrete memories was boarding a mid-budget liner for the three-week trip to the jungle planet Mi'ikenway Da Diuea for his year of experience in the field. Hundreds of scientists were living and working there, cataloguing all the flora and fauna and monitoring weather patterns. Jole looked forward to spending much of his time sampling and analysing the soil, water, and air composition, mapping the geomorphology and analysing the geology of the entire planet. This would not only give him valuable experience but would help build a comprehensive database. This year would add significantly to his overall marks at the end of his eight-year course of study.

Finding little else within his mind was such a shock to his system that at first he was unable to work out how to react or process the experience. In the absence of any real reaction, panic took over. "I can't remember anything else. What's happened to me? Why can't I remember? Oh shit, what am I to do? Isn't someone here to help me?" All these questions and many more like them echoed around the lab as he sat on a chair, hugging himself and shaking with fear. Tears coursed down his cheeks as his eyes darted around his immediate surroundings. The room swayed sickeningly as Jole hyperventilated, and when he awoke from his faint a few minutes later, dried blood caked his face. As he wiped the dried flakes from his skin with the back of his hand, a surge of pain shot up through his nose. Probing gingerly with his fingers, he was relieved to find the appendage swollen and painful, but unbroken.

Consumed with fear, Jole took a deep breath and got to his feet. Through his panic, he knew his first priority was to find help. What he needed was another person to assure him everything would be all right, to look after him and explain things. Craning his neck around to take in as much of the large room as he could, he found the immediate vicinity empty of life other than himself. Not wishing to get into trouble for trespassing in someone's laboratory, he tip toed forwards and did a circuit of the whole room. When he realised he was alone, he went over to the consoles and workstations and recognised several scientific disciplines.

"Astrophysics, cosmology, astronautics, astrobiology, planetary sciences. I guess this is a space studies establishment." In one wall was a door and he approached it slowly, scared of what he might find on the other side but driven by the need to find another person. Someone else meant an explanation for everything, reassurance, but most importantly, help. Alone, he would find none of those things. The touchpad opened the door with an audible swish and Jole jumped back in alarm, his arms leaping across his chest in a defensive gesture. Too scared to exit the lab, he remained rooted to the spot for almost a minute listening for sounds of anyone approaching but all was silent. His heart pounding against his ribs, he stepped through into the corridor, calling out for help as he did so.

"Hello? Can someone help me please? I've lost my memory and need help. Hello? Hello?" The eerie silence creeped him out and he shivered as he looked both ways down what was a curving corridor. The sight that met his eyes was not one he recognised. Although his memories aboard the mid budget liner were scant, he did not remember seeing anything like the corridor he now found himself within. "I don't remember anywhere like this on the liner," he muttered. "Perhaps it's one of the crew only parts of the ship." With renewed hope, he went to the left and crept down the corridor.

'Observation Lounge – Senior Officers only. All other personnel use the recreation room on deck five.'

Realising that he was trespassing where he should not be, Jole walked briskly until he came to a set of stairs and an elevator. A map of the ship attached to the wall caught his eye and he wandered over. Within seconds, deep furrows creased his brow.

"This isn't the liner I boarded. That was twice the size at least." Scanning the map, his frown deepened as he noticed the lack of swimming pool, concert hall, bars, restaurants, whorehouse, and library. As he studied the map, a memory floated back to his mind and the aching void grasped it, greedy to fill the worryingly empty vaults inside. He was swimming in the pool on board the liner, eyeing up a sexy blonde and laughing with some other young men his own age. Who they were he did not know, but his memory held a feeling of attachment to them, a tangible bond they shared. Where they friends? Student colleagues perhaps? At that moment, he did not know, but as he stood at the map and allowed the memory to flow back, he knew he was not aboard the liner anymore.

"What ship is this then, and how did I get here?" he mused as he checked the map and wondered where to go. Deciding that he was most likely to find help in the security section, he pressed the button for the elevator and waited. Nothing happened and after waiting for a full minute, Jole headed for the stairs and descended to deck three.

'Security,' the bright yellow letters announced. Underneath, scrawled in black marker pen, was a message. *'Inter-Galactic Elite Command, Unit 389C4 Headquarters. T Lindo Commanding Officer.'*

That sounded very official to Jole and he felt much better knowing there was someone from the Inter-Galactic Elite Command on board, although the name of the organisation caused no flutters of recognition within. He guessed it was some sort of top-secret military outfit of the kind the conspiracy theories he loved so much revolved around. He raised a hand to knock, frowning as he wondered how he knew he loved conspiracy theories. A smile teetered at the corners of his mouth when he decided that it meant he was getting more memories back. After knocking several times and getting no reply, he scratched his head at the lack of a touchpad that would afford him entry. Rather than walk away without at least trying his best, he resorted to force, pushing at the door several times and wondering how it was supposed to open. The sight of the key card slot gave him his answer.

"I guess the security section has to be secure, even if the rest of the ship isn't."

The corridor curved away in both directions as Jole stood outside the security room and wondered what to do. All the other rooms on this deck were the sort the public would not be allowed to enter, so he headed back to the stairs and the map. Taking the stairs two at a time, he went down to deck five. Crew quarters, dining room, and recreation room the map said. These were the only places on the map that ordinary members of the public might be allowed to visit. Hope still dared to beat within his heart as he entered the dining room.

The large room was empty, and by that very emptiness, creeped him out. His heart sank as he approached the counter and called out. "Hello, is anyone around? Can someone help me? Hello, anybody?" His calls echoed in the lofty room and panic again rose in his heart. "What the fuck has happened? Why am I here and why am I alone? Please, someone help me. Anyone." Brief pain gripped his fingers as he thumped his fists down onto the counter top, a mixture of fear and anger fuelling the outburst. Before his anger dissipated entirely, he used its energy to fuel the bravery to go behind the counter and into the kitchen. After noticing that it was also devoid of life, he was somewhat pleased to note an abundance of foodstuffs in store, enough to feed him for a long time. With a sudden burst of uncharacteristic courage, he helped himself to a large piece of Nolwik Cake and wandered next door to the recreation room.

This room was divided into several areas. A large vidicom screen hung down from the ceiling, its movie library handset on one of the seats facing it. Rows of seats, enough for twenty people were set out in a curve facing the screen and Jole imagined faces etched with concentration staring ahead. He imagined the sounds of movies, gunfire, men laughing together, and women screaming as monsters grabbed at them. Several gaming tables sat along one long wall and he grinned despite the gravity of the situation in which he found himself. Those tables represented fun and he knew that somewhere in his memories were good times had on machines such as these. As he went to leave, images flooded his mind. He was leaving home, his bags packed and waiting for the hover bus in the centre of a town. Deep inside, he knew this happened recently.

Opposite the gaming tables, a small stage, set up for live music, nestled beside the vidicom screen. Several musical instruments he did not recognise stood idle, waiting to be caressed by fingers or lips. In front of the stage, the dance floor echoed as he walked across. At the far end of the large room was an informal arrangement of seating and low tables and he imagined groups of people discussing topical issues, laughing and joking with each other. On the far wall, a window ten feet high by fifteen wide allowed a good view out into space, and Jole approached, transfixed by the sight. His last memory was boarding the passenger liner for travel to Mi'ikenway Da Duiea so it was not the stars gazing back at him that caused his unease. What troubled him was knowing he was now on the wrong ship with no memory of how he came to be there. He felt alone and terrified again but was unable to tear his gaze from the viewing window. That sight meant he was imprisoned as securely as if his leg were confined within the jaws of a Tiglan Trap. There was no option to leave the ship or run for help. Trapped and alone in space was a horrible way to live, but an even worse way to die, he decided as he sat down to think.

Jole sat for nearly an hour thinking about the situation and wondering what to do. Fear glued him to the seat. Fear of being alone, being abandoned, of maybe never getting help and having to live alone on the ship for the rest of his life. All sorts of horrors invaded his empty mind and gripped his heart with icy fingers. His emotions swung between self pity and blind rage. One minute he was sobbing with fear and indecision, the next he was screaming in anger at being left alone to rot. Images of his parents came to his mind, reassuring smiles on their faces and he wished with all of his being that he were back home.

"Why did I have to go and sign up for Mi'ikenway Da Duiea anyway? There were other options for my year in the field." Shaking his head in frustration, he berated himself for his stupidity, as if admitting to such lack of judgement would somehow make things all right. He sat, and continued to sit until he realised that he could not sit there forever. Knowing that action is always better than inaction, he made a mental list of the facts as he knew them so he might formulate some kind of plan. "Okay let's make a list of what we know," he said aloud without wondering who, 'we,' were. It gave him more comfort than saying, 'I,' would, which would only serve to highlight the fact that he was alone. "There seems to be nobody but me around, so it might be a good idea to go and check everywhere to make sure. There may be someone injured or holed up somewhere who also thinks they're alone." This possibility gave him a precious ray of hope and his troubled mind clung to it greedily.

By the time Jole sat back down in the dining room, he had made a quick tour of the ship and found no one around. A few of the rooms were blocked to him; the security room, bridge, and shuttle bay all had locks to which he did not have access. On deck five he found many staff quarters, all of which sported a convenient key card that hung from a hook on the outside of the door. Inside the rooms, he found clothes and washing necessities, comfortable beds, showers and toilets. Finding nothing he recognised that might indicate one of the rooms was his own, he decided to set up home in room twenty. The understated but elegant decor within the room appealed to him and the number was the same as his age, which he chose to accept as a good omen. Deck seven had provided an enormous storeroom of everything he could think of that he might need. There was enough stuff in the various crates and storage bins to keep someone in relative comfort for years, he thought to himself as he walked around.

After rummaging in the kitchen, he managed to prepare himself a meal of sorts, after which he decided to take his mind off his problems by watching a couple of movies. Afterwards, boredom quickly set in and he paced. As he strode up and down, he thought about the days ahead as they turned into weeks, then months and knew the boredom and loneliness would drive him mad if he did not find something with which to occupy himself. Not long later, he whooped as he flew along corridors, up and down staircases on one of the hover loaders he found in the cargo hangar. These machines were not built for racing by anyone's standards, but it was fun and more than once, he bashed into walls and doors. It was after he bashed in the door to staff quarters room forty-two that an idea came to him and he grinned.

Jole flew along the corridor on deck three, whooping and howling as he went. The door to the security room lay up ahead and he slowed as it came into view. Like a predator stalking his prey, he ducked his head down as he shuffled his feet into a secure position. A grin spread across his face as he flexed his fingers and gripped the controls. With a jerk of his wrist, he flung the hover loader into full power and held on for all he was worth. The machine shot down the corridor towards the security room door, closing the gap in less than five seconds. The confined space of the corridor did not allow him to approach the door head on, so he had to resort to a sudden and violent veer to the left, which sent the vehicle smashing into the door at an angle. A loud bang echoed around deck three, followed swiftly by a series of thuds and a dull pop.

"Oh shit," he groaned as he sat up and pushed the large irregular shaped piece of metal off his legs. The hover loader had successfully smashed through the security room door, which was unable to withstand the onslaught and broke into several pieces. Acrid fumes and a column of black smoke rose from the wreckage of the hover loader, which lay on its side on the floor, its engine having blown apart. Jole waved a hand in front of his face in an attempt to clear the fumes and stood up. "Nothing broken," he muttered after giving himself a quick check over. After brushing himself down, he poked around.

The security room was like a treasure cave to a bored young man of twenty, and within a few minutes, he was in the firing range he discovered through a door, testing out all the guns the lockers contained. Several of the larger rifles caught his shoulder painfully as they kicked back and he winced after his third attempt to control it failed. When the discomfort became too much to bear, he settled for a pair of impressively large handguns and was soon grinning from ear to ear as he acted the character he had seen in one of the movies earlier that day.

"Go back to where you came from, asshole," he yelled as he fired at the target, doing a remarkably good impersonation of the blonde actor. Laughing at the top of his voice, he stood back and caught his breath. He hefted the guns and knew instinctively that he had never been properly trained in handling weapons of any kind. Although fun, they felt somehow foreign to him and once he calmed down from his outburst of energy, he realised they scared him a little. For a fraction of a second, he toyed with the idea of blowing his own brains out, but the feeling was gone as quickly as it came and left him feeling vulnerable and sad again. Putting down the guns, Jole dropped to the floor in a corner and sobbed.

Swinging from suicidal depression one minute, to hyperactive frenzy the next, Jole whiled away the next seven hours and by the time exhaustion dragged him back to room twenty to sleep, his mind was struggling with the trauma. Holes and dents pockmarked doors and walls all over the ship with the evidence of his more frenzied moments as he ran naked along corridors shooting the handguns with far less care than common sense should have allowed. By a sheer miracle, he had not managed to cause a hull breech with the guns, but several computer consoles were forever beyond repair. Three times the height of a man up the right hand side of the huge clear bullet shaped engine housing was a hole the size of a man's fist.

Sleep overcame him quickly and Jole plunged into darkness. His troubled mind rested in the calming blackness and tried to piece itself back together. Once the images began however, the cracks grew ever wider. Faces, blurry and indistinct, floated in and out of his vision. Huge and terrifying, they loomed over him, undeterred by his vain attempts to recoil from their touch. Frozen with fear, he tried to shrink into the mattress beneath him but found his body numb, as if anaesthetised by some strong and poisonous chemical. Strong hands gripped his shoulders and he yelped in fear, unable to wriggle away. He tried to force his hands to move, tried to make his fingers grip the sheet and fling it over his head. Maybe if he did not acknowledge the frightening shapes that loomed and shrank above, they would go away, he thought, but his fingers lay cold and still by his side.

The bed on which Jole lay suddenly lurched and the room began to jerk and sway. Crying out in terror, he fought to escape but it was as if his body were not his own. Screaming in fear and begging for help one minute, he spat and swore in anger the next as he realised the moving shapes were taking him somewhere. From the darkness of the room, light exploded into his eyes and he counted the square pattern of illumination panels on the ceiling as they moved past. Trying hard to ignore the presence of the horrifying looming figures, he concentrated on the illumination panels above and counted them as they floated past. He found the counting strangely meditative and calming and hoped that maybe by concentrating hard on it, he might wake up from this dreadful nightmare.

Sounds reached his ears, low guttural growls and swooping cadences that boomed as they swelled up and flowed down. The sounds cut his concentration on the counting and he felt panic once again rise within. Hot tears stung his eyes and flowed down the sides of his head to his temples. Another of the huge shapes loomed towards him and he squeezed his eyes shut as he sobbed, unable to move away and hide from them. The sounds came again, and this time he noticed a strangely soothing quality to the cadences, as if someone were attempting to reassure him. Between sobs, a new sound came to his ears and he turned his head towards it. A soft ping from his right that reminded him of elevator call buttons. The gentle swaying had stopped and above, the square illumination panels no longer moved passed. Jole realised his frightening captors, whatever they were, had stopped and he wondered why. The next thing he heard was an audible swish much like the sound the doors on board the space ship made. A lurch and a feeling of leaving his stomach behind had a wave of nausea swelling up inside and he groaned as he tried to breathe it away.

Guttural growls echoed all around and he wished to put his hands over his ears and shut out the sounds. Screams filled the air and Jole felt something grip his shoulder tightly as something else wiped across his brow. Realising that the screams were his own, he tried to stem the tide of panic by squeezing his eyes shut and heaving deep breaths. The growls became the same soothing cadences once again and he listened as they gently swelled and flowed. The effect they had upon his troubled mind was swift and he felt his mind relax as the lurching stopped and he heard another soft ping before the gentle swaying began again. More illumination panels swished passed above, only these ones were circular instead of square. More sounds came, some deep and soothing, others shrill and frightening and Jole screamed, pleading to awaken from this nightmare.

Swishing sounds came and went, circular illumination panels moved passed above and as he screamed, the lighted circles moved faster and faster until they were flying past him so quickly he was unable to keep count. All of a sudden, the gentle swaying stopped and Jole noticed one single circular illumination panel stationary overhead. The moment he realised his kidnappers had stopped their flight with him, something came down over his face. Despite moving his head from side to side, he was unable to free his face from whatever it was that pressed down upon it. Before he could scream again, he noticed a nasty taste in his mouth. His eyes snapped open as a moment of total clarity hit him. He was being gassed. A fresh wave of panic swelled in his mind and he held his breath as he struggled to move.

For a few seconds nothing happened as he strained against his numb muscles. Then Jole felt himself gradually shrink until he was nothing but a spark deep within the darkest corner of his own mind. Safe at last, he allowed himself to relax as his awareness shrank away from the terrifying experience out there in the physical world and retreated into the deepest recess of his troubled mind. Without the sensuous input from his overloaded physical senses, Jole's mind became clear and he heard sounds he recognised. Gone were the guttural growls and soothing cadences, and in their place was a voice.

"Don't worry Jole. Everything will be all right. Relax and let go."

Jole listened, relaxed, and let go. Just before his awareness switched off, he heard another voice join the first and listened in horror as he waited to wake up.

"Too dangerous."

"Neutralise it."

"Wipe it out."

8

Tovis Kerral awoke and allowed himself a few precious minutes in the warmth and comfort of the bed before stirring. Snatches of dreams floated past his consciousness on their way to oblivion, and he registered the sound of wind in the trees and the vague memory of a soul crushing sadness but the reason for it evaded him. He kept his eyes closed and waited while it faded and left a gap that he knew should be filled with something. A feeling of loss swept through his heart and he frowned. Loneliness was not something he was too familiar with, but as he lay in the warmth of the bed, he suddenly felt lost, incomplete. Not being the sort of man to dwell too long on feelings and emotions, he yawned, stretched, and got up. After breakfasting lightly, he crouched by the open side of the communications station on the bridge and made himself comfortable.

The gunfire was so loud and so close that Tovis almost jumped out of his skin when the first volley started. Every muscle in his body jumped and he banged his head painfully as a result. Swearing loudly as much for the pain as for the surprise, he hastily extricated himself from the body of the comms station and looked around the bridge, exclaiming in relief when he found he was alone. Dropping the tools, he took up his guns and crept towards the door. For long seconds he pressed his ear to the door, his hand pressed against the emergency door locking switch, not wanting whoever was firing to gain access to the bridge. If any gunfire should damage the bridge viewing screen, the resulting decompression would ensure there was no chance of surviving. The only space suits he had seen were down on deck seven and with the ship decompressing around him, his chances of getting down there and into a suit were so slim as to be non-existent.

All the time he kept the bridge door locked, he knew he was safe. The door should be able to withstand all of the weaponry he had seen in the security room so he did not worry about being shot through the door. Only the lack of food, drink and a toilet made his stay on the bridge uncomfortable, and he was more than happy to stay there as long as necessary to avoid a possibly disastrous confrontation. Besides, that gunfire sounded haphazard, as though the hand on the trigger was one that was not well educated in the use of firearms. He had to endure no more than twenty seconds of silence before several more shots rang out at least one deck below, possibly two. It was difficult to tell exactly; it had been a while since he had been involved in a firefight on a space ship, and that one had been little more than a glorified shuttle. Deep furrows creased his brow as he listened to the sounds.

"How did he get down there so fast? He's maybe two decks below. Even I can't get down there in that short a time." Knowing that at least three more people were aboard with him, he briefly wondered whether one of them was pulling the trigger. Tearan Lindo was quickly dismissed as a possible gunman. He was military and therefore disciplined enough to know the danger in firing on a space ship in such a crazy manner. The engineer could be to blame, but Tovis knew how protective engineers can get with the machines they build and care for. They can become as attached to them as others do with people, or think of them as a child or a girlfriend. Many an engineer referred to an engine as, 'she,' so Tovis decided Mykus was most likely not responsible. It would be like shooting a lover. The third person was a doctor, and his job was to preserve life rather than endanger it, so Tovis was at a loss to work out which of them it was likely to be.

"Anyone can go crazy I guess, so it could be either one of them or both." Knowing that the longer he put off going to investigate, the more chance there was of the ship being damaged and that would endanger all their lives. Realising that he would have to go and sort it out, with deadly force if necessary, he checked his guns and switched his mind into working mode. "Time to party," he muttered and flung the door wide. The corridor was empty, and Tovis gradually made his way out of the bridge, following the sound of the gunfire.

To his left, right outside the bridge, the door to the security headquarters showed the tell-tale signs of laser pistol fire. The substantial security door had not been breached, but it was pock marked with blackened residue where it had taken fire. The black substance marked the surface of the door like the rays of a sun in a child's drawing, each one accompanied by a small scoop mark in the centre, and Tovis counted seven shots in total. Whoever it was, wanted very much to gain entry to the security headquarters, but had failed and was now wandering the ship firing at random. Fear coursed through Tovis's body, the kind of fear caused by the very real possibility of dying horribly in space.

"I have to stop this asshole before he kills us all."

Making his way along the corridor towards the stairs, Tovis noticed holes in the walls and doors to all the senior officers' quarters. As he approached the door to the senior officers' observation lounge, his face suddenly paled as he remembered seeing another large viewing window. If that was damaged he was done for. His mind filled with horrific images of a crack, tiny at first, creeping its gentle way across the window. As it grew, its racing became faster as it hurtled towards the opposite wall whereupon a dull explosion sent it shattering into a million pieces and drew him, gasping, to an icy death in space. Standing outside the door, too afraid to enter in case the giant viewing window was damaged, hesitation rooted him to the spot. With a growl of anger at his own indecision, he shook his head and forced his mind to think clearly. "If the window was blown through, this door would not be able to withstand the force of decompression. The fact that it's still here proves the window is still holding. It could be damaged though, so if I have to race downstairs and get into a suit, the sooner I get on with it, the better chance I have." His heart in his throat, he entered and gasped audibly at the sight of the huge undamaged window, the stars twinkling back at him serenely. Back out in the corridor, more gunfire from directly below had him running towards the stairs The map informed him that the security room was the likely location of the gunfire and he allowed himself to hope that the gunman had decided to remain within the safe confines of the firing range. Hoping that while occupied with firing his guns in so haphazard a manner, the gunman may not notice someone creeping up on him, Tovis ran along the corridor and allowed the sound of the gunfire to draw him towards it like a magnet.

Sure enough, as he approached the door to the security room, it became obvious that the gunfire was taking place at the far end of the room, in the approximate vicinity of the firing range. The main door to the room lay in pieces and the wreckage of a hover loader from the cargo hangar lay inside. The engine had blown up and the entire front of the vehicle was smashed.

"What the fuck happened down here?" he whispered to himself as he approached. The gunfire was deafening as Tovis stepped gingerly over the broken pieces of the door and winced, the sound causing him physical pain in his head. Once inside the security room, he stole forwards in silence, like a cat stalking its prey. Before he had taken three steps, the gunfire stopped abruptly, making Tovis jump. Knowing that the cessation of firing might mean the gunman was on his way out of the firing range, Tovis ran on tiptoes towards it, readying himself to open fire the moment anyone came into view.

The shadows were menacing as they hung in the corners of the firing range and Tovis was reminded of sinister images from childhood nightmares. In less than a minute, he discovered that he was the only person in the room.

"Where did he go?" he whispered as he scratched his head, bemused. There was no way anyone passed him without him noticing, so either he was imagining things or there was some secret way out of the room that he had yet to discover. Before he began tapping his way along the walls in the search for a hidden panel, another volley of gunfire exploded nearby. The sound served only to deepen the furrows on his brow and he shook his head in disbelief. "What the fuck? That's coming from below again. There's no way anyone got passed me, went along the corridor and made it down to deck four in the time. There has to be more than one person." Realising that he was very likely to be sharing an abandoned space ship with at least two gun-toting crazies, he swore again before exiting the firing range and making a swift but thorough sweep of the security room.

Tovis ran along the corridor towards the stairs and noticed the doors to the gravity field generator room, and the life support systems control centre were both blown to pieces. Curiosity stopped him outside the remains to the life support systems control centre, the sound of gunfire pushed to the back of his mind for the moment. Reaching down to one of the irregularly shaped pieces of door that littered the floor, he touched the dark residue left by the laser pistol. Fresh residue would feel hot and sticky, but Tovis' fingers touched cold metal and came away clean. Experience told him this meant the gunfire had taken place hours before, but he had heard it a couple of minutes ago. His frown deepened. The metal should be hot; it should burn his fingertips. The black residue should still be syrupy and sticky. Shaking his head, he continued down the corridor.

Gunfire rang out, the lofty heights of the main engineering section providing excellent acoustics to carry the sound throughout the entire ship. The door was intact and Tovis stood outside listening to the deafening roar within. On his initial tour of the ship, he had seen the huge bullet shaped engine and his heart sank as he thought of how it might react to being shot at. One thing he was not able to tell from the sound was where exactly in the room the gunman was standing. Squeezing his eyes tight shut, he thought back to his tour of the ship and tried to remember the layout of the room beyond the door. From what he remembered, the room opened out both right and left right inside the door, and the nearest cover was approximately twenty feet to his left. There was no option but to go in prepared to fight it out and try to find cover once he identified the gunman's position. This was the one thing Tovis hated more than anything else; going into a firefight blind without an advantage the element of surprise afforded him.

"Shit. I'm getting too old for this," he muttered as he rolled his neck around and took a couple of deep breaths. Before he could talk himself out of it, he leapt towards the door, smacked a hand to the touchpad, and waited while it swished open.

Tovis guessed it took less than six seconds to enter the room and dive for the cover of the console twenty feet to his left. He was halfway there when he realised the gunfire had ceased the moment he entered the room and peered out from behind the console, guns at the ready. From his vantage point, there was nowhere in that part of the room for anyone to hide without him seeing, so he carefully made his way to where the room went around to the right. Pressing himself against the bank of terminals, he peered around the corner and took in the whole of the long portion of the engineering section. At the far end, there was the mezzanine overlooking the engine bay and beyond that, part of the upper portion of the engine housing itself. In between, several consoles and banks of terminals offered many hiding spaces so he crouched low and dashed for the first.

Bit by bit, Tovis made it the length of the room to the railing on the mezzanine overlooking the engine housing. The huge bullet shaped object soared up through the very middle of the ship, its tip lying two feet below the floor in the bridge, while it's stubby cone shaped bottom ended just above the cargo hangar on deck seven. He was confused to discover no one in the room other than himself and shook his head in frustration. The possibility of some secret panel in the wall again crossed his mind and he did not dismiss it.

"If someone is fucking with me to make me think I'm going crazy, they're gonna be really sorry when I catch up with them," he muttered as he moved away from the railing. A gasp was followed swiftly by a loud curse as he stood rooted to the spot. Approximately three times the height of a man above him and slightly to the right was a large hole the size of his own fist. Tovis was not an engineer despite his talent with electrical and digital components, but he realised that something about that hole was weird. With a hole that size, the engine should have blown up, sending him and anyone else aboard into the waiting arms of oblivion. Yet here he was, very much alive and staring at the hole.

"That's weird. Why haven't we blown up?" Before he could begin to formulate an answer, Tovis realised he did not feel well at all. No more than a slight groan escaped him before he dropped to the floor unconscious.

Tovis snapped awake and sat up in bed. It took almost a minute before he yawned, rubbed his eyes, and believed that he had been dreaming. He had always been a practical sort of man. His job needed him to be fully focussed in the present moment of reality, and philosophical things had never been of much interest. Consequently, he had never bothered to think much about his dreams, and most of the time never remembered them. This particular dream was so real though, so vivid. The experience was like real waking consciousness and his memory of it was total, not patchy like dream memories tend to be. With a groan and a shake of the head to clear the fuzz, he climbed from the bed and went to shower.

After enjoying a light breakfast, he took the time to wash the crockery and cutlery and noticed another washed plate drying on the rack. Wondering which of his mysterious companions had been there, he put his own plate beside it to dry and went out into the corridor. Walking down the corridors and up the stairs spooked him after his dream. He half expected the residue of laser pistol fire to be visible on the walls and doors. When he climbed up to deck three, he gave in to his curiosity and wandered along the corridor to the security room. The door was intact and undamaged. With a resigned shrug, he went back to the stairs.

An angry skewer of red-hot pain sliced through his skull and he swore aloud. This was the fifth time he banged his head on the edge of the console housing and he cursed the designers who had obviously made the ship to accommodate its midget workforce. Taking care, he gingerly extricated himself from the body of the communications station on the bridge and rubbed his head. He rolled his neck around and stretched his shoulders, wincing as the knots in his muscles pulled painfully, before shifting his ass into a slightly more comfortable position. Over the course of the next three hours, he followed and identified most of the contents of the comms station and found no obvious problems. There were three bits he did not recognise and no amount of frowning and head scratching gave him any ideas as to what their function might be. He knew that all the things necessary to make the communications system work were present and seemed to be without damage, but those three extra bits baffled him. Having his entire upper body inside the comms station housing was very uncomfortable and he lost count of the number of times he banged, scraped, and trapped various parts of his anatomy. After yelling in pain for the twentieth time from banging his elbow yet again, he decided the only way to examine the three components properly would be to remove them entirely.

Twenty minutes later, he sat back and squinted as he held up the three components. In all his years working in the field, he learned to cannibalise all manner of objects for components and gleaned a substantial working knowledge of small component electronics and digitonics. Not once had he seen anything like the three small components he held in his hands as he sat on his haunches on the floor of the bridge and frowned.

"What the fuck are these?" he muttered as he scratched his head with his free hand. No matter how many times he turned them over in his hands, no matter from which angle he peered at them, their probable function eluded him. Realising that his ass was becoming uncomfortably numb, he stood and walked around to get the blood flowing again. As he returned to the comms station, his mouth fell open in shock and his eyes widened. The orange light blinked once every second from the right hand side of the control panel and Tovis leaned in to read what was painted above it.

'Ready.'

The three small mysterious components lay heavy in his hand as he watched the blinking light on the communications console. For several seconds he stood quiet, his mind trying to piece together this new information. He knew without a doubt that he had not been able to get the comms to work before this moment, not even a small blinking light would function no matter what he tried. Now, with the removal of these three components, the comms system was telling him it was ready to transmit.

"It must be some kind of inhibitor system," he said as he stared at the three components, turning them over in his hands. "But why put an inhibitor on the comms? Surely you want to be able to call for help in an emergency don't you?" Tovis sat down in the Captain's chair and debated this new development aloud. He had always found that talking a problem through, with himself acting both sides of an argument or discussion, often made answers easier to find. He was intelligent enough to realise that the most likely reason for wanting to inhibit the comms would be if hostile forces had taken over the ship. Given that he knew of only three others alive apart from himself, this seemed a plausible explanation.

"Maybe pirates boarded the ship and tried to take it over, but one of the engineers managed to fit the inhibitor before they abandoned the ship," he mused. "Or it could be a permanent but non-functioning fixture in normal circumstances. Then some emergency happened to them that made them decide to switch it on." Weighing up all the possibilities, he decided that the latter was the most likely option. This still offered no explanation as to where the crew had gone or why, but it did help him to feel a little less paranoid about the whole situation. For the first time, he had to admit that maybe it was not a personal vendetta he was experiencing after all. Maybe he had simply been unlucky enough to be in the wrong place at the wrong time.

"Just my damned luck," he moaned as he got up and wandered back to the comms. Switching to the inter-galactic emergency channel, he recorded a distress call and set it to transmit on a continuous loop. It would save him from having to sit in the chair and physically make the call himself and would give everyone time to do other things while waiting for help to arrive. He was careful not to give his name in the message; he did not want to escape the ship only to end up in custody. Smiling to himself at having made this breakthrough, he went down to deck four and along the corridor to the engineering briefing room to leave a message for Tearan and the others.

"Hi there, guys. My name is Tovis Kerral and I'm a survivor like yourselves. I managed to get the comms working today. There was some sort of inhibitor attached inside that prevented it from working. It's really weird, I've not come across anything like it before. I've left it on the table here for Mykus to take a look at. Your engineering brain might recognise it. You might even find them in other parts of the ship. I listened to your messages by the way and I was wondering if any of you are getting your memories back yet? The reason I ask is because I have no amnesia at all, which is a little weird don't you think. Why should I not have it when all of you three do? I am having weird dreams though. Anyway, maybe we should get together, we'd surely be stronger as a unit. I'll keep checking out the security room and engineering and see if I can't catch you guys there. By the way, I've set a distress call going on an automatic loop so we don't have to continuously man the comms."

After carefully replacing the recording device, he went down to deck five to make himself a meal. He was pleased with his accomplishment and gave himself an extra-large portion of meat to celebrate his ingenuity. As he ate, he wondered whether any of the ship's other systems might have such inhibitors fitted. Now he knew what to look for, he would recognise it no matter where it was situated. It would not hurt to spend some time checking out the main sensor array controls and then perhaps the ballistics and weapons control after that. If he and Mykus worked together, they might get the entire ship working again. They might even be able to fly it to the nearest system. Surely if they pooled their knowledge and experience, they could get the ship moving in some fashion? Then he remembered in one of his messages, Tearan said he thought he had navigation skills. Between the three of them, they could fix this, he postulated.

Not wanting to waste any more time now that there might be a possible way out of this strange situation, he headed up to deck three as soon as he finished his meal. The main sensor array governor was completely alien to him, but that did not deter him for more than a moment.

After giving the console and its bank of switches, dials, and levers, a quick once over, he realised none of it meant anything to him. Unperturbed, he sat down on the floor and ripped off the repair access panels.

"Wow," he muttered at the mass of components, tubes, wires, and connections. For a moment, his confidence vanished and he almost changed his mind. The dizzying mass of guts inside the body of the sensor array governor was so unlike anything he had worked with before that he suddenly doubted the logic of the whole idea. After a moment of hesitation, he shook his head and remembered the inhibitor components. "All I have to do is look for something the same as the thing I removed from the comms," he reminded himself, "and ignore everything else. C'mon buddy, you can do this."

As he had done on the bridge, Tovis gradually worked his way into the body of the sensor array governor, searching for the same three components as the ones he found in the comms. After three hours, his body ached, as did his head, and he was thirsty. Carefully extricating himself from the body of the sensor array, he wiped a hand across his brow and decided to finish for the day. He would start again refreshed after a few hours' sleep. With a groan, he stretched his back and rotated his shoulders a few times, then walked back to the stairs. A hot shower would help his muscles relax, he thought as he stripped his clothes off.

Once dressed in a change of clothes, he made his way to deck five and the recreation room to watch a couple of movies. Tovis loved movies. He was a thinker, a worrier, and sometimes found it difficult to stop his mind from working at top speed. At such times, he found himself craving movies. The often rather shallow and unsophisticated nature of them allowed the deeper levels of his mind to switch off and get some much needed rest. He found even the dullest of movies very therapeutic to watch and never criticised them as he often heard others doing. To him, it was the action of watching that he enjoyed, not the subject of his attention. They were a form of healing meditation for him. After gathering a plate of snacks and a drink, he settled down and flipped through the movie library.

Waking refreshed and with hope soaring in his heart, Tovis was ready to get back to the sensor array. The hope, the need for success, swept through his mind as he imagined seeing the lights on the control panel come to life before his eyes. For five hours, he was carried along on a wave of optimism. When his physical discomfort became too great, the hope began to struggle. His ass was cold and numb from sitting on the floor and his neck ached from craning it at all angles to peer inside the body of the console. All that discomfort and he was only a quarter the way into the huge mass of wires, tubes, connections, and components. After taking a break for something to eat and drink, he wandered along to the security room to find Tearan, then down to the main engineering section in search of Mykus. Having failed to find either of them, he went down to deck six to find the doctor but the place was deserted. His mind finally had to allow the thought he had been avoiding, to enter his consciousness and demand attention.

"Where can they be?" he asked himself aloud as he climbed back up the stairs. "Why can I never find them and why do they never find me?" No answers came and the questions bothered him. Being honest with himself, he admitted that he had been wondering about it for a while but did not want to face it. "It's not as if they can disappear, we're on a space ship for fuck's sake. We all know each other is around. Both Tearan and Mykus have mentioned getting together, so why have we not yet done it?" A thread of paranoia wound itself around Tovis' heart and clung there. Now that he acknowledged the strangest aspect of this entire strange experience, those unanswered questions raced around his head, dominated his thoughts, and sapped his optimism.

Feeling unsettled and pessimistic once again, he decided to channel some of the negative energy and work out in the small gymnasium he remembered seeing in the security room. If Tearan returned, it would give them a chance to say hello, exchange experiences and information, maybe even formulate a plan of action together. After lifting some weights, he went for a run and thought about his life as he ran along corridors and up and down the staircases. His early life in Deep Space Orphanage 1740 was not marred by cruelty or abuse of any kind, but it lacked the sort of connection that only loving parents can give a child. During his lifetime, he knew many people with memories of terrible cruelty or outright neglect as children. He was well aware that not all parents are able to love their children unconditionally. Having missed the undivided attention of parents and a family, he always yearned for it.

There were times when he considered the option of searching out his natural parents, but the possibility of them rejecting him a second time always made him hesitate. As he ran along the corridors of the space ship, he wished very much that he had searched for them. Now that his survival was not guaranteed, the absence of answers to those questions about his childhood was an aching void. He did not want to die with that void still empty and decided that if he did survive, he would seek them out and get those answers. The people who ran the orphanage were kind, but the life was by necessity a little regimented. This was largely because there were three hundred and forty two children being raised there at any one time. Tovis understood and did not blame them for any lack of individual attention he experienced. Quite the opposite in fact. Being the only thing approaching a family, it angered him when he heard people dismissing the orphanage system as flawed. "It might not be perfect," he mused, "but it did alright by me."

There were several times during his dubious career, when large sums of money came his way, all of which he anonymously donated to the governing body of the Inter-Galactic Deep Space Orphanages. They took him in as a newborn, raised him, educated him, secured employment for him, and equipped him for life as an adult as best they could. They did it all without ever beating him or abusing him in any way and until his career choice demanded that he be a little less visible, they kept in touch with him regularly. Tovis was grateful and despite feeling he missed out by not having loving parents, he knew without doubt that he had been raised by people who genuinely cared.

Shaking his head to dispel the melancholic mood, he ran up to his room on deck two for a shower.

"I have to concentrate on getting away from here," he muttered as the hot water cascaded down his back. "I can think about my life later. For now, getting off this crate is my first priority."

9

Tearan stood in the cargo hangar and examined the long racks of shelving. His task was to rearrange the stores to gain access to the long wall at the back of the large space. It seemed obvious to move all foodstuffs and related stores to the kitchen and dining room for storage. Food, drinks, condiments, crockery, cutlery, cleaning materials, and laundry products, all would be better stored in the kitchen and dining room itself. Everything would be on hand for easy resupply and there was plenty of space in the recreation room next door for any overspill.

"Okay, let's do this," he said as he walked over to the hover loaders. After noticing that one of the vehicles appeared to be missing, he frowned. He must have remembered wrong, he decided as he hopped into the nearest and started it up. Maybe Mykus has one, he thought as he manoeuvred it alongside the first of the huge storage racks. Before beginning the task of rearranging the storage, he spent an hour removing all but one of the tables in the dining room, leaving plenty of room to stack everything. Having spent several hours studying the digital manifest, he made a plan so that everything would be stored in a logical manner. This would make sure everything would be easily accessible and should help ensure nothing essential was lost or forgotten.

Specially sealed crates of preserved meat, fish, shellfish, and poultry went up first and were stored together in one area of the room. Next came crates of preserved vegetables and fruit, which he stored separately from the meat. Dried protein chunks, herbs, spices, powders, and sauces. Baking ingredients, cereals, freeze dried and powdered juices, all were stored according to their purpose and frequency of use. Anything that might be used more often was placed in front of those things used more infrequently. As he worked, Tearan entered everything into a brand new manifest so he had a running account of everything. There was no hurry to get it done quickly, time was plentiful and he wished to fill it as much as he could, so he took his time and made sure everything was done properly.

Cleaning and laundry materials were stored next door in the recreation room, as were personal washing necessities. All stock connected with the auto snack and drink dispensers were stored with the various machines. He did not bother to supply the machines in the senior officers' briefing room and observation lounge as they would not be used too often. With only three people on board, Tearan supposed everyone would be happy to stick to using the ones in the dining room, recreation room, and engineering briefing room. If they did complain, he would not mind fetching more supplies for the others, as well as those in the security room, as and when they were needed. Once the dining room was filled, he stored all the extra stock in the nearest of the staff quarters along the corridor. By the time all foodstuffs had been moved, three of the staff quarters were filled to the ceiling. Tearan guessed that they could all live to a good standard for at least five years, longer if they were careful. That was assuming rescue never came of course, which he decided to dismiss as impossible.

As he laboured, memories floated back and he wallowed in the relief as each one came back to his mind like missing loved ones and slotted into place. Many times during the day, Tearan laughed aloud as he remembered some of the antics he and his friends got up to during their seven years military training. The officer in charge of Tearan's squad, a strict disciplinarian but fair judge quickly earned all the boys' respect. There was no particular single moment when he was aware of having left boyhood behind; no one moment when he knew he was finally a man. Instead, his was a gradual transition into manhood and when he returned to his parents at the end of those seven long years, the boy they had waved goodbye to was gone. In his place was someone who looked his father in the eyes like a man, a man who his father rapidly came to respect. Tearan saw combat during his seven years but his parents knew better than to question him. His father remembered his own seven years and the traumatic battle that claimed ten of his own squad, leaving him the only man standing amongst ten corpses and held his questions back. His mother remembered the way her husband's eyes would cloud whenever she asked him about his time, the way he would shake his head and say nothing more than, "We will not speak of it my love," and held her tongue as she embraced her son.

Memories floated back as Tearan worked and by the time he sat down to a meal after finishing work for the day, he felt whole for the first time since waking up aboard the ship. Like welcoming an old friend back into his arms, he got to know himself anew and decided that he liked the man he found. The memories from his early years were strong and vibrant, as if he were remembering them from just days ago. Oddly, the more recent memories, those from the previous five years of his life had a hazy quality that made them more like dream images than memories. They were there but felt almost like the memory one has of a movie. You can remember what you have seen but there is no personal connection with the images. Then there was the woman.

Her face floated through Tearan's mind and despite not having any concrete memories of her, he felt a strong conviction that she had been a part of his life somehow. As he tried to fix upon the image with his mind, it wriggled away and the more he chased her, the quicker she escaped him. It was frustrating and his heart pounded with irritation at not being able to fill in what he felt sure was an important part of his life. The only thing he was sure of was that she was important to him at some time, and that she was gone. How or why she was gone was a mystery, but Tearan knew in his gut that she had a major impact on his life, by her presence and by her leaving. As he ate, he suddenly felt that perhaps it would be best if he never got those particular memories back.

Tearan awoke after a night of troubled dreams. Terror coursed through him as he ran, his feet heavy as lead seeming to conspire to slow him down. Angry voices followed close behind and he became terrified for his safety. Darkened streets gave way to wasteland and derelict buildings, which quickly became open fields and long matted tussocks of grass that snagged his ankles and grabbed at his feet. Leaping a river, the icy water shocked his bare feet, but still he ran, knowing his very life depended upon it. Trees loomed in the dark and he flew into their protective arms, desperate to find cover in which to hide from the throng on his heels that bayed for his blood. Leaping roots and fallen trees, Tearan raced through the undergrowth, following no particular direction or plan. All at once, a searing pain tore through his thigh and he fell, howling in agony as the voices caught him up. Dead leaves cushioned him as he wrapped his arms around his head, screamed in pain and felt himself surrounded by his pursuers.

The trees faded, to be quickly replaced by a deep circular pit in which he was held captive. The same angry voices yelled at him from the rim of the pit, twenty feet above. His naked body shivered, as much from fear as cold, his feet bound to stout wooden posts by restraints that bit into his skin painfully. Icy water sprayed down from above, a constant freezing mist that chilled him through to the marrow. Angry voices screamed from above and fingers pointed down at him from the darkness. Not knowing why he was being held, nor what he was supposed to have done, he cried and begged for mercy, waking with tears fresh on his cheeks. He sat up in bed, relieved that it had been nothing more than a nightmare.

Over breakfast, he decided that his nightmare was most likely a result of finding himself alone aboard the space ship. That, coupled with the influx of memories the day before must have upset him, he decided. This was obviously a sign that his mind was getting over whatever trauma had befallen everyone and he was relieved beyond measure. It felt like a huge weight lifting from his shoulders and hope coursed through him. He dared to hope that he might get off the ship after all, that if he and Mykus worked together they might get the ship working again so they could call for help. With fresh hope, he got up and headed down to the cargo hangar.

Tearan stopped as soon as he entered the large space and knew something was different. For several moments he stood and focussed his attention on the room, an instinctive knowing deep inside his gut telling him that something was out of place. Just as he was about to shake his head and assume he was imagining things, his gaze fell upon the hover loaders that stood against the far wall.

"What the fuck?" he muttered, his brow creasing into deep furrows. He walked over to where the vehicles stood, counting them repeatedly but always getting the same result. "There was one missing yesterday." He spent the entire previous day using one of the loaders, driving it up and down stairs and along the corridors on deck five and not once had he encountered anyone else using another vehicle. If Mykus or anyone else were using a loader, either they would have heard him on his, or he would have heard them on theirs. Not once had he been aware of any odd noises that might have signalled a hover loader in use elsewhere and the longer he thought about it, the odder it seemed. Finally, he had to admit that something about it was off. With a scratch of his head, he climbed aboard the nearest loader.

His focus for the next few hours was to move as much as possible from the long wall of shelving and put it onto the shorter rows, into the space created by moving the foodstuffs. In order for everything to be easily accessible, he was careful to mark down the changes in the digital manifest as he worked. If Mykus should need a component, wire, tool, or connector in an emergency, knowing where to lay their hands on it quickly might mean the difference between life and death. Tearan realised how grave the situation could quickly become, so he took the trouble to list everything accurately. By the time he stopped for a mid-day meal, all the available space on the short rows of shelving was filled. The next obvious task was to move the crates of medical supplies down to the medical bay where it belonged. This would create more space for engineering stuff.

By the time Tearan decided he was tired and wanted to stop for the day, all of the medical cargo was successfully stored in the medical bay, isolation ward, medical research lab, and morgue. He found no trace of Doctor Arma, but the crazy scribblings still decorating the walls gave him shivers as he read about ghosts and dismembered bodies. Reading the crazy ramblings made him wonder if it was safe down here after all. Whoever wrote it was, or had been at some point, seriously disturbed. He decided that once he had some time, he would come down and clean it all off. All this stuff about ghosts and bodies cut up creeped him out.

"I wonder if Mykus has seen this?" he muttered as he left.

After returning the hover loader to the cargo hangar, Tearan climbed back up to deck four and walked along to the engineering briefing room to leave a message for Mykus. He was surprised to find two messages already waiting for him, the first of which was from Mykus.

"Tearan. I can assure you the vidicom has been fixed by someone. That means both you and I are both nuts, or there is someone else aboard with us. I feel sure it isn't Doctor Arma though, and I have a bad feeling about him. I am willing to bet you a hundred that something horrible has happened to him. Call me crazy if you want, but I know what I'm feeling. Anyway, I found a section of wire had been cut and removed. Cut, not broken by the way. Deliberately cut out. Four inches of it including an overload connection socket, cut out cleanly. Another thing too, the engineering crawlspace has been blocked off above deck seven. Access down there is impossible, I checked for access panels but there are none. This is very odd and against all the regulations in existence. I also agree about the size of the rooms on decks seven and eight. I paced it out and you're right, there's a large area of space sectioned off down there. Now for the bad news. Despite fixing the wire, the shuttle bay emergency back up control still will not work and I cannot get those bay doors shut. Sorry. I'm going to continue my inspection of the ship's systems. Come by when you have time and talk about it."

"I knew it," Tearan shrieked, thumping a fist down onto the table. "Why block off such a large portion of the ship and try to hide its existence? I have to find out what's going on down there." Mykus' news served only to further his conviction that gaining access to the blocked off space was important. Even if it turned out to be empty and silent, he had to know. The whole idea of blocking off such a large section of two decks and trying to make it invisible, unnoticeable, was too incongruous to ignore. Mykus' apparent conviction that someone had been fiddling with the vidicom brought deep furrows to Tearan's brow. Knowing the two of them had not touched it meant that they must assume Doctor Arma had done so, or that there was indeed someone else aboard. A flush of fear coursed through him and he acknowledged the feeling of invisible eyes watching him before shaking it off and listening to the next message.

"Hi there, guys. My name is Tovis Kerral and I'm a survivor like yourselves. I managed to get the comms working today. There was some sort of inhibitor attached inside that prevented it from working. It's really weird, I've not come across anything like it before. I've left it on the table here for Mykus to take a look at. Your engineering brain might recognise it. You might even find them in other parts of the ship. I listened to your messages by the way and I was wondering if any of you are getting your memories back yet? The reason I ask is because I have no amnesia at all, which is a little weird don't you think. Why should I not have it when all of you three do? I am having weird dreams though. Anyway, maybe we should get together, we'd surely be stronger as a unit. I'm in room ten on deck two. I'll keep checking out the security room and engineering and see if I can't catch you guys there. By the way, I've set a distress call going on an automatic loop so we don't have to continuously man the comms."

Tearan's eyes widened in surprise when he heard this new person introduce himself and as with Mykus and Doctor Arma, there was something about him that seemed familiar. Try as he might, he was unable to pinpoint what it was and he shook his head in frustration. He seemed friendly enough though and keen to pitch in and help. Having working comms helped their situation and it might not be long before someone hears the call and comes to rescue them. He glanced over at the table but found no components, so guessed Mykus beat him to the message. This was the best news he had since waking up on board and he was smiling as he felt his earlier paranoia disperse. Relieved to have another person with usable skills, Tearan recorded a response.

"Hi there, Tovis, Tearan Lindo here. Welcome to umm, well wherever we are. I can't see any component on the table here, so I guess Mykus is already checking it out. I hope he finds and removes one from the shuttle bay emergency controls so we can get those bay doors closed and have access to those shuttles. I've noticed something odd about the size

of the rooms down on decks seven and eight. The rooms as they appear on the maps are much bigger than they actually are and I estimate there's a substantial amount of space hidden away down there. Take a look at the maps and pace out the cargo hangar and shuttle bay. Then go and pace out the hazardous waste store, you'll see what I'm talking about. I'm shifting some stuff in the cargo hangar so I can gain access to the far wall that should be the boundary wall of the spare space and if it comes to it, I'll crash through it with a hover loader. I won't rest until I've found out the reason for the discrepancy in the sizes of those rooms. Have either of you come across Doctor Arma yet? And have either of you seen that crazy shit down in the medical bay? Go take a look if you want to be creeped out. It makes me wonder if it's safe down there. He could be a crazy hatchet murderer for all we know, waiting to leap out on us and hack our heads off. Be careful down there until we know for sure where he is and what condition he's in. Oh, by the way. I got the rest of my memories back over the past couple of days, all except some of the more recent stuff. I've started having some nightmares too, so I guess this is all part of the process. Come by the cargo hangar and find me, I'd like to meet you both."

With renewed hope, Tearan went up to deck three and the security room to shower. His mind was fully engaged upon buttoning up his shirt when a sound made him snap his head up and spin around, eyes wide with shock.

"Tearan Lindo? Hello, anyone home? I came to introduce myself to a fellow survivor. Hello."

"Hello?" Tearan called in reply, walking towards the main entrance area to greet the visitor. "Come on in. Is that you Mykus? Tovis? Doctor Arma?" After doing a tour of the whole security area and not finding anyone, Tearan stood and frowned. "Jeez, he didn't wait long did he? I could've been taking a shit or something. A little patience huh?" He ran into the corridor and looked both ways. "Hello?" he yelled. "I'm here." No boot steps echoed other than his own as he returned to the security room.

His reflection gazed back impassively as he combed his hair and contemplated the situation.

"I guess whoever it was that came to visit was in a hurry. I told them I'm working in the cargo hangar at the moment, so maybe they didn't expect me to be here anyway. It won't be too...what the fuck?" Tearan's musings were abruptly halted by a loud crash that shook the items on the bathroom shelf in front of him. His dental cleanser fell into the basin as the mirror shook against the wall. Not wanting to be covered in broken glass, Tearan steadied it with both hands until the shaking subsided. When all was still, he ran from the bathroom into the main area of the security room, expecting to find himself in the midst of devastation. Everything was as it should be and he frowned. That crash had sounded like it was right inside the room, like an impact or something smashing through a wall or door. He sniffed as an acrid smell wafted past his nose and recognised the smell of an engine.

"That smells like a hover vehicle engine." He walked around, allowing his nose to guide him towards any possible source of the smell, but found nothing except the familiar security room he now called home. There was no doubt in his mind what caused the smell, he owned many hover bikes over the years and knew how to tune their engines and keep them running smoothly. All of those memories, along with many others, came back to him the previous day. The acrid fumes caught his throat and he put a hand over his mouth, knowing that such fresh fumes meant that a hover engine was nearby. "That's the smell of a hover engine in trouble, big trouble." There was no vehicle to be seen and Tearan knew the only hover engines aboard were on the cargo bay loaders. He had been using one for the past two days and knew they were the only possible sources of that smell. He had no idea what the ship's engine would smell like if it blew apart, but he was smart enough to realise that if he did smell it, it would mean the ship was falling apart and he would likely be dead already.

He then remembered one of the loaders had been missing on his first day working in the cargo hangar. He assumed Mykus was using it and when it reappeared the following day, he thought nothing more about it. "But why should there be such a strong smell of a hover engine in here now? If someone came in here on a hover loader I would have heard the engine ticking over." Shaking his head in confusion, he ran a hand through his hair and examined the floor. Any hover vehicle in enough trouble to cause such an acrid smell would leave oily marks on the ground. It was pristine and his frown deepened. Crouching down, he reached out a hand, letting his sensitive fingertips caress the metallic tiles. As he was about to bring his hand away, his fingers registered an irregularity and his mind snapped into full focus. Sweeping his hands back and forth across the area, he let his fingers tell his mind what it was.

"Scratches," he muttered under his breath. Lying flat on his stomach, he turned his head and put his cheek to the floor. The angle of light playing on the tiles showed up the two sets of scratches clearly. From the doorway, all the way into the room for around twelve feet or so, where they ended in a large irregular worn area. There was also a slight dent approximately a foot in diameter, which looked like something having come to rest after skidding across the floor. Tearan got up and frowned. What did this mean? There was no evidence of anything untoward having happened within the past couple of minutes and he had to admit that he had not noticed the damage to the floor before. He had not been looking for it though and it was sheer luck that he found them at all.

"I'm going crazy and paranoid," he announced as he stood and shook his head. "I did hear a crash though, it shook the whole room. I didn't imagine that." One hour later, he stood in the kitchen and wondered what to make himself to eat. After a quick tour of every room on board, there was nothing to account for the crash he heard and no obvious damage to the ship to worry about. "I wonder if the other guys heard it," he muttered as he took off his jacket and washed his hands. Whilst waiting for his meal to cook, he thought about his plan for the next day of labour in the cargo hangar. Now that all the food and medical supplies were out of the way, he could shift more of the crates. This would free up more of the long wall of shelving.

Despite wanting to get to the task of examining that long wall, Tearan knew how important it was to know where everything in the cargo hangar was. This was especially true of anything connected with engineering or the working of the ship itself. If the ship should suffer an engineering emergency, a hull breech from a small particle of space debris, a problem with the engine or some electrical fault, Mykus would need to know exactly where to find every component, connector, clip, valve, and length of wire. Wasting valuable time searching for something only hastens a nasty death. Safety was paramount, so he decided to spend the next day rearranging all the crates and storage bins so that everything connected with engineering or the running and repair of the ship was together. Although desperate to get away from this isolation, he had to admit he was getting used to it. It was becoming familiar and easier to cope with so one more day delay would not hurt.

Tearan spent the night running from unseen pursuers, begging the angry voices for mercy, and walking the perimeter of the circular pit. The woman's face floated beside him as he circled and he grew frightened. Her accusing glare bore into him no matter how hard he tried to ignore her presence and he awoke screaming at her to go away and leave him alone. Sweat beaded on his brow and glued the sheet to his body. He ripped the sheet aside and sat up, breathing hard as he watched the remains of his dreams fade. His conviction that the woman was someone known to him would not go away and he frowned.

"Who the fuck is she? I'm certain I know her somehow. Dammit, why won't the memory come back?" he spat, jabbing the flat of a palm to his forehead. With the burden of frustration weighing heavily, he got up and went to work out before having a hot shower and going down to the kitchen for breakfast. He walked the corridor, heading for the stairs but something made him climb instead of descend. Without warning, his mind cried out for company and he knew it was time to address the need to find one of the others, to finally make a connection with at least one of them. Too many weird things were happening and he did not wish to be alone for much longer. The dreams, the sounds of gunfire, footsteps, and the crash in his room the day before; there was no explanation for them and that worried him. With no exception, the last thing he wanted was to lose his mind so soon after getting it back. Tovis said he was staying in room ten on deck two, he remembered.

"Tovis?" Tearan called as he knocked on the door to Senior Officers' Quarters Room Ten. "Tovis Kerral? It's Tearan Lindo here. I came by to say hello. Are you awake? Hello." There was no answer and Tearan swore. "Fuck." Giving himself no time to change his mind and walk away, he fumbled in his pocket and drew out his own key card. Fully expecting it to be rejected, he slammed it into the slot and waited for the mechanism to spit it back out at him with an angry beep. The door swished open and his eyebrows shot up to the top of his forehead. Remembering that his key card came from the locker in the security room, he assumed it was a master key. The security personnel would need to have access to everywhere on board, so it stands to reason they would have master keys. With a shrug, he entered, still calling out but getting no reply.

"Hello, Tovis. Are you here? It's Tearan Lindo." He called as he entered the room to find it empty. The room was a cut above those on deck five where Mykus said he was sleeping and afforded much more classy living standards than his own arrangements in the security room. The bathroom was empty, so he allowed his curiosity to get the better of him and decided to investigate. Tovis was a tidy person; that much was obvious right away. The bed was pulled back neatly, the sheet folded down and over the end of the bed to allow the mattress to air. An extra blanket lay neatly folded on a chair to one side. The closet revealed ten shirts, all the same grey and green camouflage pattern that Tearan realised instantly would be perfect for someone on a stealth mission. Three pairs of pants hung below them, all uniformly dark grey and very hard wearing. Drawers revealed underwear that was comfortable rather than stylish and sturdy boots that matched his own stood to attention by the door. In the spacious and luxurious bathroom, the washing necessities were arranged with precision and everything was spotlessly clean. One drawer contained laser pistol power cells, placed in rows of five, each with the identification label facing to the left and each with the security tab torn off.

Tearan's eyebrows lifted once again at the sight of those power cells and he realised what Tovis Kerral was. Placing the cells with the identification labels facing left ensured extremely quick reloading. The only people who needed to be able to reload so quickly were military, security, or criminals. The security tab on a laser pistol power cell makes sure that it cannot discharge without first being fully engaged within the pistol. The action of engaging the cell into the pistol automatically tears the tab off, which folds back against the body of the cell housing as it sits within the cell chamber. It is an offence in the military and all law abiding security forces to remove the security tabs before loading and is a clear indication that the bearer is a gun for hire.

Living and working in the shadowy world between legality and illegality, these men and women have a reputation for being without morals. They do not choose a side as most people do. Their side is the one that pays the most and you may find them fighting alongside you one day, then hunting you the next. The vast majority of high profile murders are committed by such people and very few are ever brought to justice. They are masters of invisibility and one of Tearan's newly returned memories was being eight years old and telling his father that he wanted to be one when he grew up. His father laughed and asked him how he knew of such men. Tearan told him that his friend from the next street told him about an uncle of his that was one. His father told him there were plenty of other fine things to devote his life to and plenty of time to do them. The next day, his father went out for an hour, telling Tearan to remain at home and clean the house with his mother. When he went to play the following day, the boy and his family had moved away and Tearan never saw them again.

Now he was an adult himself, Tearan sat down on the bed and thought about that memory. It had never occurred to him at the time to connect his father going out with the family leaving town, but now he did and it seemed odd. Maybe the boy's family were cross that he had told about his uncle and had to move away to keep their secret. Now he thought about it, he realised that his own father's behaviour was strange. Why would he go and visit the family whose boy joked with his son about being a gun for hire when they grew up? Surely it was normal small boy stuff and not something to get worked up about? He wondered whether the reason his dad had gone around to his friend's house was not to complain, but to warn them their secret was out. Tearan shook his head slowly and grinned.

"Dad, was there something you weren't telling me, old man?" He laughed aloud and got up from the bed. If Tovis was indeed a gun for hire, which Tearan was convinced was true, his priority would be his own safety first and foremost. If anyone got into difficulty in the meantime, he could not be relied upon to help. Yes, he had skills that Tearan intended to make full use of for as long as possible, but he would try not to put himself in a position where he would need to rely on Tovis for help. He also knew it would be a very bad idea to ever bring up the subject of his career.

"I'm not going to be asking you what you do for a living, that's for sure," he muttered as he left the room and went down to deck four to find Mykus.

10

Mykus sat on the edge of his bed for many minutes. The dream was still vivid and did not fade as dreams usually do. As his conscious mind absorbed the images, the memories flooded back and he wailed with grief. They first met as children and she never knew how much he loved her until their brief affair during their late teenage years. When she left him after falling in love with Dosmik Lolien, another of their mutual friends, Mykus' heart broke but he remained silent and stayed that way while watching them become a couple. He was present at their marriage, was amongst the first to be told when both their children were born, and always kept his broken heart a secret. When Dosmik went crazy and murdered her and their two children, Mykus berated himself for letting her go and wished that he had said something to prevent it. He felt as guilty for their deaths as Dosmik was. If he had spoken up, she might not have fallen for their friend at all and she would not have met such a gruesome end.

"Elestra Millay," Mykus whispered to the empty room as he finally remembered her name. With a moan of anguish, he dragged his heavy heart from its melancholy and went to shower. First priority on his list was the investigation of the stanchions that hold the engine housing in place within the engine bay at the very centre of the ship. He knew that if there were a problem with them, or the gas supply tubes and valves that ran along the top of two of them, he would not be able to fix it alone. Each of the stanchions weighed several tons and Mykus was confident that even with Tearan and Doctor Arma helping, their combined strength would be inadequate for the task. When the ship was built, the stanchions were put into place using computer controlled robotic cranes. Not having power to the ship meant such help was unavailable and all work would have to be done by man power alone. No, if the stanchions, gas supply tubes, or valves prove to be faulty, it's goodbye to their dreams of getting the ship going.

How can there be so many different hues of the colour green? Mykus asked himself this question every time he encountered this type of engine. When working at optimum, there were so many greens they defied his attempts to count them. The silently swirling liquid gases within were mesmerising. Like a slowly churning maelstrom, it drew his gaze and held him in its hypnotic grasp. A galaxy in miniature, he reckoned that if he concentrated hard enough, he might watch stars form, planets encircle them while their own moons orbit gracefully. As quickly as these solar systems formed, they disappeared, to be replaced seconds later with more. Mykus was always transfixed and appreciated the engines not only for their efficiency, but also for their hypnotic beauty. Forcing away his daydream, he rolled his neck around before climbing into the safety harness.

Once he was safely attached to the topmost stanchion, Mykus fixed the Snail in place and switched it on. The ring shaped device is designed to detect minute cracks and flaws in metal rods and tubes. Nicknamed the Snail because of the slow pace at which it crawls along the rod, its digital readout displays what its range of sensitive detectors are seeing. If the Snail picks up a flaw or minute crack, it stops its slow creep along the stanchion, a light flashes and an alarm sounds. Best of all, the device is battery powered so the ship's lack of power was not an issue. Mykus would not have to hang there in the harness twiddling his thumbs for hours watching the Snail creeping along each of the stanchions. That would be slightly less interesting than watching paint dry. He would be able to occupy himself with other tasks, but he would have to remain within earshot of the alarm.

Once the Snail began its slow creep along the first of the stanchions, Mykus climbed down to check the third most likely source of any problem on his list. The collector, fitted inside the base of the engine housing, is a ten-foot high rod that sticks up through the centre of the swirling mix of liquid gases. Its tip is coated with a substance that attracts the Quasic particles produced by the mixing of the two liquid gases. Once attracted to the tip of the collector, the Quasic particles are channelled down its length and into the base where they are stored prior to passing through the Quasic Modulator on their way to be used by the ship's various systems. Checking the operation of the collector and modulator should be relatively simple tasks and Mykus would normally be finished by the time three of the stanchions had been checked. The collector has a built in diagnostic system that checks the efficiency of the particle collection, the integrity of the storage module, and the calibration of the modulator. Having no power to the engine meant that he was forced to rig up a bypass circuit to power the diagnostic from the Life Support System power feed. So long as his bypass held, the diagnostic would function normally. All he had to do was set the diagnostic programme going, then sit back and wait until the Snail had finished its slow creep along the stanchion.

By the time he stopped for a meal, he was pacing. Having run the collector and modulator diagnostic programme and found them both working perfectly, he spent some time tidying the engineering section before finally sitting down to wait it out. Now he knew without doubt that three of the stanchions were undamaged, two of them being the ones carrying the gas resupply tubes and valves. In an effort to be optimistic, he allowed himself to predict that all the others would prove to be undamaged too. Despite the job of checking the engine taking so much time, everything needed to be checked in the right order to be sure of finding the problem. Once he knew for sure that the whole of the engine assembly was functioning normally, the next thing to check would be the supply tubes that ran from the Quasic Modulator, to all corners of the ship wherever power is needed. The task would be labour intensive but there was no other way to find whatever the problem might be. Besides, there was nothing else for him to do whilst stuck aboard an abandoned space ship, so why not? It would save him from going crazy with boredom.

Deciding on a whim to go along the corridor to the engineering briefing room to leave an update for Tearan, he yawned and stretched as he left the main engineering room and headed left. His interest was immediately piqued as his eyes fell upon three small components on the large table that dominated the room. Reaching over to scoop them up, he recognised what they were and frowned.

"An inhibitor array. What the hell is this doing here?" Hoping the recorder would yield an explanation, he went over and played the messages from Tovis and Tearan.

"Hi there, guys. My name is Tovis Kerral and I'm a survivor like yourselves. I managed to get the comms working today. There was some sort of inhibitor attached inside that prevented it from working. It's really weird, I've not come across anything like it before. I've left it on the table here for Mykus to take a look at. Your engineering brain might recognise it. You might even find them in other parts of the ship. I listened to your messages by the way and I was wondering if any of you are getting your memories back yet? The reason I ask is because I have no amnesia at all, which is a little weird don't you think. Why should I not have it when all of you three do? I am having weird dreams though. Anyway, maybe we should get together, we'd surely be stronger as a unit. I'm in room ten on deck two. I'll keep checking out the security room and engineering and see if I can't catch you guys there. By the way, I've set a distress call going on an automatic loop so we don't have to continuously man the comms."

Mykus was delighted to learn they had a new companion and hoped to meet him soon. He examined the inhibitor array in his hands, glad that there was someone else with some electrical and digitonics expertise aboard to help him out. He listened to Tearan's message and frowned.

"Hi there, Tovis, Tearan Lindo here. Welcome to umm, well wherever we are. I can't see any component on the table here, so I guess Mykus is already checking it out. I hope he finds and removes one from the shuttle bay emergency controls so we can get those bay doors closed and have access to those shuttles. I've noticed something odd about the size of the rooms down on decks seven and eight. The rooms as they appear on the maps are much bigger than they actually are and I estimate there's a substantial amount of space hidden away down there. Take a look at the maps and pace out the cargo hangar and shuttle bay. Then go and pace out the hazardous waste store, you'll see what I'm talking about. I'm shifting some stuff in the cargo hangar so I can gain access to the far wall that should be the boundary wall of the spare space and if it comes to it, I'll crash through it

with a hover loader. I won't rest until I've found out the reason for the discrepancy in the sizes of those rooms. Have either of you come across Doctor Arma yet? And have either of you seen that crazy shit down in the medical bay? Go take a look if you want to be creeped out. It makes me wonder if it's safe down there. He could be a crazy hatchet murderer for all we know, waiting to leap out on us and hack our heads off. Be careful down there until we know for sure where he is and what condition he's in. Oh, by the way. I got the rest of my memories back over the past couple of days, all except some of the more recent stuff. I've started having some nightmares too, so I guess this is all part of the process. Come by the cargo hangar and find me, I'd like to meet you both."

Tearan said there were no components on the table, but they were right there, he only found them a minute ago. How did he not see them? A dark cloud of fear came to life within his gut; fear for Tearan. So far, he seemed to be someone Mykus felt comfortable relying on and he was grateful that his only travelling companion was so dependable and sensible. Now he seemed to be losing it. Either that, or Mykus himself was and that thought did not exactly please him. He had also been wondering about Doctor Arma for days now and this news from Tearan did nothing to allay his fears. A doctor was a very useful addition to any group of people struggling to survive and for him to have not kept in touch was a further worry. Also of concern was Tearan's point about whether it was safe for anyone to venture around the ship without knowing what had happened to the doctor. It was entirely possible that this strange and traumatic experience was too much for his mind to cope with. Mykus shuddered at the thought that he might be sharing an abandoned space ship with a crazy assed axe murderer and decided it would be prudent to arm himself at the earliest opportunity. Trying not to panic, he recorded his own update.

"Hello, Tovis and welcome to this crazy ass nightmare. It's Mykus here. I have the inhibitor array you found and will check it out in more detail this afternoon while waiting for some stanchion integrity tests to finish. Tearan, I've only just found the inhibitor, so I've no idea why you couldn't see them when you recorded your message. Are we time travelling here now as well as everything else? That's a joke by the way; please

don't let that be actually happening, I don't think I could cope with that on top of all this other weird shit. Anyway, I can now confirm that the engine housing itself is intact and working perfectly, as is the collector and modulator. There are six more stanchions to check, but I have a hunch they will prove to be undamaged too. It looks as if I'm going to have to start checking the supply tubes that lead out from the modulator. That's not a job I'm looking forward to, but it's the obvious next step on the journey. Also, it'll be the first thing I will actually be able to fix if there is a problem. If it had been a problem with the engine, we would have no hope of getting the ship going again. I'll check the emergency shuttle bay control for an inhibitor this afternoon too. Now we know one was aboard, there may be more. I'll keep you updated. I'm worried about the situation regarding Doctor Arma and I have to admit it makes me nervous not knowing if he is okay or if we need to be careful. I'm an engineer not a soldier and I don't like violence. Oh, before I go. I've got my memories back too, but like you guys, the very recent stuff is still missing. The nightmares too, I'm having them now so I guess it's part of the process. It's better than not knowing anything though; that would definitely have driven me round the bend if it had continued for too long. Can we finally make a concerted effort to meet up now? You both know where to find me. Anyway, keep in touch guys."

Mykus was preoccupied throughout his meal. The combination of worry about the Doctor Arma situation, coupled with curiosity about the inhibitor array meant he was unable to concentrate on the pleasure of eating. Before leaving the dining room, he returned to the kitchen, took down two large carving knives, and hefted them from hand to hand. Jabbing and thrusting at thin air, Mykus practiced defending himself despite not knowing whether he would have the courage to stab a living person if it came to it. He hoped never to find out.

Once the Snail was busily making its way along another stanchion, Mykus turned his attention to the inhibitor array. With the aid of a pair of high magnification goggles, he examined it carefully before taking the small components apart piece by piece. It did not take him long to realise that the situation he had found himself in was even more strange than all of them thought. Once he was sure of his findings, he raced back along the corridor to the briefing room and snatched up the recorder.

"Hey, guys, it's Mykus again. It's now just over two hours since my last message and I've taken a close look at that inhibitor array you found, Tovis. I took it apart and checked it thoroughly and it makes this whole crazy situation even more crazy than any of us could have thought. That specific type of inhibitor is high end stuff. Extremely high end actually. In fact, it's a military component, I recognised the serial numbers on the inside and those prefixes are used for military components only. I'm not sure what this means for us and our part in this, whatever this situation is, but it just got a whole lot weirder. I have to get back to engineering, but I thought you should both know."

The afternoon dragged by, the passage of time marked by the slow progress of the Snail making its leisurely way along each of the remaining stanchions. Mykus stuck it out until all of them were checked and found to be without flaw, which meant he was late finishing but the thought of waiting for the Snail again the next day was too much. He was glad to get it all done in the one day and headed down to deck five and his room for a shower before making himself a meal. The following day, he would begin the huge task of gradually following each of the supply tubes that led out from the Quasic Particle Modulator. The supply tubes ran along under the floors and behind the inner hull inside the crawlspace. As he stripped off his clothes, he thought about the logistics of following each of the supply tubes throughout the entire ship. Should he follow each tube from the Modulator in engineering to its destination, or should he check each of the supply tubes on each floor and work down deck by deck? Deciding to think about it after a few hour's sleep, he stepped into the shower.

Wrapped in nothing more than a towel, Mykus stood before the mirror in his small bathroom and rubbed a hand over his chin. Stubble scratched his fingers and he frowned. Shaving was a chore he hated, but his hatred of facial hair was greater, so he took the time to do it. Worried blue eyes stared back at him as he gazed at his reflection and realised that he seemed different somehow. It had been a long time since he had studied his reflection and it was almost as if he did not recognise himself any more. He was about to turn away when he heard a voice call his name. It was Tearan; he recognised the voice from the recorder. Without warning, another face appeared behind him in the mirror. Gasping in shock, his hand went to his mouth as he felt adrenaline course through him. Shaking with the shock, Mykus was rooted to the spot as the pounding in his chest throbbed in his ears. Mykus knew he should confront him, but he was startled almost out of his wits by the sudden appearance of a face from so long ago, a face he should not be seeing again. Terror and surprise held him firm, preventing any action on his part so he stood, transfixed. It may have happened years ago, but Mykus knew he would never forget that face. No matter if he forgot everyone he had ever known, that face was forever etched upon his mind.

"Dosmik Lolien?" he whispered. This was the last thing he would ever expect to happen. What the fuck was Elestra Millay's murderer doing here on board this abandoned space ship with him? No, it was not happening. It was impossible for one obvious reason; Dosmik Lolien had been sentenced to death for murdering Elestra and their two children. This meant either he was imagining it, or Tearan bore an uncanny resemblance to the murderer. Mykus spun around to find no one behind him, but the distinctive swish of the door to his room caught his attention and he leapt from the bathroom just as the door to the corridor closed. Thoughts raced around inside his mind, so many questions that he found himself temporarily rooted to the spot unable to decide what to do. With a shake of his head, he screamed and ran for the door, leaping out into the corridor and looking both ways as he yelled at the top of his voice.

"Hey, Tearan. Or should I say, Dosmik? Come back here and talk to me. Hey, hey." Mykus stood in the corridor wrapped in the towel and yelled his head off for almost a minute until his throat dried and he coughed. Reluctantly he returned to his room and dressed hurriedly, before running along the corridor to check the kitchen, dining room and recreation room for Tearan. When he did not find him, he raced up to deck three and along the corridor to the security room and hammered on the door, yelling Tearan and Dosmik's names and demanding to be let in. He remained there for several minutes, hammering and yelling and finally slammed his own key card in the slot and marched into the room, not caring whether anyone was waiting there with a gun aimed at his head or not. He searched the entire security suite, even the lockers and cupboards and punched the wall in frustration when he had to admit that no one was there. Growling with anger, he marched back down to the kitchen to make his meal.

Although he tried to push all thoughts of Dosmik Lolien from his mind, Mykus allowed his dinner to burn, so consumed was he with questions about this strange new occurrence. Dosmik and he were friends since they were both at school, there was no way Mykus would mistake him for someone else. The years of their friendship, the days he spent at his trial and sentencing made sure his countenance was forever burned into his memory. Despite having dreams about Elestra and her murder at Dosmik's hands, Mykus did not believe he imagined seeing that face in his bathroom mirror. He distinctly heard Tearan calling his name moments before Dosmik's face appeared in the mirror. Then there was the sound of the door closing. If he was imagining the whole thing, why would the door open and close? Mykus frowned as his mind settled on this question, and then realised that he did not hear the door open, only the closing.

"The sound was probably covered by the running water in the shower, or the noise of my shaver." This was the most likely explanation and nothing changed the fact that he heard and saw the door closing, so someone had been in his room. "It had to be Tearan," he said to the empty room. "There's no other explanation for it. But, Dosmik Lolien? How can that be? Shit." He dropped his head into his hands and let out a frustrated howl of anguish while the questions still raced despite his attempts to push them away. It was not too much of a stretch to imagine that Dosmik escaped custody. Mykus agreed that such things do happen, but for him to be here on this ship with him, how could that happen? He wondered what the chances were for himself and Dosmik Lolien to be amongst the only five survivors of some deep space disaster, but had no idea how to begin working out the odds. The whole idea seemed preposterous and so completely out there that Mykus knew he would not believe it if someone else reported it. After trying and failing to take his mind off the situation by watching a movie, Mykus decided to go to bed and try to sleep it off. Maybe he would feel more at ease after some sleep, he thought as he made his way back to his room.

Sleep evaded Mykus. His mind was stuck in overdrive and refused to switch gear no matter how hard he tried to force it to quieten. Despite it being such a crazy experience, he could not move past the solid fact that he recognised Dosmik Lolien's face. Sitting up in bed, he tried one last time to get the facts as he knew them, straight inside his mind in order to have a chance at sleeping. It was a fact that he heard Tearan calling his name; he recognised his voice from the messages on the recorder they all used. Mykus turned this first fact over inside his head several times until he was sure he had not missed anything before moving on to the second. The next unalterable fact was that he was familiar with Dosmik Lolien and would not mistake his face. They were friends since childhood and his face was permanently burned into his mind. This second point was placed neatly beside the first, then he turned his attention to the third fact. Although present when Dosmik was sentenced to the death penalty, he did not witness the execution personally. This meant there was a chance he escaped. Finally, he heard and saw the door closing, which meant someone else had been there. Despite having to admit he might have imagined the face as belonging to Dosmik Lolien, he did not imagine the closing door.

Now too restless to remain in bed, Mykus walked the corridors of the empty ship, the strange occurrence swirling inside his mind until the anguish became too much. It was only when he put two facts together that things finally started making sense. Dosmik murdered Elestra and their two children and had known Mykus still had feelings for her. He tried to use this fact as an excuse during his trial, saying that Elestra was planning to leave him to return to Mykus and take their children with her. Although knowing this to be untrue, Mykus was somewhat surprised to find out Dosmik knew his feelings had not diminished since Elestra left him. In his twisted mind, he might wish to seek revenge for him still loving his wife. Mykus realised that it was a real possibility that Dosmik escaped and somehow caused whatever befell the ship on which he was either travelling or working, to have his revenge. The one thing he was unable to make sense of was why the voice he heard was Tearan's when the face was Dosmik's. Finding no answer to this conundrum, he wanted to assume that Tearan just happened to bear an uncanny resemblance to his childhood friend, but his mind was too troubled to accept that. As time wore on, events became mixed up inside his troubled mind and he grasped at one crazy idea after another until one remained. Dosmik Lolien was posing as Tearan Lindo in order to get revenge.

"I wonder why he's never bothered to come and introduce himself," Mykus muttered as he paced. "Why not get his revenge and be done with it. What's the point in pretending to be Tearan? What possible explanation was there for choosing now to reveal himself?" There was no way to know of course. Whatever motivated Dosmik might never be revealed and he found this undeniable fact troubling. His mind was one that needed precision. Unanswered questions and vague possibilities did not fit with him at all. This need for clarity made him the perfect candidate for life as an engineer and knowing that there was an aspect of this whole situation that he may never understand was like rubbing an open wound.

Worry weighed heavy inside the troubled mind of Mykus Romin and as the hours wore on, he paced the corridors of the abandoned space ship, trying to make sense of everything. Times without number, he went through the whole situation event by event, fact by fact, but always ended up with the same thing. Dosmik Lolien murdered Elestra and her two children and was here on board the ship posing as Tearan Lindo and trying to fuck with his mind. This angered Mykus and the more he acknowledged that anger, the more of the old anger he felt rise within. Emotions he thought he had dealt with at the time of Dosmik's trial came up from somewhere dark that he was not even aware existed within his soul and with a ferocity that scared him. This was not a straightforward case of lost love, nor even stolen love, or crime of passion. No, at the heart of this whole thing was self reproach for not trying harder to work things out with Elestra when they were breaking up. Tears coursed down Mykus's cheeks as he finally realised that he had more anger towards himself than for Dosmik.

Mykus was not truly aware as he began to scream. Obscenities flew from his heart and out of his mouth as he stalked the corridors. Feelings, many of which had never been acknowledged let alone voiced, were now given names, purpose, and direction. At some point in the early hours of a new morning, in those misty few hours that make it difficult to know whether you are alive or wandering in some other ethereal plane on your way to the afterlife, Mykus's mind crumbled. He was not aware of slipping from the world of order and sanity into one of dark chaos and you may think it a blessing that he be spared the cruel knowledge of that moment of ultimate loss. The screaming stopped and the ship became quiet, those misty ethereal early hours closing around it once again.

A light flickered red, beating regular time to a silent musical score that was echoed in the peaks and troughs of the readout waveform on the screen below. The light stopped flickering, the wave became a line and a deep voice echoed. A hand reached out and flipped switches.

"As predicted then, good."

A nod of acknowledgement. "Yes."

Soft footfalls turn heads and bring smiles. "Hourly update on M253016-143B. Everything within acceptable parameters, Sir."

The smiles broaden. Chests puff with pride. The man with the pale eyes nodded to the thin young man. Both men acknowledge the curvaceous woman warmly. All the hard work was paying off. The years of research studies and computer modelling, followed by years of ethical debate and argument before real experimentation began. Pale eyes had been with the project since the very beginning when his own friend and mentor had first put the idea forward as a legitimate possibility. Pale eyes took over when he died from a broken neck after a space shuttle crash and now his thoughts turned to the memory of his old friend. Sending a thought, he hoped the old man was proud, wherever he was.

A tall young man joined them. Pleasantries were exchanged and pride in the project was expressed. He handed over a digital console.

"Costings for you, Sir. Up to date as of this morning, as well as costing predictions for the next six months."

Pale eyes perused the information and nodded. Taking up the pen, he signed and handed back the console. The tall young man went to walk away, but hesitated.

"Oh, by the way. Remember your meeting tomorrow with the Protocol Committee."

"Thank you." Pale eyes shrugged to the thin young man. "The sponsors are pushing for a time scale and operation schedule."

The thin young man's eyes widened. "So soon? We're nowhere near that stage yet."

"I know, Julian, but they're paying for everything so if they want to know when they can make use of it, it's up to us to give them an answer they're happy with. We need them to keep paying for everything a while longer, so it pays us to indulge them."

"I understand, "Julian replied. "What do you need from me?"

Pale eyes sat down beside Julian. "Melissa, call my wife and let her know I'll be late please?"

Melissa made a note and walked away. Pale eyes and Julian discussed for an hour before being joined by the same tall young man as before. During the next hour, they studied readouts, watched security footage and listened to audio recordings. When they smiled, shook hands, and went their separate ways, Pale eyes was confident and proud.

11

Tovis Kerral stood and stretched his back. He was not an especially big man, but spending four hours hunched half in and half out of the sensor array was not conducive to his comfort. Despite not being able to identify most of what he found within the body of the machine, he felt sure there was no inhibitor in there. If there was, it was different to the one he found in the communications station. The possibility that a different type of inhibitor lurked within the seething mass of components worried him. His engineering skill was limited to cannibalising electronic and digital components. What he found within the sensor array was beyond anything he had ever worked with and he doubted the wisdom of his decision. For the first time, he contemplated giving up the search for more inhibitors. After putting the access panels back onto the body of the sensor array, he left the room and went next door to ballistics and weapons control.

Knowing that a distress call was going out continuously made him feel better with his predicament. The ability to call for help was the most important thing beyond basic survival needs. Although useful, a sensor array was not the most vital part of a survival kit, so he decided not to worry whether another inhibitor was hiding somewhere inside it. Weapons though, they are important. If those with ill intent discovered the ship, a chance to defend themselves meant a chance to survive. Then again, even those on the wrong side of the law would mean a way off the ship and any way off would be preferable to staying on board forever. Tovis spent years of his life in the company of people whose regard for the law was not that high. Such people did not faze him. In his opinion, laws are created by people and often tend to benefit only the rich. Many laws seemed to him to have little purpose other than to restrict the freedom of the masses, to keep them from fucking things up for the elite. The fact that upkeep of those laws was done by people with their own agendas and interpretations of their individual power engendered little respect from Tovis.

A non-conformist and dissenter at heart, Tovis was not one to actively rail against the accepted dogma of the society in which he plied his trade. He had his own view of imposed law and societal doctrine and lived by his own code of morals rather than the ones expected of him by those in power. The last thing he wanted was to start a revolution, he would never be found waving banners or shouting from rooftops. That sort of behaviour tended to result in nothing more helpful than gaining a criminal record that would forever cast a stain upon the lives of those who were least able to bear such a burden. More can be achieved, Tovis believed, by living his life according to his own values, whether they agreed with imposed precepts or not and if a direct action against a law is required, doing so quietly and without fanfare. His career often broke imposed laws and ideology, but never his own true values and he was fine with that. It was far more important that he be able to look himself square in the eye, than for someone with a power they do not deserve and cannot wield sensibly to do so.

Tovis knew how to be patient. His chosen career often demanded it. People were seldom predictable and even when he knew their habits and routines he never relied on them. People often think they do things to a fixed routine, but that is seldom true. They might think they leave the house at the same time every day, follow the same route to work, take lunch at the same time and place, and return home the same way at the same time. There are many differences in the tightest of schedules, which mean little to most people but can mean the difference between success and failure to people like Tovis Kerral. One person's clock might be set a couple of minutes slower or faster than another person's. What one person thinks of as eight thirty might be eight thirty three to someone else. Public transportation can run early, or late, or it might not turn up at all, throwing a schedule into complete chaos. A pretty girl can catch a man's eye, delaying his progress down the street enough to save his life, or sign his death warrant. Mouth watering cakes call from shop windows and you go inside to make an unscheduled purchase. You then miss your usual hover bus or return to work a few minutes later than usual.

Most of these discrepancies mean nothing to the vast majority of people, but for those like Tovis Kerral, they mean failure to connect with the right target. Since the cost of hiring someone in his line of work is rather high, Tovis learned the value of patience early on in his career. Shooting the wrong person not only goes against his own personal code but tends to infuriate whoever is paying him. So does not shooting the intended target at all. Tovis knew how the little variances in time change a person's routine, so he learned to wait and observe. Haste never served him well and he had never experienced a situation where he felt panic would be appropriate. Forcing himself to think slowly and carefully, he mentally assessed his situation and came up with a plan of action. The process took no longer than five minutes and consisted of four statements and one decision.

'I don't know how I got on this ship but I can't get off it yet.'

'There are a couple of others here but they haven't made real contact yet so I'm effectively alone in this.'

'There are plenty of supplies, enough to enable me to live reasonably comfortably for years so there's no immediate need to get away.'

'There is a distress call going out on continuous auto loop.'

'I will therefore dig in and wait it out until the situation changes.'

Having made the decision, there was nothing more to do other than decide how to fill the time until the situation changed. Knowing this could be either days, or years in the future, he knew he needed to fill his days with a schedule that not only used up time but kept him sharp physically and mentally. He would work out each morning before breakfast, then spend the day checking as many of the ship's systems as possible to check for inhibitor arrays. This would help keep his electrical and digitonic skills up to scratch and keep boredom from driving him crazy. Tearan Lindo seemed like a proactive kind of man who would no doubt be trying to find out what was going on and Tovis made the decision to aid him as much as possible. Now that he had a plan of sorts, he relaxed and returned to his room on deck two for a shower.

Once showered and dressed in fresh clothes, Tovis decided his first job was to find out if any of the others had left messages for him on the recording device, so he jogged down to deck four and along the corridor to the engineering briefing room. He was surprised to find himself pleased when he noticed three messages waiting for him. The first was from Tearan.

"Hi there, Tovis, Tearan Lindo here. Welcome to umm, well wherever we are. I can't see any component on the table here, so I guess Mykus is already checking it out. I hope he finds and removes one from the shuttle bay emergency controls so we can get those bay doors closed and have access to those shuttles. I've noticed something odd about the size of the rooms down on decks seven and eight. The rooms as they appear on the maps are much bigger than they actually are and I estimate there's a substantial amount of space hidden away down there. Take a look at the maps and pace out the cargo hangar and shuttle bay. Then go and pace out the hazardous waste store, you'll see what I'm talking about. I'm shifting some stuff in the cargo hangar so I can gain access to the far wall that should be the boundary wall of the spare space and if it comes to it, I'll crash through it with a hover loader. I won't rest until I've found out the reason for the discrepancy in the sizes of those rooms. Have either of you come across Doctor Arma yet? And have either of you seen that crazy shit down in the medical bay? Go take a look if you want to be creeped out. It makes me wonder if it's safe down there. He could be a crazy hatchet murderer for all we know, waiting to leap out on us and hack our heads off. Be careful down there until we know for sure where he is and what condition he's in. Oh, by the way. I got the rest of my memories back over the past couple of days, all except some of the more recent stuff. I've started having some nightmares too, so I guess this is all part of the process. Come by the cargo hangar and find me, I'd like to meet you both."

Tovis was pleased that he had accurately summed Tearan up. The man was obviously observant, which was always an admirable quality in a person and his theory of unused space down on decks seven and eight was intriguing. This was definitely something he wanted to be involved in. What possible purpose was there for such a hidden space? As his thoughts developed, he frowned. One fact made the whole thing suspicious as far as he was concerned; the furtiveness of it all. Unused space on its own was not something to be worried about. There could be all sorts of reasons for cordoning off part of the lower two decks and making the existing spaces smaller. Damage to the outer hulls, bringing the inevitable decompression of decks seven and eight was the first thing that came to mind. The crew might have needed somewhere in which to remain hidden from something or to remain safe from something. Some ultra-secretive military unit might be using the space for whatever their secret mission is. It was possibly a simple case of miscalculation by the creator of the maps, although Tovis thought this was probably the rank outsider of all his theories.

The thing that worried him most was the time necessary to do such a rebuild. It would take a substantial amount of time to rebuild two decks to create additional rooms, whether those additional rooms be indicated on the maps or not, and that smacked of an agenda. A response to an emergency would result in the job being done quickly and quality of workmanship would not be the first priority. If the ship were decompressing, the crew would need to make the environment safe as quickly as possible and would not be too worried about the aesthetics of the job. Tovis decided he needed to go and assess the whole thing for himself. If Tearan's theory was right and the size discrepancy was not a mistake by the map's creator, the workmanship of the job would tell him a lot. A hasty and obvious rebuild would indicate it was done quickly, which could hint at some emergency having befallen the ship. A quality rebuild that was not obvious, even on close inspection, would take time to achieve. That would hint at the job having been planned beforehand. That indicated the one thing Tovis hated more than anything else, a committee.

He closed his eyes and registered a shudder of annoyance ripple through him. Few things had the power to cause him more irrational rage than groups of bureaucrats and their agendas. Images of ageing men in robes, their beards brushing their knees as they argued back and forth the merits of this or that change being forced onto the poor unwitting masses flashed through his mind. To Tovis, they spend so long arguing back and forth that nothing positive ever gets done and what changes they do decide upon are always for the worse. If the changes to the ship really did exist, and the quality of the workmanship was good, Tovis knew this meant a committee was behind it. This obviously meant its purpose was negative for someone, and experience had taught him that usually meant those with the least power and zero choice. Yes, Tovis was a cynic but life had taught him to be. He groaned aloud and listened to the next message.

"Hello, Tovis and welcome to this crazy ass nightmare. It's Mykus here. I have the inhibitor array you found and will check it out in more detail this afternoon while waiting for some stanchion integrity tests to finish. Tearan, I've only just found the inhibitor, so I've no idea why you couldn't see them when you recorded your message. Are we time travelling here now as well as everything else? That's a joke by the way; please don't let that be actually happening, I don't think I could cope with that on top of all this other weird shit. Anyway, I can now confirm that the engine housing itself is intact and working perfectly, as is the collector and modulator. There are six more stanchions to check, but I have a hunch they will prove to be undamaged too. It looks as if I'm going to have to start checking the supply tubes that lead out from the modulator. That's not a job I'm looking forward to, but it's the obvious next step on the journey. Also, it'll be the first thing I will actually be able to fix if there is a problem. If it had been a problem with the engine, we would have no hope of getting the ship going again. I'll check the emergency shuttle bay control for an inhibitor this afternoon too. Now we know one was aboard, there may be more. I'll keep you updated. I'm worried about the situation regarding Doctor Arma and I have to admit it makes me nervous not knowing if he is okay or if we need to be careful. I'm an engineer not a soldier and I don't like violence. Oh, before I go. I've got my memories back too, but like you guys, the very recent stuff is still missing. The nightmares too, I'm having them now so I guess it's part of the process. It's better than not knowing anything though; that would definitely have driven me round the bend if it had continued for too long. Can we finally make a concerted effort to meet up now? You both know where to find me. Anyway, keep in touch guys."

Tovis liked Mykus despite not having met him yet. There was something about his manner that put him at ease right away. Tearan seemed likeable and trustworthy but he lacked something that Mykus had and it was a few minutes before he realised what it was. Mykus displayed a subservience that told him he would never be a threat to his authority, whereas Tearan did not. This did not surprise Tovis, a good soldier will automatically try to take control when separated from his unit and while forced to work alone. Mykus was a civilian and as such would be used to taking orders from all sorts of other people. Besides, Tovis surmised, his focus was the engine and as he admitted in his message, he hates violence. Tovis knew he could control Mykus but not Tearan. He was not unduly worried about it yet but he registered it in his mind. If things should change aboard the ship and turn into a situation where team unity is needed, Tearan was a threat to his authority, Tovis thought and he had to acknowledge the possibility of a pissing contest up ahead. He was glad Mykus was working on the inhibitor and hoped he would be able to give them all more information about it. If they found and removed more of them, the ship might be usable again. He was also glad to find out both of the others had their memories back and were having a similar experience as he was. It calmed his worries about how his mind might be coping with the whole crazy situation and gave him hope that everything might turn out okay in the end. Relieved, he turned his attention to the last of the messages.

"Hey, guys, it's Mykus again. It's now just over two hours since my last message and I've taken a close look at that inhibitor array you found, Tovis. I took it apart and checked it thoroughly and it makes this already crazy situation even more crazy than any of us could have thought. That specific type of inhibitor is high end stuff. Extremely high end actually. In fact, it's a military component, I recognised the serial numbers on the inside and those prefixes are used for military components only. I'm not quite sure what this means for us and our part in this, whatever this situation is, but it just got a whole lot weirder. I have to get back to engineering, but I thought you should both know."

Tovis frowned and replayed Mykus's last message several times. "What the fuck?" was all that came to mind by way of a verbal reaction and his mind's inability to make immediate sense of this new information frightened him. He was not a product of a military upbringing, despite being Arlenikan. Having been raised by the orphanage system, he missed the seven-year military training that Arlenikan boys experience, but it had never been an issue before. Tovis knew Tearan would have had his seven years and would have reaped all the rewards such an experience would bring. Jealousy flushed through him before he decided that having spent many subsequent years in the military to get into whatever secret operation the Inter-Galactic Elite Command was, might make Tearan a little fixed in his reactions, predictable even. The one downside of military life was the predictability it engendered within the minds and reactions of its subjects, he decided. Although part of the reason for its popularity and appeal, it did not help a person react to sudden change with spontaneity. Tovis comforted himself with this judgement and realised that this new information would be as much of a worry to the soldier among them as it would to him. A hired gun he may be. Untrained in military discipline and team tactics he definitely was, but he learned over the years to react to change quickly, to take in new developments and adapt his plans to suit as situations evolved. He felt confident his skills were of as much benefit to them all as Tearan's and Mykus's would be. People always regard hired guns as nothing more than the lowest of the low, uneducated killers with no sophistication or standards. Well he would prove them wrong.

Picking up the recorder, his mind working overtime as he thought about this new development, he left a reply to Tearan and Mykus.

"Hi, guys, Tovis here. Thanks, Mykus for taking a look at that inhibitor. That news does put a different face on things here doesn't it? We need to think about this carefully now we know there's a military connection, but this ship doesn't look like a military vessel to me. I admit my experience of the military is somewhat limited though. Tearan, what do you think? Is this ship a military vessel? If not, then we have to wonder why a civilian ship would contain high end and possibly secret military components, how it

obtained them, and for what purpose. We need to discuss whether that purpose has been fulfilled or not and what part we might be playing in it. What side are we on, guys? We need to think about that too. Mykus, my feeling is that you should concentrate more on looking for more inhibitors or other obviously military involvement in the engineering side of things, rather than strictly on getting the ship going again. I suppose the two can go along in tandem for part of the way. If the military has been doing secret stuff, they might be planning to erase any evidence of their involvement. There could be bombs or devices attached to the engine that blow up when we try to fly the ship out of here or something. Maybe you should check that out first huh? Tearan, I'm going to go and take a look at decks seven and eight and check out your findings. I'll help you gain access to that wall if I can. My only question about it is what if it was done because of damage to the outer hull or something? If those two decks suffered damage and decompressed, removing that wall could be dangerous and I can't hold my breath for long enough to get up to deck six and close the emergency airlocks, even if you can. I don't even know if there are any. Maybe I'll take a look for some before doing anything else. Anyway, those are my thoughts, what do you think?"

Tovis raced down to deck six and found the emergency airlocks situated at strategic intervals throughout the corridors and was relieved to see them. Situated within grooves set into the walls, when in place they would seal off the corridor, effectively forming a brand new end wall. He had walked passed them for days without having noticed them, the grooves in the walls and slots in the floor passing him by as he struggled to understand his new environment. The relief was short lived however, when he found no obvious way of operating them. Deep furrows crept along his brow as he wondered whether they were automatic, being triggered by decompression and accompanied by a countdown alarm. Images of people screaming in fear and running along the corridors as the countdown boomed through the ship filled his mind and he shuddered. Whatever it must be like to be trapped on the wrong side of those metallic slabs, he did not wish to discover. Shaking his head to dispel the imagery, he hoped Mykus would be able to tell them how they operated, should Tearan's plan to get through the cargo hangar wall prove dangerous.

Tovis knew that if decompression were to occur, they would not survive long enough to make it back up the stairs to deck six in time to operate the emergency airlocks, but it gave him hope to know such safety systems were at least in place. With renewed hope, he went back to the stairs but remembered both Mykus and Tearan talking about the Doctor and some crazy stuff that was going on down on deck six. Now that he had found himself down there, he might as well take a walk around, he decided. Laser pistol in hand, he crept along the corridor and into the medical bay.

Half an hour later, Tovis walked back into the engineering briefing room and picked up the recorder.

"Hi, it's Tovis again, just over an hour later than my last message. I've been down to deck six to check out the emergency airlocks and found them. They're set into grooves in the walls, ceilings, and floors. I've been walking passed them without noticing them all this time. Maybe you guys already know this, but have you any idea how they operate? There is no obvious mechanism on the walls down there, so I'm guessing they're either automatically triggered or manually engaged. Mykus, can you figure this out and let us know? If they're triggered automatically, how long do we have to get back up the stairs? If they're manual, where is the control and does it work? Also, if one of us should get stuck on the wrong side, can they be opened? The other thing is that I've seen the Doctor's crazy rantings on the walls down there, and wow, that's some creepy shit. I don't feel comfortable knowing someone is around who has that kind of shit on their mind, do you? He could be anywhere aboard so I vote we take care wherever we go. Maybe we should meet up and only move around together until we can find him and restrain him if necessary. I would guess the security room offers us the most secure accommodations, so if we all hole up there and work as a team, we can ensure each other's safety. How do you feel about that, guys? Until I hear back I will be on full alert, so remember that if you should come across me in a corridor. I'm armed and won't hesitate to fire on anyone until I know you're not a crazy hatchet murdering doctor who thinks the ship is haunted. I suggest you two do the same until we can team up."

Tovis tried to put thoughts of a mad hatchet murderer to the back of his mind and went back down to deck seven to check out the size of the cargo hangar. A frown creased his brow when he quickly discovered that Tearan had been correct in his observation. The map showed the room to be much larger than it really was, indicating a substantial space hidden beyond the long wall at the back of the room. His interest piqued, he wandered over to examine the wall more closely. This was not a rush job, that much was obvious right away. Haste was not evident in either the manufacture or construction and Tovis realised that if Tearan had not found the discrepancy in the map's account of the room sizes, he would never guess it was a false wall. There was a substantial area that had been cleared by Tearan and Tovis found something that proved the construction had been done with extreme care.

There were no obvious joins between panels, and Tovis knew this meant that they had been mould-welded panel by panel. In such a wall, the joints between wall panels are melted together in such a way as to make a single continuous wall without joints that might fail. This not only makes a stronger wall but ensures no gaps that might let dangerous gases in or life giving air out. Drawing his fingertips gently over the surface, he registered the slightly textured surface and frowned. There was something odd about this wall, apart from the fact that it was apparently in the wrong position, but he could not decide what it was that captivated him about it. As he was about to lift his fingertips from the surface, he felt the slight vibration and his eyes widened in shock as he snapped his hand away.

Tovis stumbled backwards a few steps, his mind reeling as he took in what his fingers told him. The ever so slightly rough texture of the wall, almost smooth but not quite, was a clue but on its own not significant. If he had lifted his fingertips a moment earlier, he would have been none the wiser and in a way, he wished he had done so. The knowledge that now raced around inside his mind was not only weird but its ramifications scared him. The slight vibration told him what he really did not want to know and coupled with the texture of the wall, made only one explanation possible.

"It's a Q-Wall," he gasped in a half whisper. "What the fuck is one of those doing aboard a civilian space ship?" The question went unanswered as

Tovis bumped into the rack of shelving behind him and stood there staring at the wall and what it meant. A Q-Wall, or Quantum Interference Particle Wall to give them their correct name, are constructed of two types of particles. One of the particles, Xanthomelium type A, forms a strong and hard wearing, flat, metallic surface that is ideal for walls, floors, and doors. The second particle, Xanthomelium type B, works in tandem with type A and when excited by an interference wave of a specific frequency, form themselves into a grid pattern. This grid pattern renders the whole wall insubstantial enough for a person to traverse through it without harm to either themselves or the wall. Switch off the wave generator and the type B particles lose their grid pattern, returning the wall to a solid structure once again. This, coupled with Mykus's discovery about the inhibitor array being high end military hardware told Tovis that whatever was going on here was more than just a bunch of unfortunates being left on a becalmed space ship after a pirate attack.

Q-Walls are only ever seen in military or corporate situations where the utmost secrecy is required. When they were first invented for general use, several accidents occurred which resulted in people being caught halfway through the wall when the interference wave generator either failed, or was switched off. The deaths almost spelled the end of the Q-Wall business and laws against their use were quickly brought in wherever they were produced and sold. After several more years of rigorous testing, they were deemed safe for general use so long as strict guidelines were followed. They are often found in bank vaults, scientific establishments, military and security environments, and wherever the existence of a room needs to be kept secret. Failsafe measures are required by law wherever they are used and yearly maintenance checks are a legal requirement for the licence that allows their use. Their presence on board meant that something secret was going on. The ship did not look like a military vessel, so Tovis assumed the Q-Walls use was a corporate or scientific one. The presence of the military inhibitor components placed within the communications system indicated that the military were involved somehow. His experience told him that the military would only ever be interested in one thing – something that gave them more soldiers or made the existing ones last longer or cheaper to maintain. He had heard many tales of soldiers being used in horrific experiments and had once met someone who claimed their brother had been a victim of such experimentation. He clenched his fists, digging the nails into his palms so the pain would allow him to focus on something other than fear while he waited for his mind and body to relax. When he felt calm, he ran a hand through his hair and berated himself for almost losing it.

"Get a grip for fuck's sake. So the military is funding something scientific they didn't want the crew and passengers to find out about, so what? It might've been experiments on making water last longer, or to enable soldiers to go without food or water or sleep for longer. They might've wanted to find a way to make cryo sleep safer or they might've invented a new kind of gun. There are many possible reasons. Stop thinking the worst and calm the fuck down."

Once he had got over the initial shock of his discovery, Tovis decided he really should tell Tearan. Climbing back up the stairs to deck four, he quickened his pace while climbing past deck six and raced along the corridor to the engineering briefing room.

"Hey, Tearan, it's Tovis again. Sorry for the third message but this is important. I've been down to the cargo hangar to check out what you said and you're right about the size. I took a look at the wall and discovered something weird. That long wall you're uncovering is a Q-Wall. Yeah, weird right? With the information Mykus gave us about the inhibitor being high end military hardware, this confirms military involvement. It's probably just something benign like making rations taste nicer and I'm probably being unduly paranoid, but something about it feels sinister to me. Why the fuck have we four been left alone here on an apparently civilian ship that has military components and secretive Q-Wall technology? What was it they wanted to hide behind there? Think about it before you go busting through there. There could be some germs behind there that will kill us if we breathe them in. That might be what happened here, a breakout of some virus or something that killed everyone else but us. Maybe we're immune. Anyway, think about it and get back to me okay?"

Tovis put down the recorder and sat down. His had ached and he felt nausea welling up inside. Deciding not to bother making a meal that he might not be able to keep down, he made his way towards the stairs. Hoping he would feel better after some sleep, he began to climb. He fell into bed and closed his eyes, never to open them again. There was no awareness of slipping from life to death, no painful gasping or regrets at what he failed to achieve. He simply stopped being.

The man with the pale eyes looked at his companion, Julian, who nodded in response. "So here we are again, Julian."

"Yes, Sir. Everything is as you predicted."

"How is M253016-143B?"

"Still within accepted parameters. Everything is as we hoped so far."

"And the Limbic System, how are the readouts?"

"Emotions are high but the subject is coping fine at this time. Nothing to worry about yet."

"Good. Let me know as soon as anything changes."

"I will, Sir, sleep well."

12

Tearan ate his breakfast slowly, chewing and swallowing robotically, the flavours doing nothing to please his palate. Meat, once rich and mature, now caught in his throat as he forced down the tasteless mush. What were once delicate, subtle vegetables now lay in his mouth like straw as he fought the urge to gag. Thoughts raced around his head, the nightmares, the woman's face, Tovis Kerral, and those laser pistol power cells. Worry creased his brow as he chewed and the more he dwelt on the thoughts, the worse he worried. He had not felt this unsettled since waking up with no memory other than his own name, and did not know what to do about it. There was no way to answer his questions other than to hope more memories came back. At least then he might identify the woman whose face haunted his dreams so. Tovis Kerral being a hired gun was not so much of a worry; it was more of a shock than anything else. The man had made contact freely enough and his voice carried a ring of authenticity that Tearan found himself trusting without a second thought. This last thought had his fork stop mid way between his plate and his mouth as he dwelt upon Tovis Kerral's voice.

"I know that voice," he whispered. "His voice is familiar. Where have I met him before?" The answers refused to come and he jabbed his temples in frustration. Tovis himself had not mentioned any similar feelings of familiarity in his message, so Tearan had to assume that either he was mistaken or Tovis did not share the feeling. He let his thoughts drift back over his years in the military and knew of a few ex-soldiers that were said to have become hired guns. Maybe Tovis had been a colleague in the early years of his service. Shaking his head in an effort to clear the fuzz that lay within his mind where he knew memories should be, he thumped a fist down onto the table. He closed his eyes and listened, extending his awareness as far throughout the ship as he was able. All around him the ship slept, the silent leviathan neither dead nor alive but kept in a state of permanent half sleep. Only those systems necessary for life were still working. Like a comatose animal, the lungs breathed and the heart pumped but everything else was asleep. Tearan, unable to wake the sleeping dragon, was forced to watch it sleep and listen to its breathing. And hope, there was always hope. There was little more than that and he felt reluctant to let it go just yet.

He listened to the silence and aching loneliness washed over him. He was sure he heard the empty air echoing along the corridors and bouncing from lofty ceilings. If there were three others aboard with him, why had none of them ever met each other? Why did they each ask the others to meet, but then not do so? What was keeping them from each other, and why? Tearan tried to expand his mind into all corners of the ship, probing for life, any life other than his own but found none. If he shared the ship with others, why did he feel so alone? Why did the ship feel so empty?

"I have to find the others before I go mad," he moaned as he got up from the table and left the room without bothering to wash the dishes. Starting at the top of the ship, Tearan walked the corridors and rooms, floor by floor, yelling for the others by name as he went. By the time he found himself inside the hazardous waste store with a sore throat and headache, he knew he was in trouble. He had yelled himself hoarse in every room and corner of the ship, but not one of the others responded. This meant either they had not heard him, or they were ignoring him. Neither of these options delighted Tearan and he began to question himself.

"Maybe there are no others at all," he muttered as he headed towards the stairs to climb back up to the security room on deck three. "Maybe they don't exist and those messages are a hoax or a fabrication made up by my mind as it slowly goes mad." When he reached deck four, on a whim he decided to go to the engineering briefing room and listen to all the recorded messages again. Picking up the recorder, he saw three new messages were waiting and raised his eyebrows.

"Hi, guys, Tovis here. Thanks, Mykus for taking a look at that inhibitor. That news does put a different face on things here doesn't it? We need to think about this carefully now we know there's a military connection, but this ship doesn't look like a military vessel to me. I admit my experience of the military is somewhat limited though. Tearan, what do you think? Is this ship a military vessel? If not, then we have to wonder why a civilian ship would contain high end and possibly secret military components, how it obtained them, and for what purpose. We need to discuss whether that purpose has been fulfilled or not and what part we might be playing in it. What side are we on guys? We need to think about that too. Mykus, my feeling is that you should concentrate more on looking for more inhibitors or other obviously military involvement in the engineering side of things, rather than strictly on getting the ship going again. I suppose the two can go along in tandem for part of the way. If the military has been doing secret stuff, they might be planning to erase any evidence of their involvement. There could be bombs or devices attached to the engine that blow up when we try to fly the ship out of here or something. Maybe you should check that out first huh? Tearan, I'm going to go and take a look at decks seven and eight and check out your findings. I'll help you gain access to that wall if I can. My only question about it is what if it was done because of damage to the outer hull or something? If those two decks suffered damage and decompressed, removing that wall could be dangerous and I can't hold my breath for long enough to get up to deck six and close the emergency airlocks, even if you can. I don't even know if there are any. Maybe I'll take a look for some before doing anything else. Anyway, those are my thoughts, what do you think?"

Tearan listened to Tovis's first message. He had a point; the ship was most definitely not built as a military vessel and did not look like a passenger liner either. It was not big enough for one thing, and the lack of facilities for passengers was another clue. Military vessels had mess halls, parade rooms, dormitories, armouries, lecture rooms, a brig, and a weapons system with big balls. Passenger liners had shops, beauty parlours, vidicom theatres, bars, restaurants, whorehouses, and all sorts of other delights to entertain the fee-paying masses. This crate had nothing of that nature and Tearan guessed it was either a freighter or some kind of research or exploration vessel. The military were obviously involved somehow, his presence here as a member of the Inter-Galactic Elite Command proved that, as did the inhibitor array. Exactly what their involvement was though, was a mystery Tearan had no idea how to explain. He agreed that it was probably sense for Mykus to concentrate on the search for more inhibitors or other unusual hardware that should not be there and the possibility of explosive devices was very real. If whatever the military were involved with was either illegal or sensitive, they would probably want to erase all evidence of it when it had served its purpose. He switched the recorder on to the second message and listened.

"Hi, it's Tovis again, just over an hour later than my last message. I've been down to deck six to check out the emergency airlocks and found them. They're set into grooves in the walls, ceilings and floors. I've been walking passed them without noticing them all this time. Maybe you guys already know this, but have you any idea how they operate? There is no obvious mechanism on the walls down there, so I'm guessing they're either automatically triggered or manually engaged. Mykus, can you figure this out and let us know? If they're triggered automatically, how long do we have to get back up the stairs? If they're manual, where is the control and does it work? Also, if one of us should get stuck on the wrong side, can they be opened? The other thing is that I've seen the Doctor's crazy rantings on the walls down there, and wow, that's some creepy shit. I don't feel comfortable knowing someone is around who has that kind of shit on their mind, do you? He could be anywhere aboard so I vote we take care wherever we go. Maybe we should meet up and only move around together until we can find him and restrain him if necessary. I would guess the security room offers us the most secure accommodations, so if we all hole up there and work as a team, we can ensure each other's safety. How do you feel about that, guys? Until I hear back I will be on full alert, so remember that if you should come across me in a corridor. I'm armed and won't hesitate to fire on anyone until I know you're not a crazy hatchet murdering doctor who thinks the ship is haunted. I suggest you two do the same until we can team up."

Tearan frowned as he listened. Tovis sounded as if he were getting a little off track and this was worrying. The man's sudden preoccupation with safety suggested he was succumbing to the kind of fears that inhibit a man's effectiveness. Tearan knew it was sensible to be conscious of safety, but anyone who had spent any time on board a space ship would have undergone at least a basic safety lecture before take-off. Even passenger liners are required to give them and Tearan knew Tovis should have realised that decompression would have triggered the emergency airlocks. The fact that they had not been triggered indicated that no decompression had taken place beyond the false wall. This was spaceship safety 101 and Tovis's lack of common sense enough to realise it, was a worry Tearan did not need. A hired gun on full alert, armed to the teeth and willing to kill was not a prospect he relished. With a heavy heart, he listened to the third message.

"Hey, Tearan, it's Tovis again. Sorry for the third message but this is important. I've been down to the cargo hangar to check out what you said and you're right about the size. I took a look at the wall and discovered something weird. That long wall you're uncovering is a Q-Wall. Yeah, weird right? With the information Mykus gave us about the inhibitor being high end military hardware, this confirms military involvement. It's probably just something benign like making rations taste nicer and I'm probably being unduly paranoid, but something about it feels sinister to me. Why the fuck have we four been left alone here on an apparently civilian ship that has military components and secretive Q-Wall technology? What was it they wanted to hide behind there? Think about it before you go busting through there. There could be some germs behind there that will kill us if we breathe them in. That might be what happened here, a breakout of some virus or something that killed everyone else but us. Maybe we're immune. Anyway, think about it and get back to me okay?"

"What the fuck?" Tearan said aloud, his mind immediately alert. Tovis had gone from a potential problem to the bearer of interesting and useful information and Tearan was grateful. This news was easily the last thing he would have expected to hear and it certainly did take things to a whole new level of weirdness. "Hell yeah that's weird all right. Q-Wall? What the fuck do they want with that on board this crate?" He agreed with Tovis completely, the whole business now felt entirely sinister and he was not sure how he should proceed. As a soldier, his duty was to upkeep military rules and those of the Inter-Galactic Elite Command were slightly different to those of the regular military. Keeping secrets was what the IGEC was all about, the fact that something covert might be going on aboard the ship did not bother him. Military secrets did not worry Tearan, that was his job and his life. No, what bothered him was the existence of secrets that had not been shared with him, a member of the most secretive military unit in the galaxy. Whatever those secrets were, Tearan knew it went beyond making rations taste nicer. His mind working overtime, he recorded a reply, the excitement evident in his voice.

"Hi, guys, Tearan here. Tovis, are you sure about that Q-Wall thing? If you're right, it gives this whole operation a totally new face, one that will make me feel more than a little uncomfortable. It worries me that as a member of the Inter-Galactic Elite Command, I know nothing about it. Maybe I was told but can't remember. Perhaps those memories still haven't returned. It's equally possible that I wasn't told at all, which makes the level of secrecy worryingly high. Having only just heard your message a couple of minutes ago, I haven't yet had time to figure out how this changes our plans, or even if it should. This is so fucked up I get a headache just trying to understand it all. I thought it was maybe pirates or something, an engine failure perhaps. I hoped we just had to get the word out and wait for rescue. Now things are so weird I'm beginning to think I'm going crazy. Despite all of us asking to meet up, we never do and I've just been over every inch of this crate and yelled my head off. Either you're all deaf, you're ignoring me, or you don't exist. There are no more messages from Doctor Arma and there's all that crazy stuff down in the medical bay about ghosts and bodies. We're all having nightmares and I for one keep thinking I see shadows moving around but when I look, there's no one there. I heard a massive crash in the security room and when I rushed out to look, there was no damage but some scratches have appeared on the floor. There's the time discrepancies too. Remember when you found that inhibitor array, Tovis? I recorded my message before Mykus and it was definitely not on the table. Mykus did his message after mine, but he made a point of saying he'd only just found it. How can that happen? I know it wasn't there, I'm not going crazy. I don't like the way this business is making me doubt myself. All I know is that I'm Tearan Lindo, I'm a soldier with the IGEC and I'm from Arlenika Prime. No matter what happens here, those are unalterable facts. Mykus, I

agree that it is probably best that you concentrate on looking for inhibitors and any other stuff that you feel shouldn't be there and remove it if you can do so without blowing us all to oblivion. I don't know how this Q-Wall business affects us, but I have to get into whatever empty space is hidden down there. I have to know, I just have to. You're welcome to join me if you want."

Tearan closed his eyes as he replaced the recorder on the counter and acknowledged all the questions racing around his mind. Why was he here in this crazy situation? What series of random events trapped him within this nightmare? Had he chosen to be here but was unable to remember why? Was he right to feel as unsettled as he now did as he leaned his backside against the edge of the briefing room table and rubbed his eyes. It was now hours since he ate breakfast and he would normally be making himself a snack, but he had lost his appetite and decided to wander the corridors to think. He found it easier to concentrate the mind whilst walking. Sitting and relaxing tended to encourage his mind to wander, whereas the exercise of walking made the act of disciplining his mind, easier.

At one point, he found himself in the Senior Officers' Observation Lounge on deck two and stared out at the inky void. Points of light from distant stars made him feel trapped and lonely in this strangely becalmed hulk and he hugged himself. It was a vain attempt to find some comfort, which did nothing to quell the chill of fear that gripped his insides with icy fingers. He was no longer a man, a serving soldier fighting for the liberty of others for the common good. Now it was his own freedom he feared lost and the fight to regain it felt insurmountable. The incongruities of the situation added up to one extremely weird experience and Tearan begged for it to stop.

"I want to enjoy my life and work hard, to do things few others get to do, and have a laugh with my friends. Is that too much to ask? I don't want to have amnesia and speak to people I can't see and who I can never find anywhere on board. I'll go mad if I'm trapped here for the rest of my life." Tearan did not know whether he felt anger or self pity, but had to admit that whatever his feelings were, he was not enjoying them. With a growl of frustration, he thumped a fist onto the table before getting up and heading down the corridor to the stairs. Downstairs, he washed the dishes from his breakfast and wondered what to do to fill in the endless days that might possibly lie ahead. Until a few hours ago he was fired up with enthusiasm for clearing the cargo hangar to get access to the wall he believed hid a secret room. Thanks to the information given to him by Tovis, the knowledge that it was a Q-Wall that divided the room sapped his energy for the task.

"What I need is a change of routine," he said aloud as he mentally shook himself from the self pity he felt rising within. Before he changed his mind, he raced up to his security room on deck three and stripped the linen from the bed. Before leaving the room, he gathered all his discarded clothes and trudged back down to deck five. Through a door in the recreation room was a large laundry area and Tearan put one of the machines on for the bed linen and another for his clothes. In thirty-five minutes, the items emerged washed, dried, ironed, folded, and wrapped in a thin protective paper covering.

'Research Vessel Novosentia.'

Tearan read the paper label printed onto the protective covering that surrounded his bed linen and clothes. After re-reading it several times, he stared wide eyed as the significance of his discovery hit home.

"So this ship is called the Novosentia huh? What a weird name. And it is a research vessel after all." He was pleased that he now had a little more information about his prison, despite it bringing yet more questions that he was unable to answer. One thing he knew right away was that the vessel was not known to him. There was no way for him to know whether the IGEC's involvement with it was recent or not, nor whether any other branch of the inter-galactic military was also involved. Simply having a name for his prison gave him more emotional relief than he would have anticipated. It was as if by giving it a name, he made it more solidly real and therefore easier to cope with. After the nightmares, shadows, and unexplained noises that made him worry about his sanity, the solidity offered by that name was a huge relief.

After taking the cleaned items back up to his security room, Tearan left the paper with its printed label on the table in the engineering briefing room and left a new message on the recorder for Tovis and Mykus. That done, he returned to the security room and spent a couple of hours cleaning it from one end to the other. Finding considerable emotional comfort in the familiarity of mundane tasks, he then turned his attentions to the kitchen and then the dining room. Having missed eating in the middle of the day, he ate his late meal with more than his usual appreciation and then spent a couple of hours watching movies on the Recreation Room vidicom screen before deciding to go to bed. As he lay and listened to the silent ship, he said its name over and over.

"Research Vessel Novosentia. I have to know what is behind that wall. Even if getting through it kills me, I have to know what they're hiding. I can't live like this for much longer and I'd rather die trying to find out what's going on, than live alone in ignorance for the rest of my life and slowly go mad." The decision now made, Tearan's mind relaxed enough to allow him to fall asleep.

Tearan stood before the wall in the cargo hangar and examined it closely. After a good night's sleep, he awoke with fresh determination to explain the mystery of the wall and decided it was his first and only priority now. He ate a hearty breakfast, believing that an adequately fuelled body helps maintain a balanced and healthy mind. One thing was without question, he needed his mind to be clear and objective. With all the weirdness he had endured recently and the subsequent worry about his state of mind, he did not intend to neglect his mental health any more. During breakfast, he allowed his mind to dwell on the question of whether the others actually existed or not and came up with a couple of possible explanations, none of which pleased him. When he considered the fact that Mykus, Tovis, and himself had all separately requested they all meet up and work together, yet they had not done so, his heart sank. Then he remembered his trip around the ship, yelling his head off for the others. No reply had been forthcoming from either of them and his frown deepened. There was also the uncanny sense of recognition he felt whenever he listened to the messages Mykus and Tovis left, and it was this fact that helped him make up his mind. Despite being the explanation he wanted least, Tearan had to admit to a definite possibility that the others did not exist other than in his own troubled mind. Once he finished washing up his breakfast dishes, he made his way down to the cargo hangar to begin the process of working out what kind of weird shit was actually going on.

"Maybe whatever caused my amnesia is causing me to think there are others aboard. Perhaps my feeling of recognition is my mind beginning to realise they're not real. If that's true then it's a sign that my mind is recovering."

Another thought that had occurred to him while he showered before breakfast, was that Mykus and Tovis were working for whatever secretive operation was running the ship. Maybe they had been planted on board to watch him and report to whoever was in charge. If the memories from the time leading up to blacking out returned, he felt sure some of his questions would be answered. Forcing his mind back to the time before waking up, his last memory was sitting with other soldiers in a lecture hall and listening to a sector commander talking. The subject of the lecture was lost but he had no idea how long before his blackout the lecture took place.

"It could be the day before or ten years before," he said and ran a hand through his hair as he prepared to shave. It was becoming more and more likely that his unit had been connected in some way with some kind of secret research. The most likely scenario was that his unit was being used in a security capacity, given the secrecy of whatever had been going on. Something might have happened that overwhelmed their security measures. He had not found a single dead body aboard anywhere and this told him that either everyone survived whatever happened, or the dead had been taken away when the survivors fled. Somehow, he had been left behind, either accidentally or on purpose and now, here he was awake and alone. One thing he knew for certain was that if his unit thought he had died during whatever the event had been, they would not be coming back for him. If they believed there was a chance he was still alive, they might do, if they were able.

"Maybe they all got amnesia too, so they might not remember I exist at all." This thought made his heart sink even lower as he realised that in such a case, he had no hope of rescue. "They have to come, they have to."

Standing before the wall in the cargo hangar, Tearan was pleased with his efforts. A quarter of the entire length was now cleared. He remembered using Q Walls a couple of times during his time with the IGEC, and knew from his experience that somewhere there should be a control pad. He also knew that the control pad was normally situated on one side of a Q Wall, not both. Such walls are usually built in places where either secrecy or security are paramount and control of the wall tends to be carefully guarded. Tearan knew it was likely that the control for the wall would be on the other side. Despite this likelihood, he was going to check anyway. The gravity of his situation demanded he be thorough, so he decided to make sure before taking further action.

He noticed immediately that there was no wall control panel on the end of the wall he had cleared, but he checked up close anyway. Sensitive fingers tapped and slid along the edge from floor to ceiling but he found no secret panel or hidden compartment that might hide a control panel. Experience told him the panel would be at a height easily reached by a man; an emergency would demand they use the wall quickly and they would not want to waste time climbing up to the top to press the switch. Nevertheless, he checked all the way up, climbing the now empty shelving just to be sure. Only when he was satisfied the control panel was not there, did he walk to the other end of the wall. This end had not been cleared of cargo, so he was forced to shift boxes and crates to reveal the end of the wall where it joined the adjacent one. He hopped into a loader to shift the higher shelves and after an hour, began another search for a control panel. Finding none, he stood back and scratched his chin.

The lack of a control panel told Tearan that it had to be on the other side. This went some way to confirming that there might indeed be people through there. Why put the only control for the Q-Wall on the other side if no one is there to use it? Furthermore, this told him that they had the upper hand, by design rather than by accident. Thoughts raced around his head and he made a conscious effort not to express his thoughts aloud. Striding back down to the empty portion of shelving, Tearan walked right up to the wall and pressed the side of his face against it while touching it with all five fingertips of his right hand. Closing his eyes to heighten his concentration, he allowed his other senses to tell him what his eyes alone, were unable to. The ever-so-slightly rough texture of the wall and the almost-not-there vibration confirmed what Tovis said. This was indeed a genuine Q-Wall.

Tearan stepped away and ran a hand through his hair as he tried to get the ramifications of this new information into some sort of order. Q-Walls are expensive. Not the, give up the booze for a few weeks and put the money in a jar, sort of expensive, but the, beyond all comprehension, kind. The, it would take you seven hundred years of saving every penny, kind of expensive. They are way beyond the means of the majority of companies. Their use is still not readily accepted by the mainstream, despite modern safety advancements making them almost completely safe. Ninety nine percent of Q-Walls are used in either secret military installations, or equally secret research establishments. Knowing the Novosentia was a research vessel, Tearan wondered what kind of secret research they might be hiding. Was it some kind of deadly virus they were mutating for bio weapons, a new type of fuel maybe, medical experimentation perhaps?

'Maybe that's it. Maybe some medical experiment went horribly wrong,' he thought to himself, not daring to talk aloud in case the room was bugged. He knew that if whatever was going on was so secret they needed a Q-Wall, secret filming and bugging was to be expected. For this reason, he kept his mouth shut and discussed the situation with himself in the confines of his own mind. The level of secrecy indicated by the presence of the Q-Wall made him wonder if he had been observed since the moment he awoke. Was he being filmed, listened to? His mind raced as he tried to think back to anything he might have said or done to make things dangerous for himself and he remembered speaking aloud about the inhibitors Tovis found. Now he understood perfectly why high end military inhibitors were on board and he mentally kicked himself for being so vocal about them with Tovis and Mykus. His two colleagues then filled his mind and he knew he had not imagined them after all. They were not hallucinations conjured by his troubled mind, they were real and in as much danger as he was. Maybe this explained the absence of Doctor Arma and his crazy rantings written on the walls of the medical bay. They might not be such crazy rantings after all. There was every possibility that what the doctor thought was a haunting was actually the people from behind the wall.

All sorts of odd things fell into place and Tearan pieced the jigsaw together inside his head. The missing doctor, the apparent absence of Mykus and Tovis, the crash he heard in the security room and the scratches on the floor, the shadows seen in the corner of his eye that disappeared when he tried to focus on them. Even the time discrepancies. Everything fell into place as he stood before the wall.

'We're the experiment. Tovis, Mykus, Doctor Arma, and me. They're on the other side looking at us, probably listening too. They've captured Doctor Arma, maybe even Mykus and Tovis because they found out too much and they're probably going to come for me soon for the same reason. They've been doing secret experiments that they don't want people to know about so they get the military to guard their secret and dispose of anyone who finds out.' Tearan gasped as the realisation hit home. 'Oh shit, they're gonna be after me too because I know as much as Mykus and Tovis. I'm a dead man walking.' This final piece of the jigsaw fell into place and Tearan fought to retain control over the emotions he felt fighting to rise within. After less than thirty seconds, he clenched his jaw and balled his fists, determined to fight to the very end, whatever form that might take. With one last sweep of his eyes from one end of the wall to the other, he yelled at the top of his voice.

"I know you're there assholes. Can you hear me?"

13

Tearan paced up and down the room as he yelled into the lofty silence. Inside himself, he knew such an emotional display would not yield the results he wanted, but it served to relieve the anguish that had grown to uncomfortable proportions within his mind. Shrieking demands and yelling insults was not going to worry people with the money and power to have created this whole situation, but he did it anyway, to make himself feel better. Tearan was not a man for tears; he always found explosions of anger a far more effective way of relieving emotional pressure.

There were so many questions needing answers and he shrieked them all at the wall, which stood impassive and undaunted. The most burning question was what was going on and the absence of an answer lay in his gut like a rock. Every fibre in his body ached to know the reason why he had found himself without memories in an apparently abandoned space ship. Worry for the others in his unit, for Mykus, Tovis, and Doctor Arma came next and he yelled at the wall, demanding to know they were alive and unharmed.

Knowing there should be seven beside himself in his IGEC unit, with Mykus, Tovis, and Doctor Arma, that made ten others now unaccounted for. Experience told him his unit was probably there originally as security. This meant that he was, at least originally, supposed to be on the same side as those running whatever was going on. The absence of the other men in his unit told Tearan that something must have happened to make the unit change sides. Either that or everyone else believed that he had done so. This was rapidly dismissed as a possibility. Over the years, Tearan learned to keep an emotional distance between himself and whatever his unit were guarding, despite seeing many things that sickened him. Without that detachment, he could not function in his duty as a member of the IGEC. Turning a blind eye was a painful lesson everyone in the unit learned, some more easily than others and Tearan knew his ability to step back from whatever was happening would not have deserted him.

'If we were brought here as security, why would they turn on us?' The question forced its way through the melee inside his head to the front of his consciousness. 'If we were guarding them from something, why has my unit disappeared?' Tearan had done many such highly secret security missions and he knew that there were only two possible answers to his question. Either his unit had been killed by whatever they were guarding against, or they switched their allegiance for some reason and paid for the mutiny with their lives. If indeed they were killed by something, whatever that something might be was anyone's guess. Tearan labelled this unknown quantity, 'the bad thing.' Maybe the bad thing had somehow got out and killed everyone but himself, Mykus, Tovis, and Doctor Arma. The subsequent disappearance of Doctor Arma suggested that the bad thing was still very much alive and functioning, which meant if Mykus and Tovis were still alive and hiding somewhere, all three of them were still in danger from it.

Knowing the ship was a research vessel, as confirmed by the writing on the paper label wrapping the clothes he laundered, Tearan wondered what sort of bad thing he was dealing with. Horrific visions of laboratory created fiends flooded through his mind unbidden and a frisson of fear coursed through him. Words on walls, telling of ghosts and dismembered bodies floated across his perception. Words written by a man driven almost insane by what he saw; words Tearan and the others had not believed. As he stood before the wall, lost in the melee of thoughts and images that raced around his mind, he was no longer so quick to disbelieve. Perhaps Doctor Arma was not crazy after all. Maybe he knew what the people behind the Q-Wall were trying to keep secret. He was now sure the Doctor had indeed seen something and that seeing it was the cause of his disappearance.

'Shit. What the fuck is happening here?' A moment of panic gripped him and he closed his eyes while he waited for it to go away. From the messages he had exchanged with Mykus and Tovis, none of them had actually seen anything so far, other than fleeting shadows that were gone the moment you tried to focus on them. He had heard things, heard his name called. There was the crash he heard in the security room, and the scratches on the floor, but that was not sufficient to cause him to want to write anything on walls about hauntings or dismembered bodies.

'Maybe the bad thing got out by accident and roamed the ship for a while until they caught it. Maybe Doctor Arma encountered it and they had to get rid of him so he couldn't talk about it.' Tearan reasoned with himself, trying to embrace all possible sides of the situation to avoid allowing paranoia to take control and send him crazy. 'Damage control. That's most likely what happened to the doctor. Something got out by accident, Doctor Arma knew about it and was afraid, so they had to make sure he can't tell anyone.' It was with extreme relief that his mind, eager for everything to make sense, grasped this most benign of explanations. Such things happen all the time and he thought back to a few missions where he and his unit had been tasked with, 'securing a target for safe keeping,' which he knew meant capturing them for execution. Such missions had never bothered him until now. He had always chosen to believe his commanders assurances that the acquired targets were treated well and that many were given new identities. Now he doubted the truth of those assurances.

Tearan learned to obey from the first day he joined the military, when he left his parents to begin his seven-year journey to become, 'a grown man proud and true.' Obedience was something he had been good at; his unquestioning loyalty to his superior officers' had borne fruit in his acceptance into the Inter-Galactic Elite Command. There were many times when he knew his mission called upon him to step beyond normal military remit and into a grey area where different rules apply. His superior officers' always assured the men that what they were doing was for the good of all people in the galaxy, that they were helping to save millions of lives, that so much good was to come from what they were doing. A little step over the line now would pay dividends later, they said. As Tearan stood before the Q-Wall and immersed himself in his thoughts, he realised with dismay that his unwavering belief in his superior officers' had probably been misplaced.

This thought then led his mind to the second likely explanation for this situation and he pondered it for a while. If his unit decided that what they were doing was beyond what they were comfortable with and mutinied, it would be the first such occasion Tearan ever heard of. Not once did he ever hear anyone talk about an IGEC unit going against orders and switching sides. It was unheard of but although unlikely, he knew the men in his unit each had a strong personal code of ethics. People sometimes got hurt at the Unit's hands and they all knew they were sometimes sent to catch people that were then quietly executed without trial. People can be conditioned in such a way that the normal boundaries of acceptable behaviour are skewed and stretched. The training Tearan's unit and the others like it received involved a rearrangement of those boundaries and they never questioned orders. If something occurred on board the Novosentia that caused them to question their obedience, it would have to be something awful. He was used to guarding the secrecy of others and not asking questions. IGEC personnel often had to do things that other people would not be comfortable with. The secrecy and cover-ups, things that would be distasteful to the general population. None of that ever made him consider going against orders though. In order for it to do so, it would have to be something even worse than what he had so far experienced and he was confident the rest of his unit would feel the same.

If his unit had mutinied, they would now be in control of the ship, of that Tearan had no doubt. Such was his confidence in the unique skills of himself and his men that contemplating their failure was not an option. IGEC units are the most highly trained soldiers that exist. Their status as an, 'above top secret' unit means their skill base is wider than a normal soldier's is. No matter what resistance they met, an IGEC unit in operational mode would have control of a ship like the Novosentia within a few hours. Their training, along with the weaponry and tools available to them make them the most feared and respected military force known. The possibility of Tearan's unit trying to mutiny and failing to achieve their goal was not one he considered worthy of contemplation.

'Unless whatever they've got behind there is even deadlier than we are,' he mused within the confines of his mind. 'If that's true, then the universe is fucked.' A force more deadly and effective than an IGEC unit was something Tearan automatically feared and he shivered as a new feeling of vulnerability swept through him. 'If they created a monster behind that wall and it got out and killed my men, we're totally screwed.' He swore then shook the thoughts away. They would serve only to keep him awake at nights and he wanted to concentrate on what he knew and was able to deal with, not fantasise about monsters. Scanning the wall and empty shelving for clues, he brought his mind back to his immediate needs.

There was no response to his yelling that he was aware of and the sequence of thoughts he had subsequently experienced told him it might not be a good idea to continue. He chose to assume that whoever was in control of the situation was filming him and probably had been doing so since he woke up. If this was indeed the case, he was doubtful that Tovis's distress signal would be allowed to go out. Feeling suddenly paranoid at the thought of his every movement possibly being filmed, he decided to play them at their own game and see who gave in first. Unable to stop himself from grinning, he grabbed a hover loader, then went back up to deck three and the security room to pack.

After parking the hover loader alongside the others, he unpacked and within an hour had set up home in the cargo hangar. With the aid of several seating cushions from the recreation room on deck five, he made a comfortable bed on the floor facing the Q-Wall. The gym equipment stood at one end of the large room and afforded him plenty of space to work out and keep his fitness levels at optimum. After fiddling with the vidicom handset control, he found that music could be piped throughout the whole ship, so he set the handset down beside his new bed. Several guns and hundreds of power packs were stacked within easy reach should he need them and a line of motion triggered alarms spanned the room. Setting these across the width of the room in front of the Q-Wall, anyone trying to sneak through would set them off and give him the chance to arm himself. On a whim, he decided to put another one facing the door that led out into the corridor and two more outside the door facing both ways down the corridor. Anyone approaching from any direction would set them off and he would not be caught unawares. If they were indeed filming him, he wanted them to realise it would be futile to try to sneak up on him.

The cargo hangar's small office contained a drinks dispenser, nutri-vend, and an auto snack so he would not want for food. The small staff bathroom at the far end of the office would ensure he would not have to leave the cargo hangar unless he wanted to cook a proper meal in the kitchen or watch a vidicom movie. The stores manifest yielded a personal library console, which meant he had ten thousand books, articles, and magazines to read, all contained within a small device four inches square and half an inch deep. After making himself a hot drink, he switched the vidicom handset control to random shuffle and cranked the volume up loud. The cargo hangar throbbed to the beat of some teenage boy band whose song consisted of little more than three completely unintelligible phrases, which they shouted repeatedly at the top of their lungs. He inwardly winced at the cacophonous noise and hoped whoever was behind the wall was doing so too.

All there was to do now was to settle in and wait it out for as long as possible, or until someone revealed themselves. Tearan was used to digging in and waiting, sometimes for many days and he was disciplined enough to be able to withstand the boredom. He could work out, read, listen to music, clean the cargo hangar, and even move stuff around the shelving with the loaders to stave off boredom if he was suffering. Not having something to do would not be too much of a problem. No, that's not what worried him at all. He knew the only thing he would find difficult was not having anyone to talk to. When his unit had to dig in and wait it out on missions, having each other's company helped keep them sane and focussed. There was no one with whom to share his fears or lighten the loneliness and he knew the solitude was already taking its toll on him.

Having missed a mid day meal, Tearan approached the nutri-vend in the cargo hangar office and perused its menu. Military personnel use these machines all the time, so he knew what to expect. These machines deliver a variety of hot and cold meals, all made with a nutritionally balanced, food grade, synthetic puree. With the addition of equally synthetic flavourings and some processing, something safe, healthy, and edible is available to those in situations where cooking or real ingredients are not an option. The puree is highly concentrated and stored with all the air taken out. The high concentration means a little goes a long way and when air is reintroduced through the extrusion nozzle as it exits the machine, it fluffs up to fifty times its volume. Used by a single individual, a fully stocked nutri-vend machine can go for a thousand meals before needing a refill cartridge.

Tearan knew what he was going to choose, but he always took the time to peruse the menu anyway. All nutri-vend machines offered the same fifteen item menu of well known dishes from a variety of planetary systems. With many different savoury and sweet dishes on offer, most soldiers knew the menu by heart and had tried them all, with the exception of one. Yamelian Pie is one of the sweet dishes offered by all nutri-vend machines galaxy wide and is a popular dessert from the Canorly system, right out in galactic sector 83583-3340P. The Canorly system has three large inhabited planets, all of which are the only known location of Mexahedralonium X4. All three Canorly planets produce it in abundance, via the unique mineral make up of their molten cores. With an abundance of volcanoes on all three planets, the bright pink lava flows yield a constant supply, which is sold all over the galaxy at enormous profit for use in the production of a high specification space ship fuel additive. The substance makes Trans Wave Flow Core engines run cleaner and enables them to gain up to twenty-four percent extra speed. Because of the cost of this rare substance, it is used exclusively by the military, where extra speed and agility in the theatre of war can save countless lives.

The Canorly people love Yamelian Pie passionately. As a token of gratitude from the military for providing them with Mexahedralonium X4, they were promised that wherever a Canorly soldier should find himself, no matter what dangers he may be placing himself in for the good of others, he would always have a taste of home to keep up his spirits. Thus, Yamelian Pie will always be on the nutri-vend menu. The only problem for everyone else is that no one other than Canorly people like it. Everyone else unanimously agrees that it is the most disgusting substance known. Tearan was not about to break with tradition, so he plumped for his usual Wassalen Toka, then Noma Curd for dessert.

After spending a couple of hours reading, he decided it was time to start stirring things up a little. This would not only give him something to do, but it would hopefully annoy the hell out of whoever was keeping watch from behind the wall. If so, that would amuse him no end. He was done trying to avoid getting involved in whatever was going on and did not care that he was making it plain he knew of their existence. Whether there was any danger to him from knowing about the Q-Wall, he did not know, but he was beyond caring. He had to change things and if they proved dangerous, so be it. Remaining on board alone, possibly for years to come would send him insane with loneliness. That was worse than death and he would rather die than endure it.

He switched off the music and began to sing aloud. If the men in his unit were still alive and watching him, he knew they would be wetting themselves laughing. Tearan, a strong and dependable soldier, a highly trained elite operative with many awards for marksmanship and for his ability to focus in extremely stressful situations, was most definitely not a natural singer. Being tone deaf meant that if he ever sang a note on key, it was by accident rather than by design and his friends teased him mercilessly about it. During training, when he and his men did twenty-mile training runs with seventy five pound kit packs on their backs and full helmet air masks on their heads, they sang various songs to help keep their spirits up and their feet in step. The men in the unit got together and taught Tearan to sing these songs all on one note, as a sort of harmonisation for their own voices and it worked reasonably well.

In the cargo hangar, he let rip with as much force as his voice would give, only this time he did not sing the songs all on one note. His attempts to sing reverberated around the lofty space and he knew he could keep it up for hours, as he used to on those training runs. Singing at the top of his lungs, he let his mind drift as he jogged back and forth up and down the room. By going through each song a certain number of times, Tearan knew he had run up and down the cargo hangar for something approximating twenty miles during the three hours and twenty-five minutes he had been singing. One of the songs had one hundred and seven verses, each one telling the story of a fictitious person from an equally fictitious Arlenikan village. A terrible tragedy befell the village and many different forms of the song exist in different military units. The one Tearan and his unit sang had the villagers suffering a flood, with each verse telling the story of one of the village's one hundred and seven inhabitants. Although the tragedy that befell the village tended to change with whomever was singing, the ending was always the same. Each of the inhabitants died and their spirits remained to haunt the now abandoned and forever uninhabitable village. Tearan decided that if his men were still alive and listening, he hoped they were joining in.

Warm water cascaded down his back as he stepped into the shower and closed his eyes. Anguish slowly melted away with the water as he stood there, eyes closed and motionless. He always indulged in a few minutes like this every time he showered. There was something about warm water gently flowing from above that calmed him like nothing else could. Whenever he felt especially stressed or anxious about something, a warm shower would float it all away. When he was finished, he wrapped a towel around himself and realised he felt uneasy at being half naked while someone was secretly filming him. It made him feel self conscious and he thought of the others behind the walls as voyeurs, getting off on watching him go about his daily life. This annoyed him and the annoyance drove away his blushes. Striding into the cargo hangar, he ripped the towel from himself and strode around stark naked. At one point, while feeling particularly vengeful, he had to physically resist the urge to wag his penis around flamboyantly and ask if they were enjoying the spectacle. Suddenly struck by the humour of that scenario, he laughed aloud, his guffaws echoing around the cargo hangar and reverberating from the walls. He realised it might seem to outsiders as if he had finally lost his mind. Tired from his workout, from the run, and now relaxed by the warm shower, he turned his back on the wall, lifted his right knee sideways and broke wind loudly.

He slept surprisingly well and awoke refreshed. He was ready for another day of being extremely annoying whilst preventing anyone from using the Q-Wall without him knowing about it. Whilst he was intelligent enough to realise that there were probably other ways in and out of wherever they were, he figured it must be something of an inconvenience to have this cargo hangar Q-Wall unavailable for use. He spent the day working out, moving boxes and crates around with the loaders, jogging, singing, eating his nutri vend meals, and reading. It was while in the shower on the second evening that he realised he was losing his grip. Thinking back to earlier that afternoon, he remembered spending well over an hour trying to build a pyramid out of cans of some oil he found in one huge crate. Once built, with all the blue labels facing the same way, he leapt into the air, kicked it with his right boot and sent the cans to all corners of the room. He then remembered making the decision to try to make a bigger one the following day and he shook his head.

'I'm losing it,' he thought to himself, still too afraid to speak his thoughts aloud in case they incriminated him. 'If something doesn't change around here soon, I'm going to be smearing my own shit on the walls and drawing pictures with it. Someone save me from that, please.' His mind was too traumatised to function properly, so he went to bed. By late afternoon the next day, Tearan had not got out of his bed, other than to pee and get drinks of water. When he did get up, he did not bother to shower or dress, workout or do anything at all. After having a bite to eat from the auto snack, he paced up and down the room while his mind raced.

'I can't keep this up for much longer. I'm supposed to be part of a unit but where are my men? Where are Mykus, Tovis, and Dr Arma? Are they dead or are they being held somewhere and hoping for me to come and rescue them? They weren't my friends as such but we helped each other out here, even though we never met up.' This thought stopped him in his tracks and his eyes widened as pieces of a puzzle came together. The picture the pieces made was so horrific he did not at first know how he was going to cope. All those times he asked the others to meet up but they never did and he could never figure out why. At one point, he wondered if his mysterious companions were figments of his own troubled imagination but he had dismissed the idea. Now he revisited this troubling scenario and it was no easier to face than it had been the last time. 'Mykus, Tovis, and Dr Arma don't really exist. They pretended to be them, those scientists or whatever they are; they left the messages pretending to be them. They've been filming me all this time and listening to me leaving messages and talking aloud. They pretended to be on my side to get me to talk. They're worried about how much I know or if I'll tell anyone about what's going on.' Sure that both Mykus and Tovis had been made up by the people behind the wall, Tearan felt more alone and lonely than ever and despair filled his heart. 'I'm what they're experimenting on. It's been me all along. Shit, how do I get out of this?'

Without bothering to dress, he strode up to deck four and the engineering briefing room. The recording handset was still there on top of the drinks dispenser and he snatched it up angrily. There were no new messages and he decided he was not surprised. This was proof that none of the other three had ever existed at all. It had all been so believable; he accepted the existence of Mykus, Tovis and Doctor Arma without a second thought. Despite their apparent unwillingness to meet up, Tearan refused to wonder if this might be because they were not real people. He always chose to assume they were too busy or wanted their privacy, or maybe they weren't quite sure he was trustworthy. So desperate was he to believe he was not alone, he happily accepted even the most tenuous evidence of their existence.

Anger boiled inside Tearan, but he fought the desire to throw the recording handset at the wall. 'Yeah you'd love that wouldn't you assholes? Getting off on seeing me go crazy are you?' Forcing himself to appear controlled, he walked back down to the cargo hangar. There was no way for him to know the exact nature of whatever experiments these people were doing on him and with escape impossible, he despaired for his future. An uncertain future as a lab rat was not a prospect he relished, but he was stuck on the ship. He did not have the skills to repair it, nor the ability to fly it if he did miraculously get it fixed. He was a soldier not a mechanic or pilot. Navigation was familiar to him, he realised that when he first visited the Bridge. Now he decided he would rather not know all the places he was unable to get to. Rubbing salt into his wounds would do nothing for his mental state, so he decided to stay away from the Navigation station. Feeling ill from keeping his emotions inside, he went back to bed and dozed fitfully until he awoke in the small hours knowing his ability to endure the situation was at an end.

Being experimented on for however long he had left to live was something he had no intention of submitting to, especially without anyone to talk to or be friends with. With no way off the ship, he was stuck in a place he did not want to be. The soldier in him came to the fore and took control. Picking up the recording handset, he approached the wall and swept his eyes from one end to the other. With frightening speed, he flung the device at the wall, which broke apart on impact, sending small components flying in all directions.

"Hey you. You lot behind the Q-Wall. I know you're experimenting on me for something. I know you've been pretending to be Mykus, Tovis, and Doctor Arma. I reckon you're probably doing experiments on how to drive people insane. Maybe that's some kind of twisted weapon you've invented and you want to know how a man's mind can withstand it. I don't know how I got here, nor if I even consented to this. You lock me up in this prison with no one to talk to or hang out with and expect me to carry on my daily life. Dammit, I'm a person not some lab animal that can't think. For years I've served the galactic military, put my life on the line to keep your dirty secrets and overlook your mistakes. Times without number I've turned a blind eye when you've lied to whole worlds and I've probably taken innocent lives to cover up for you. So this is where that loyalty gets me huh? At least afford me the courtesy of some company while you drive me insane as payback for my service. There's no way I can get off this crate alone, I realise that, but I can't simply remain here like this and wait for the walls to start talking back to me. I'm taking control of this situation here and now."

Tearan walked to his makeshift bed, an idea having found its way to the forefront of his overactive mind. 'If I'm the subject of some kind of experiment, they're gonna want me alive so they can keep doing whatever it is they've been doing. Maybe if they think I'm a danger to myself they might reveal themselves in order to save their investment.' Taking up the nearest of the laser pistols, he faced the wall.

"What I do now, I do with a sound mind and as a man of clear conscience and spotless record. I have no control over you or whatever it is that you're doing, but I do have ultimate control of one thing, my life. I choose to exercise that control now. I will no longer allow myself to be subject to your experiments and I will not walk these corridors as a mindless husk of a man whose mind has been driven from him, for countless years into an unknown future."

He lifted the pistol and held it against his temple. "I am Tearan Lindo of the Inter-Galactic Elite Command, Unit 389C4. I am thirty-three years old and from Arlenika Prime. I go to the afterlife with a full heart and a clear conscience." Squeezing his eyes shut, he prayed it would be a painless end and tensed his finger on the trigger.

"Hello, Tearan." The voice made Tearan almost jump out of his skin. His eyes snapped open and he found himself looking into the pale eyes of a middle-aged man. Lowering the gun in shock, he squeezed his eyes shut, then opened them again. The man was still there and offered a reassuring smile. "I assure you I am real."

14

For several seconds, Tearan stared into the pale eyes of the stranger, who continued to gaze at him benignly. Wide eyed and open mouthed, he did not at first believe that what he was seeing was not a hallucination. Conflicting emotions battled for control. On the one hand, he was so happy to see another real live person that he felt tears pricking at his eyes, and the urge to rush over and hug the man was hard to resist. On the other hand, all his pent up anger and frustration fought to burst out now that there was someone at which to aim it and the urge to shoot the man was equally hard to resist.

Shaking himself from his daze, he straightened his shoulders. "Who the fuck are you?"

"I am Doctor Hunter and I am in charge here. I am happy to answer any questions you have."

Tearan was immediately suspicious and looked the man up and down. "You're the one who's responsible for me being imprisoned here? It's you who gave me amnesia?"

Hunter held his gaze. "Yes."

Quick as a flash Tearan lifted the gun once again, this time taking aim at Hunter's head. "Then this is for you."

"If you kill me I can't answer your questions can I?"

"There must be others with you. You can't do whatever it is you're doing, all alone. They can talk, you can die."

"Is that really what you want to do, Tearan? Is this what you've come to after all this, a killer?"

"I'm in the IGEC; we kill to cover up for assholes like you. It's what I do. Killing you will be therapy."

"Will it really make you feel like justice has been served to you? After killing me, this place, this work will still be secret and will still go on. You will be executed and everything else will go back to being as it was. Killing me will achieve nothing other than relieving this present moment of anger. I thought IGEC personnel were more disciplined than that."

Tearan bristled, annoyed at the man's logic and the way his words made him feel stupid. Furrows creased his brow as he struggled to regain his composure. Trying not to appear as if he had been caught off guard, he swiped a trembling hand across his forehead and dropped the gun to the floor.

"A moment ago you were going to shoot yourself, then you were going to shoot me. Neither of those actions would get you the answers you've been seeking. At least give me time to explain things to you before you decide if either of us is to die."

"So talk. How the fuck did I end up here and what is going on?"

"Come with me and I'll show you. Perhaps you'd like to umm, get dressed first?"

Tearan remembered he was naked and blushed. "Shit," he hissed and rummaged around for his clothes.

Two minutes later, Hunter motioned towards the Q-Wall. "Down there between the racks of shelving is a gap just wide enough for one man. Follow me." He walked down the cargo hangar, glancing back twice to make sure he was following. Tearan had noticed the gap in the shelving many times but never noticed anything different about this portion of the wall. He scanned it closely but there was nothing that caught his eye as being out of place.

Hunter took a small device from his pocket. "This is a mobile Q-controller. It is calibrated in such a way that allows us to open a limited portion of the wall, big enough for one person to walk through. It allows us entry and exit without having to activate the whole wall, which would be harder to defend. Here, you try. Press the button at the top and hold the unit towards the wall." Tearan took the device from Hunter and examined it. It was a rectangular box about twice the size of a cigarette packet, and had five buttons, a rotating dial, and a small one-inch square screen. A regular quiet blip was coming from it and a constantly moving waveform was flowing across the screen. "I would advise you don't fiddle with that rotating dial or we will both be stranded on this side. The button at the top makes the wall traversable. The next one down makes it a solid wall again. The other three are a locking mechanism, an alarm, and an intercom that allows us to communicate with those on the other side. That rotating dial alters the calibration, so unless you're an expert in quantum mechanics, I'd leave that one alone. Go ahead, press the button at the top and I will show you where we've been hiding."

Tearan held the device towards the wall and pressed the button. He heard a low hum and a noise like a small stone splashing into water and the surface of the portion of wall in front of him changed. Gentle undulations flowed over the surface, a glowing radiance emanating from between the individual cells that made up the wall.

Tearan frowned at Hunter. "Why do Q Walls always glow like that when they're activated?"

The hint of a smile played on Hunter's lips, as if he were delighted that Tearan were taking an interest in the science. "It's a by-product of the quantum interference process. Without getting too scientific, cells that make up structures bind together through the actions of special cell adhesion molecules."

Tearan's frown deepened. "You mean special sticky molecules?"

"Yes, that's one way of describing it. These special sticky molecules stick cells together in various different ways, some of which allow liquids or gases to pass between the cells. In order for a person to pass through a structure, we had to make a brand new kind of special sticky molecule that allows us to pass through the structure, and then makes the cells bind together again without our passage having caused damage."

"And they glow?" Tearan asked.

"Yes. When they're activated by a sound wave, they glow. When we pass through, the cell bindings are broken, but our special binding cells automatically re-bond again without damage. You're interested in science, Tearan?"

"Yeah. Oh, I would never be in a position to take your job or anything, but I'm interested in how and why stuff works. When I was a kid, I wanted to invent things when I grew up. A relative of my father invented a fuel valve that made engines use half the fuel without loss of power output and I used to love tinkering with things whenever we went to visit. I wanted to be like him when I grew up, but I didn't have his brain."

"You make your own contribution to life," Hunter said. "One that's just as valuable as any other. Let's go shall we?" He indicated the wall ahead. The wall glowed, its surface gently undulating and Tearan swallowed. Although he had traversed Q-Walls a couple of times before without adverse effect, it still made him hesitate for a moment.

"You will feel a tingling sensation," Hunter said from behind him. "It's a little like strong pins and needles but it fades within a few seconds once you're through."

"Yeah I know," Tearan replied. "I've done Q-Walls a couple of times. It's so unnatural that's all. It's not the physical part of it that bothers me, it's the fact that we're not designed to walk through walls. It kind of, goes against nature I guess. Stupid I know."

"I understand completely. Many people feel the same way. I felt that way when I first started working with them. Believe me you get used to it and don't worry, you won't get stuck halfway through. Those special sticky cells we invented won't stick when living tissue is passing through. It's a safety feature we built into the process. Go ahead, the rest of my staff are waiting to meet you."

Tearan stepped into clean white surroundings. Several men and women sat at workstations in front of bleeping computer consoles, readouts, display screens, and flickering lights. A group of men in overalls stood at one end and Tearan thought they were probably manual labourers.

Another group of men in security uniforms stood at the far end and stared unseeing into the middle distance.

"Hello, Tearan," a thin young man approached him, a polite smile on his lips and his hand outstretched. "It's good to meet you at last. My name is Doctor Julian Danvers."

"Another doctor," Tearan remarked as they shook hands. "Is that the medical kind of doctor or the scientist kind?"

"The scientist kind," Danvers replied.

Hunter came up and joined them. "First things first eh? You haven't eaten properly in the last couple of days, so would you like a proper meal?" Tearan hesitated, tempted to say no. He was hungry and now that he finally made it through the wall, there was no immediate need to do without. Hunter read his hesitation as acceptance. "Right then, follow me. Danvers, would you like to join us?"

Hunter and Danvers led Tearan along several corridors and up three flights of stairs before they entered a reasonably sized dining room. From the areas he had so far seen, he was even more confused about the size of this missing portion of the ship. From the maps on the walls, this missing space should be almost the same size as the cargo hangar on deck eight, and a similar sized area above it on deck seven. From what he had seen so far, this whole space was way too big. Something was off and he frowned.

Hunter noticed his frown. "It must be confusing, Tearan. Don't worry, the moment you've got a decent meal inside you, we'll take you down to meet everyone and tell you everything. Now, what would you like?"

Several people were staring wide eyed and Tearan felt the weight of their stares. It made him feel self conscious and he blushed. Turning away from their stares, he squared his shoulders as he forced himself back into IGEC mode. During the meal, he fired questions at the two doctors, but both skilfully avoided answering them. Halfway through a delicious steak, Tearan slammed his knife and fork down and growled. Everyone in the room stopped talking and turned to stare. He felt their gaze burning and anger flared into life.

"What are you looking at, assholes?" he yelled. Everyone snapped their heads away and pretended to be continuing with their own conversations.

"Please try to be patient, Tearan," Hunter said. "I've promised you all the answers you want, but it would not be fair to prevent the other staff here from contributing to that discussion. They are all experts in their own fields, all of us have an interest in you and what you've experienced."

"You've earned the right to enjoy a decent meal that you don't have to cook for yourself after what you've been through," Danvers added.

Tearan closed his eyes, trying to force his anger back down. When he opened them, he looked down at his plate. "Okay, I apologise for yelling but I've been imprisoned back there for days on end, lost my memory and still haven't got it all back. Why this happened to me and what I did to deserve it is a mystery. I've always done my job to the best of my ability; kept the secrets, done the dirty work, turned the blind eye and never questioned orders. I've earned the truth if nothing else."

"You'll have it, I give you my word," Hunter said.

"Hello, Tearan," the pretty brunette said with a genuine smile that crinkled at the corners of her eyes. "I'm Doctor Melissa Frost."

"Hi," Tearan replied.

Once the large briefing room was full and everyone seated around the oval table, Hunter looked at Tearan. "Okay. We are all here to explain what's been happening and why. It will seem unbelievable to you but I promise you everything we are about to tell you is the truth. You can ask questions at any time, if you don't understand or if we get too scientific."

"Good, so what the fuck have you done to me and why?"

"This ship," Hunter replied, "the Novosentia, has been the home of the Dreamspinner project for the past six years."

Tearan frowned. "Dreamspinner? I've never heard of it."

"That doesn't surprise me in the least," Hunter said. "In fact I'd be worried if you had. It's above top secret and always has been. You consented to be a part of this project. That's why you're here."

"That still doesn't tell me anything and why should I believe you that I consented? Anyone could claim that. What part have I been playing in this little game of yours?"

Danvers leaned forwards. "You're one of our test subjects. As you figured out for yourself, we've been filming you and listening to you since you woke up, but this is so that we can observe how you react to the procedure."

"Procedure?" Now Tearan leaned forward. "What procedure?"

Danvers and Hunter hesitated and it was Melissa Frost who spoke. "The Dreamspinner project was set up to do research and testing into personality alteration."

"Personality alteration? What the fuck is that?" Tearan frowned and closed his eyes. When he felt calm, he opened them and apologised. "I'm sorry for my language but you're all still holding out on me and it's damn annoying."

She nodded. "I know, but you've been so successful that we don't want to risk anything going wrong. We are a little afraid that if we dump all the missing bits of information onto you now, you won't be able to cope and the test will fail."

"If you don't tell me, I assure you all here and now that this little test of yours will fail spectacularly, because I will go insane with frustration." He let out a howl of anger and banged both fists down onto the table. "Please, tell me what the fuck is going on. I'm an honest and hard working man and I deserve the truth if nothing else."

"We've given you a new personality," she replied, her eyes never leaving his own. "There, I said it."

"You what? A new personality?" Tearan let out a cry that was halfway between a laugh and a sob, and leaned back in his chair as he ran a hand through his hair. "That's crazy. You're crazy. I am who I am."

"Actually, you're not. At least you weren't, but you are now. Sorry, now I'm getting confused." She shook her head and gave an attractive giggle of embarrassment. "What I'm trying to say is that you came to the Dreamspinner Project voluntarily. We then implanted you with a totally new personality, with its own identity and its own sense of self. We've been observing you so that we can keep a check on how well you take to being Tearan Lindo."

Tearan listened, the words floating into his brain but making no sense whatsoever. "That's nuts." He leaned forward, scanning the faces around the table. "That's impossible. Isn't it?"

"Not any more it isn't," Danvers replied. "That's the reason why you can't remember the time spanning a week before you came here, and a week after. That portion of time will always be gone. We've found that it's the only way a subject can ever hope to accept the newly implanted personality. The newly implanted information needs that little window of time as a sort of, clean slate, on which to set down its initial roots."

Tearan was wide eyed by now and so amazed by what he was hearing that questions evaded him. He was so stunned he did not know how to reply.

"The exact process goes like this," Hunter said as he switched on a vidicom screen. "You are given an anaesthetic and then a small computerised chip is implanted into your brain." He pointed to the various photographs, diagrams, and film footage as he explained. "After this is done, we keep you sedated while we activate the chip remotely from one of the consoles in the room by the Q-Wall. What this does is erase a small amount of your short term memory, from around a week before, and prevents new memories from embedding for approximately a further week, give or take a day or so either way. Into this memory free patch of your mind, we download the information that forms the basics of the new personality. After another week or so, when your wound is healed and our readouts show the new personality has implanted, we take you through to the ship and leave you to wake up naturally. All we then have to do is observe and be ready should anything untoward happen."

"What do you mean by anything untoward?"

"Sometimes the new personality refuses to implant," Melissa said. "Sometimes it starts to implant and then stops for some reason we can't yet explain. Sometimes the original personality is too strong and rejects it."

"And what do you do when that happens?"

"We bring the patient back here and start over," Hunter said.

"So you don't kill them or anything," Tearan asked.

Hunter gave a snort of surprised laughter. "Good heavens no. Why on Earth would we do that? Our patients are valuable assets. We don't get many people volunteering, so we look after those who do."

"So anyone who had this thing go wrong, they would get another go around?" Tearan asked.

"Yes," Hunter said.

"So all my memories, are they fake?"

Melissa shook her head. "No. Everything you remember is part of the new personality, part of Tearan Lindo's life. They are his memories, and now that you are he, they are yours."

For some reason that Tearan was unable to fathom, this knowledge upset him greatly and he was unable to stop hot tears from flowing down his cheeks. "So I'm not who I think I am?"

"On the contrary," Danvers replied. "You are who you now think you are. All of the things you remember doing, all the skills you remember having, are now part of you. Even though you've never actually been Granyar hunting on Perialan 7, if you went there today, you would be a skilled hunter because your brain now accepts that it is Tearan Lindo, expert Granyar hunter."

"So you can program people with skills they never had before?"

"Yes," Melissa said. "So long as the memory of those skills are part of a whole new personality. We cannot yet add just the skills, but who knows where this technique will be in twenty years."

"That is one of the reasons why volunteers like yourself are so valuable to us," Hunter said. "What you're helping us with will enhance the lives of so many people in the not too distant future. You're a brave pioneer, Tearan, not a prisoner."

"So what happens now?" Tearan asked. "Do you wipe me out because I forced my way in here? Do you start me over again?"

"No," Hunter laughed. "We will continue to observe you here and now that you know we're here, we might as well leave the wall open so you can have the run of the whole place. There's the firing range you've come to enjoy using, the vidicom and music. I umm, would hope you might lower the volume a little though, and perhaps sing a little quieter?"

Tearan laughed aloud, delighted that he had given them a hard time. "How many other people like me are there?"

"Forty seven at this moment," Melissa said. "Eighteen women and twenty nine men."

"So we all take turns at being the lab rat huh?"

"No," Danvers replied. "All but four of you are active at the moment. One has caught an infection that we are treating, and the other three are in the process of receiving a new implant. They'll be active within a few days."

"Look, out this window," Hunter said as he pressed a button. A blind rose up, revealing a large viewing window. Tearan got up and went over, his mouth open in shock. The structure was immense, a tall cylinder from which pods protruded. Each of these pods was shaped like a space ship docked at a space station or deep space refuelling station. Below, the enormous curve of a planet hung serene in the void. The intense blue of the huge ocean he gazed at was reflected by the hue of his own eyes and was the most beautiful colour Tearan had ever seen.

"Wow, what is this place? I thought it was a space ship that had broken down. None of this is visible from any of the windows I've seen. And that planet. What is it? It's beautiful."

"That is our home world," Hunter replied. "We call it Earth, but the galactic registration has it down as Solar 4. The Dreamspinner Project began in a small lab down there fourteen years ago, when my friend and mentor wondered if it were possible to change a person's personality by wiping memories and uploading newly manufactured ones. This is a controversial project as you can imagine, so we're discreet about what we're doing. The space ship you lived in is one area of the Novosentia. There are one hundred pods like the one you're familiar with, and there's room for sixty more if the number of volunteers should ever increase that far. The reason you can't see any of this from the windows in your pod is because the windows are vidicom screens on which is displayed a generic space view. We have switched them off now you know about it."

Tearan sat down again and dropped his gaze to his hands. There were two questions he wanted to ask more than anything, but now he had the opportunity, he found himself afraid to do so.

Danvers noticed he seemed worried. "It's a lot to take in I know. I've no idea how you're feeling about all of this, but if you can open up to us as much as possible, it will help us fine tune the process and make it easier for future participants."

"I don't really know how to feel about it, and that's the truth. I feel angry at having this done to me. I know you say I agreed to it, but because you wiped that part of my memory, it feels like it's been forced on me."

"Don't worry," Hunter said. "We have your signed consent papers and vidicom footage of you signing them. They show you clearly stating that you understood what you were volunteering for and that you gave us permission to go ahead. We will show you the film at the earliest opportunity."

"Okay. Can I ask a couple more questions?"

"Of course, ask anything at all," Hunter replied.

"Why did you pretend to be the other guys, Mykus, Tovis, and Doctor Arma? It felt like I had friends in there and that made me feel like I wasn't alone, abandoned."

Everyone shuffled in their seats as an uncomfortable quiet descended on the room. Tearan guessed he had asked something they did not wish to answer, but he did not care. He glared at Hunter.

"We didn't pretend, Tearan."

This took Tearan by surprise and it showed. "Oh. So they're real? They're other volunteers? Are they okay? Where are they? Can I meet them?"

Hunter hesitated for a split second and Tearan got the feeling that he was not going to like what he was about to hear. "Okay, let me explain about them as clearly as I can. If you can't follow me, stop me and I'll try to explain better." He coughed nervously. "Mykus Romin, Tovis Kerral, Doctor Soval Arma, and Jole Smoy were not real people."

Tearan frowned. "Huh? But you said."

"I said we didn't pretend to be them."

"So what do you mean they aren't real people? They're not volunteers like me?"

"This process involves implanting a new personality into your mind, which we hope integrates with your mind successfully and becomes the new you."

"You told me that already. Get to the point please."

"I'm trying to make sure we explain the whole picture to you. It is our experience that around twenty-seven percent of procedures do not implant successfully. They are rejected and the original personality remains the stronger one. In order to overcome this problem, we have had considerable success by implanting more than one new personality at a time. This seems to help one of them to implant quicker and more successfully. It's as if having others to compete with enhances the strength of one, which then becomes the one that fully integrates."

Tearan felt his head sway a little as he took in Hunter's words. "So you're telling me that the other guys, they were me too?"

"Yes, Tearan," Melissa said, again holding his eyes with her own. He gazed back at her, feeling instinctively that above all the others around the table, she was the only one to trust. "Mykus, Tovis, Doctor Arma, and another called Jole Smoy. They were also implanted alongside the personality of Tearan Lindo."

Tears coursed down Tearan's cheeks. "So what happened to them?"

"They failed to implant. Tearan Lindo was the strongest personality and implanted successfully."

Tearan let out a loud cry and stumbled to his feet, sending his chair toppling to the floor behind him. Covering his eyes with his hands, he battled with the emotion that flooded his soul. Anger whirled him around to face the scientists, his face red with rage as he banged his fists onto the table top. "They felt like people I was going to be friends with and now it feels like I killed them. I feel like a murderer. You shouldn't have made it possible for us to speak to each other."

Hunter wrote furiously on a pad as Tearan yelled at them. When quiet once again filled the briefing room, he looked up. "Okay, thank you for being open about it. You formed a bond with the other personalities and now they're gone, you're grieving. I'm sorry this has caused you pain. Your candour will help us fine tune the process so that future volunteers won't suffer the same way."

"Where did the other personalities come from?" Tearan asked. "Were they invented or are they somehow uploaded from real people?"

"It's a mixture of both," Danvers said. "Volunteers who agree, allow us to implant a chip into their brains, similar to the one you have. This collects information from their brain and sends it to us, where we collect it, alongside a full written record of the person's life and information. After they die, our sophisticated computer programs clean and recombine all the collected information into a format we can then upload into a volunteer like yourself."

"So the other guys, Mykus, Tovis, Doctor Arma, and the other one, what did you say his name was?"

"Jole Smoy."

"Yeah, him too. So they were once real people who are dead now."

Hunter's eyes widened as he understood what Tearan was saying. "Yes, so we can show you their information if you'd like. Would that help you feel better? It would enable you to say goodbye to them, sort of."

"Yeah. I would appreciate that."

"No problem at all. We will arrange that as soon as we can collate the information together." Hunter indicated to one of the men around the table, who wrote on the pad in front of him.

"Thanks. There's just one other question."

"Of course, fire away."

"Who was I? You know, before."

Silence fell upon the room once again, so thick it almost choked him.

Hunter ran a hand through his hair. "Oh, Tearan, that is the one question we really don't want to answer right now."

"Why not?" Tearan demanded, an edge to his voice that was not there previously.

"For a couple of reasons. First, you haven't long integrated as Tearan Lindo. It is our experience that the original personality retains a strong hold over the mind for quite a time after it has been subjugated by another. To confront a newly integrated identity with the original one would undoubtedly result in the process failing. Tearan Lindo needs time to fully bed in and take control enough so that you will feel as if you've always been him. You will know when this is happening because you will dream of yourself being him. At the moment, your dreams are likely to be either unpleasant or missing completely. Tearan's dreams will contain images that you remember from his memories. Smells will spark a memory, a song perhaps. All of these things will show that you are fully becoming Tearan Lindo. The second reason we don't want to face this yet is because it's like a death has taken place for you and it has, in effect. It's as if you died and were reborn as someone else. You will go through a grieving process for the person you used to be. You can't remember him yet you feel guilty for abandoning him. These are all natural parts of the process. We've learned this through the brave efforts of people like yourself. You need time to come to terms with losing your old self, losing the other guys you thought were real and to fully become Tearan Lindo. Once you reach that comfortable place in your head, you will be ready to learn about your old self. Please trust me on this."

"Yeah, I umm, I understand," Tearan said. "It makes sense I guess."

"Of course you're curious," Danvers said. "That is totally normal. We get that and we will help you all we can."

"How long will all that take?"

Hunter shrugged. "Well, how long is a piece of string? Obviously this isn't something we can pin down to a definite time frame. Every person is different and every race of people takes the process in a different way. The quickest we've ever had someone reach that point of total integration was seven weeks. The longest was eleven months and two weeks. All I can tell you is that of the two other Arlenikan volunteers we've had, one took nineteen weeks and the other took twelve."

"So I have to keep living here like I've been doing?"

"Yes. You won't be on your own now though. There are lots of people to talk to and hang out with. You'll have access not only to your own familiar pod, but many areas in this part of the vessel too. There are state of the art recreational and sports facilities were you can meet people, keep fit, and relax. You've already sampled our restaurant. There is a vidicom theatre, library, and even an educational facility if you wish to expand your knowledge and skill base."

"That reminds me," Tearan said. "Why were the vidicom screens not working? What harm could there possibly be in letting us, I mean me, watch a few movies?"

Hunter grinned. "That was done to encourage the personality of Tovis Kerral to remember his electrical engineering skills, which he did."

"Oh, okay. Do I still have to sleep back there?" he asked, pointing behind him.

"Not if you don't want to," Danvers said. "We can give you a room here if you'd prefer."

"I would."

"Okay, I'll fix that up."

"We try to make your time here as comfortable as possible in exchange for your indulgence in our testing and monitoring," Melissa said. "We will want to monitor your brain functions every day, which will involve you lying down for two hours and answering questions. There will be simple tests to check your motor and cognitive function as well. It will be boring but painless. We will also ask you to sleep with a brain monitoring cap on at night. It's like a light cap; it's not uncomfortable. It sends us your brainwaves while you sleep and your implant performs certain functions while you're asleep that it can't do while you're awake. We like to keep a check on how the implant is performing. Other than that, your time will be your own. We'll introduce you to two others who are both at the same stage as yourself, so you can exchange experiences."

"Okay. It will be good to have company at last."

Hunter leaned forward. "The only facility we do not provide here is alcoholic refreshment. You will have to abstain until you're fully integrated. Once you reach that stage, we will gradually reintroduce it and monitor how you cope. Alcohol affects the brain in many ways, one of which is memory retention. Whilst your new personality is still embedding itself, it is at great risk from anything which can impair memory function or retention. We've found in the past that even a small amount can result in a total breakdown of the new personality and a breaking through of the old one. Arlenikan males have quite a low tolerance anyway, so you might find you have to abstain even when fully integrated."

"I don't drink," Tearan said without thinking, then blushed. "At least I think I don't. Is it the old me, or Tearan Lindo who doesn't drink? I'm not sure who I am now."

"That is a perfect example of why we don't want to deal with who you used to be just yet," Hunter said. "Tearan Lindo is who you are. All your thoughts, memories, desires, likes and dislikes, and personality foibles are his and therefore yours. When you said, I don't drink, you were being

Tearan Lindo perfectly. Don't question it, be natural and let yourself be yourself."

"Okay. Well I don't drink so abstaining from alcohol won't be a problem."

"That's wonderful. Now would you like to meet the other two volunteers who are at the same stage as yourself? My colleague will collate all the information on Mykus, Tovis, Doctor Arma, and Jole for you to read later today."

15

"Are you sure this isn't going to fuck things up?" Tearan asked as he sat down.

"On the contrary. Seeing the others as individuals separate from yourself will help cut any lingering threads of attachment that your mind might be harbouring towards them. Your sub conscious mind will know beyond doubt that those people are not you. It will help Tearan Lindo to fully take over."

"Okay, thanks."

"No problem. Take your time. You're familiar with a library console?"

"Yeah." He watched as Hunter left the room before turning back to the console in front of him. With a couple of clicks he was staring into the face of a man labelled Donor number P848902-693L – Mykus Romin. Tearan's eyes widened as he gasped in shock. Even if there had been nothing to identify the man as Mykus, he would have known it was him. A wave of emotional recognition flowed through him and he smiled at the face that gazed up at him.

"Hey there Mykus, I'd know you anywhere." Another click and the photograph became animated as the vidicom footage began. Tearan watched the thirty-minute film in silence, emotion overtaking him as he listened to the man he thought of as his friend, speak about himself.

"Hello there. I am Donor number P848902-693L and for the purpose of the Dreamspinner Project, its aims and objectives, I will be known as Mykus Romin. I am at the time of joining the project, twenty-eight years of age, single, and from Arlenika Prime. I joined Dreamspinner as a donor of my own volition, and hereby give the project's scientists and doctors, full permission to carry out whatever procedures they may deem necessary. I understand that I will be required to undergo a surgical procedure to implant a chip into my brain and that the aforementioned chip will remain in place for the rest of my life. The rules are that I state all of the aforementioned clearly, along with my assurance that I am a willing participant and donor. I've also been asked to explain why I decided to donate, and I know it sounds like a cliché, but I want to make a difference y'know? A good difference if possible and this seems like a way to do that."

Tearan grinned as he watched Mykus. The sense of recognition was uncanny; he felt a tangible bond despite never having met the man before. It was as if he were watching his brother on film. Mykus then recounted the major details of his life and Tearan nodded his way through them. Once the film was over, he read the additional details in the file and was dismayed to read that Mykus had taken his own life a year after joining the Dreamspinner Project. Details of his suicide were scant, all it told Tearan was that his friend took his own life due to emotional stress caused by the death of a friend. Tears coursed down his face as he read and re-read the file and the sense of loss was as genuine as if his own flesh and blood had died. Fuelled by grief, Tearan got up and strode from the room.

Doctor Hunter ran down the corridor, the screams drawing him along. Tearan Lindo lay on his stomach, pinned to the floor by four security guards. Another guard sat propped against the wall to his left, blood spouting from his nose as a nurse fussed over him. Tearan screamed and struggled.

"What the hell happened here?" Hunter demanded. "Why is Tearan being restrained?"

"He went crazy, Sir," the guard with the bloody nose said. "He ran from the office, screaming and yelling his head off. We approached him and asked him to calm down and tell us what was wrong, but he lost it and attacked us."

"He attacked you without provocation, are you sure? It's very important that you be as accurate as possible. His future depends upon it."

The guard blushed and his mouth flapped as he fought his embarrassment. "Well, he was screaming and yelling. We were worried what he might do. We couldn't let him run around like that, not with all the people living and working here."

"So you manhandled him first and asked questions later," Hunter snapped.

"I'm sorry, Sir. We were only thinking of everyone's safety."

"Let him up, now," Hunter demanded. The guards hesitated for a second. A glare from Hunter and they backed off, leaving Tearan on the floor. His screams calmed to sobs now that he was not being forcibly restrained and he looked at Hunter as he sat up and leaned against the wall.

"Thanks," he sniffed and wiped his eyes.

"I'm sorry my security personnel acted like a bunch of Neanderthals. Believe me when I say they will answer for their actions. Come to my office and tell me what's wrong." He held out his hand to help Tearan to his feet and with another glare to the security guards, led him down the corridor. After sitting him down and offering him a cup of coffee, which he accepted but obviously did not like, he asked him to explain.

"I'm sorry, Doctor Hunter. I was reading about Mykus and watching the film. It was uncanny, the feeling of recognition I mean. Everything he said about his life, his memories. It was as if I already knew it, except I know I didn't know any of it. I even recognised his face and the sound of his voice. It was like he's my twin or something. When I read he killed himself, it was like someone kicked me in the gut. I'm sorry for hurting that guy, but they grabbed me like I was a dangerous criminal or something. They didn't ask me what was wrong or if I was all right. They jumped on me and pinned me to the floor."

"That feeling of recognition happened because the personality of Mykus was the second most compatible with you. He nearly took over control, but Tearan Lindo won out in the end. You might feel a similar feeling of recognition with the other personalities too, although probably not to such a strong degree. You might want to think about whether you wish to know any more about them."

"I want to continue," Tearan said without hesitation. "I have to. I want to know who they were. Out of respect for them y'know? We shared something, them and me. Something people don't normally share. I feel I need to acknowledge that, make a gesture to the universe or something. It may sound stupid to you but you're not going through this, you haven't experienced this weird bond."

"It doesn't sound stupid at all," Hunter said. "Those feelings of recognition are the way your brain copes with the memory of you having been him for a while. Although his face is distinctly different to yours, despite his voice being unlike yours, your brain sees and hears them as your own. Another thing to remember is that the individual personalities controlled their own voices. The pitch, speech impediments, accents and inflections, all are slightly different when under the control of the individual personas. There are many incongruities of the brain that we're still trying to understand. Listen, we have a room set out as a non-denominational place of worship. It's open all the time, day and night for anyone to visit. We have furnished it with everything necessary for all our volunteers and staff to demonstrate their religion in the way they need to. You will find the four bells and scrolls of the Arlenikan faith in there and a member of my staff is fully licenced by the Arlenikan Council of Belief and Culture to administer to you while you pray, should you wish for witness."

"Thank you. By the way, I've thought of something else that was very odd. Can you explain it to me?"

"I'll do my best."

"There were a couple of times during the past few days when weird things happened that almost made me think the ship was haunted or something. I heard noises of someone else nearby, the sound of gunfire and a loud crash in the security room. Then there was all that weird shit down in the medical bay about ghosts and bodies. We all thought, I mean I thought, shit it's hard to explain."

"Don't worry, say we if it helps."

"Thanks. Well, we all thought Dr Arma was going crazy, but I guess I wrote all that stuff, didn't I?"

Doctor Hunter nodded. "Yes, you did it while the persona of Dr Arma was struggling under the weight of Tearan Lindo's dominance."

"What about the stuff I heard though, the fleeting shadows out of the corner of my eye. It spooked me, I admit it."

"They were brief flashes of memory your brain experienced, during which you almost remembered being one of the other personalities. You see, Tearan, you flitted from one personality to another; it was most interesting to watch. Sometimes you were one of the guys for several days, other times it was just a few hours. As the others began to fail under Tearan's dominance, those moments of being the others became shorter and shorter."

"So when I heard gunfire, footsteps, heard my name called a couple of times, and that crash, that was me remembering doing it while I was being the other guys?"

"Yes. That's it exactly."

"What was that crash all about? It sounded like the ship had crashed or something."

"That was Jole Smoy playing at being a racing driver with one of the hover loaders. He was curious about what lay behind the security room door, so decided to crash through it."

Tearan grinned. "So I wasn't imagining those scratches on the floor."

"No, you weren't. Top marks for observation."

Tearan sat on the floor of the small room and breathed in the heady incense. Naked apart from a white cloth around his genitals, his pale skin shone from the spiced oil the administrator had rubbed into him. The administrator, whom Tearan was pleased to discover was Arlenikan, had the job of helping him get ready for prayer, to lead him in prayer, and to be witness to his act of faith. An administrator was not necessary for every prayer session, but is there when the devotee wishes for a deeper connection with his deity or if they wish to make a greater than usual gesture of faith. After ringing the bell for the first of the prayers, he listened intently to Tearan's words.

Arlenikans believe in a single all-knowing deity they call Almistra, which means a genderless omniscient creator. Almistra has four faces, a baby, an adult, an old person, and a skull. The number four is sacred to Arlenikans, who believe that life is made up of four phases, birth, adulthood, old age, and death. Four principles rule their daily lives, the pursuit of knowledge, personal growth, compassion, and the keeping of faith. Four major sins, apathy, deceit, cruelty, and greed, must be avoided in order to keep one's soul clean and ensure entry into the desired level of afterlife upon death. The lowest level, a cold place without light is inhabited by the souls of the very worst of Arlenikans. No one wishes to go there, and all are afraid to end up there. The second and third layers are where the majority of souls end up, with the fourth and highest level reserved for those who demonstrated extreme and lifelong goodness and compassion. These rare souls usually suffer greatly in life whilst remaining without anger or the wish for vengeance. They spend their lives striving to make life better for everyone else before serving their own needs. Those who find themselves alighting on the golden shore of Ramojistra upon their death know that they never have to live another physical life. They can spend their eternity as spiritual teachers reaching out to those in prayer or via the dreams of those who sleep.

Tearan rocked back and forth as he chanted the words, each one coming from the depths of his heart. As he listened for the administrator to ring the bells, each one symbolising one of the four stages of life, he prayed for the lives of Mykus Romin, Tovis Kerral, Doctor Soval Arma, and Jole Smoy. He also prayed for his own soul, the one he had given up by becoming Tearan Lindo. By turning his back upon his own true born self, he committed a grave sin that meant there was a very real chance that he would find himself washing up on the dark shore of Omdook upon his death. He acknowledged and accepted this very real threat and hoped that by living a good and honest life for however long he had left, he might atone a little. When his prayers were done and the Administrator finished giving his acknowledgement of witness, he placed the four lifebloods into the flame that burned from the hearth in the centre of the room. The four substances necessary for physical life, water, blood, food, and air are offered at the end of Arlenikan religious devotion. A cup of water is first poured into the glowing embers of a small fire, the resulting smoke symbolising air. A drop of blood from a pricked finger sizzles in the embers and a piece of meat fills the temple with delicious smells. All that is necessary for life comes from Almistra, and is given back by these symbolic offerings.

Tearan felt at ease as he showered the spiced oil from his body and hair. This was the first time since waking up that he had given any thought to faith. Up until now, he had not even been aware of having any particular belief. The scent of the oil as the Administrator rubbed it into his skin, brought memories of a strong and enduring faith rushing back into his mind. Tearan opened his heart to them and realised as the hot water cascaded down his body, that it gave him a sense of peace he never realised was missing. Once dressed, he went in search of a meal and met Doctor Melissa Frost in a corridor.

"Hello, Tearan, how are you feeling now?"

"Better, thank you. I thought I might have a meal if that's okay."

"Of course. I will escort you to the restaurant if I may; I have a couple of things to tell you."

"Sure."

Red digital numbers flashed as the elevator rose up through the immense structure. Melissa Frost handed Tearan a key, the number seventy-eight carved into the rounded top.

"Your room is on the seventh floor. We've put washing necessities in the bathroom for you and there are two pairs of overalls and a couple of changes of underwear in the closet. You can retrieve things from your pod if you wish; the Q-Wall has been left open for you to go back and forth whenever you want."

"Thank you. I'd like to continue using the firing range."

"No problem. The other thing I need to ask you is to report to the lab guys when you're ready to go to bed. You'll find an intercom in your room. Press button three and it will connect directly with the lab. Someone will come and fit you with the electronic cap."

"Okay, sure." Tearan indicated for Melissa to exit first and then followed her into the restaurant.

"Ahh, your two companions are here. Let me introduce you." Tearan followed her over to a table at one side of the large room. Two men sat talking and seemed to be firm friends. One was huge and had the blackest skin Tearan had ever seen. His bright yellow eyes regarded him as Melissa introduced him, and the corners crinkled when he smiled.

"Hi there, Tearan, welcome to the club. My name is Rajfar Ki Qenway, but everyone finds it easier to call me Qen. This is Eishlo." He indicated the thin man beside him who smiled shyly.

"Hello, Tearan, sit and eat with us won't you? Tell us how you're coping with all this."

"Hi, guys. Thanks. I'll go get something to eat and join you."

"You mean you really stood there naked and threatened to shoot yourself?" Qen asked, his eyebrows raised in disbelief. Tearan nodded and the three men laughed.

"That's hysterical," Eishlo grinned. "I think I'm going to like your style."

They spent the next three hours comparing experiences and feelings about what they were going through and all three found considerable comfort in having others who understood. Qen and Eishlo were envious when Tearan took them on a tour of his spaceship pod and showed them the firing range he enjoyed using.

"This is wonderful, Tearan," Qen said as he turned a large laser pistol over in his hands. "I did my military service back home and used a sidearm there, but not since."

"I've never even handled a gun," Eishlo said. "I'm a librarian not a soldier. I've always fancied having a go though. My father frowned upon the use of firearms and I learnt very early to keep quiet about my desire to familiarise myself with them. Between you and me, I think he was a raving pacifist."

"I'd be very happy to teach you," Tearan said as he handed Eishlo a small laser pistol. "It would be fun to have others to compete with."

"Yes it would," Qen agreed.

"Okay then," Eishlo said. "When I was a boy, my friends and I used to secretly play Mercs and Convicts. We'd carve bits of wood, use them like guns and take turns being the Mercs. I never told anyone, but I had more fun being the Convict."

"My friends and I used to play those games too," Qen laughed.

"Y'know, I find this whole multiple personality thing, most disquieting," Eishlo said.

"So do I," Qen agreed.

"Did you communicate with your umm, others?" Tearan asked.

Qen was wide eyed at the question. "What? Of course not."

"No way," Eishlo shook his head. "That would be too errm, weird."

"I did." Tearan said quietly and blushed as his new friends stared at him.

Qen gaped. "You're joking surely."

"I wish I was. There was a digital recording device in the Engineering Briefing Room and we left messages for each other on it."

"Wow, that's real umm, wow," Eishlo exclaimed in surprise.

Tearan nodded. "Yeah, it was for me too when I found out they weren't real people."

Qen frowned. "So you heard their voices on this recorder and you never realised it was your own voice?"

Tearan shook his head. "No. They all sounded different to me. Doctor Hunter told me that I used different voices when I was being them. He said it's normal and that each new personality affects speech and physical behaviours as well as memories and thoughts. Stuff like voice, accent, speech impediments and pronunciation are an intrinsic part of a personality, so he says."

Eishlo scratched his head. "That's kind of interesting, you have to admit. If I weren't so personally involved, I would find this stuff fascinating."

Qen ran a hand through his hair. "It's creepy is what it is. And wrong. Whatever their noble reasons for doing this might be, it goes against the natural order of things. That's what I believe anyway."

"On a personal level I agree," Tearan said. "Hunter told me something interesting though. He said that one day this procedure might help people with psychological illnesses. He also said they hope to use it as a method of treating violent criminals."

"That makes good sense," Eishlo said. "To rehabilitate such people would be of great benefit."

Qen sniffed. "Execution does that very effectively and costs less."

Tearan did not want to get into a moral argument, so he steered the conversation away. "I did find it hard to swallow though, when Hunter told me the guys I'd come to think of as friends were really me with other personalities." He blushed as he felt a swell of emotion within. "It was like my friends died and I couldn't save them. It was like I killed them myself."

"That's rough, sorry," Qen said.

"We're here if you want to talk about it," Eishlo added.

"Thanks." After a few seconds of awkward silence, he coughed. "So, you want to watch a movie or something?"

Life became routine. After waking early and enjoying breakfast with his new friends, Tearan was subjected to three hours of tests. Lunch was followed by two hours in the gym Tearan had set up in his security room, then the three showered and took a nap for an hour. Their evenings were spent watching movies, or playing several rounds of Flatchet, a ball game with extremely complicated rules from Qen's home world. Every evening, Eishlo would grin as he listened to Tearan and Qen arguing some rule or other. He often secretly agreed with Tearan that the rules seemed unnecessarily complicated. One or two of the crew joined them on their nights off and the three friends learned basketball, football, and tennis. All three quickly agreed that they were not made for tennis, but it was a laugh and laughter lifted the monotony of their lives a little.

Tearan did as he was asked and allowed himself to be tested and re-tested, questioned, probed, and interrogated without a fuss. Qen and Eishlo's friendship helped him cope with the boredom and heal his heart of the grief of losing Mykus, Tovis, Doctor Arma and the silent one, Jole Smoy. He had never been aware of Jole, so the bond was not as strong but he held him in his heart alongside the others nonetheless. Knowing these men had once been people, alive and vibrant with life who had donated their personalities, their memories, in the hope that one day, troubled minds might be eased, helped him keep things in the proper perspective. Little by little, as the grief subsided, Tearan had to admit that something troublesome had replaced it. Knowing all three were being filmed and listened to by Hunter and the other scientists made it hard for him to know how to deal with his frustration. Eishlo presented him with the perfect solution one evening when he offered to show Qen and Tearan the spaceship pod where he had spent his time before being allowed through the Q-Wall.

"I got something neither of you two got," he grinned as he led them down corridors and up to a door marked with some writing neither Tearan nor Qen understood. Flinging open the door with a flourish, Tearan gaped at the state of the art steam room that lay before them.

"Whoa, you got a steam room?" Qen said. Eishlo nodded proudly.

"What's it for?" Tearan asked.

Qen and Eishlo gaped at each other, then at Tearan. "You're serious?" Qen asked. Tearan nodded. "You don't have steam rooms on Arlenika?"

"Nope."

"Man, you need an education fast," Eishlo said and Qen laughed.

Tearan wiped the hot sweat from his brow and sighed. He was sure his bones were melting within his body, but Qen and Eishlo assured him this would be good for his health, so he bore it with as much grace as possible. Every few seconds, a loud hiss would herald a fresh burst of steam and he began to wonder how much longer he could bear it. Hot condensation covered everything within the small room and he was glad he had followed Qen's instructions to leave all of his clothes and belongings outside. This heat and wet would ruin anything and he was relieved that he did not own any electronic or digital devices. Boiling steam and electronics do not mix well; even Tearan knew enough about electronics to know that. Eishlo noticed Tearan's wide eyed stare and frowned.

Tearan waited for the next loud hiss before speaking softly. "I doubt they can film or record us in here." Eishlo opened his mouth to reply, but a hand appeared across his mouth. Qen shook his head at Eishlo as he held a deep black hand across his face. Eishlo nodded and Qen took his hand away.

"Tearan, you're a genius, man," Qen said during the next hiss. "We talk only when the steam hisses okay?" Tearan and Eishlo indicated their agreement.

As he waited for the next hiss, Tearan struggled to construct his next statement. The duration of the hisses was short, no more than five seconds, so they needed to get to the point whilst getting all relevant information across. Raising his hand to signal he intended to speak, the three waited for the hiss.

"Did they tell either of you two about who you really are?"

Qen and Eishlo exchanged a glance, then both shook their heads. Tearan felt immense relief flood through his body and he almost cried out with the strength of it. To be singled out to be kept in the dark would make him extremely paranoid and he did not wish to think about how he would react in such a situation. At least all three of them were being treated the same, which helped to bond them as a unit. Tearan felt less alone and took strength from their shared experience. Qen raised his hand to speak, so they all waited in silence. "Hunter said it would make my new personality fail to integrate."

Eishlo furiously pointed to himself, indicating that he too had been given the same explanation. Tearan followed his example and then raised his hand.

"Am I the only one who finds this whole thing a little sinister?"

Eishlo raised his hand for the next chance to speak. "I find the theory sound, but the execution is flawed." Tearan and Qen frowned so Eishlo raised a finger. Everyone waited for the next hiss. "The old me might have been mentally ill and now I have a chance to be cured, but." He raised the finger again to wait for the next hiss. "But the way they're doing this is not good."

Qen raised his hand. "Agreed. A brilliant idea poorly executed." Keeping his finger raised, everyone waited. "I'm curious to know but worried about the outcome."

Eishlo mouthed a silent "Yes." Tearan nodded and pointed to himself. The heat was getting to him, and he wiped a hand across his brow for the hundredth time and groaned.

"This heat is getting to me," he said in a normal voice. "I'm going to pass out if I stay here much longer."

"Let's go and cool off," Qen said as he got up and headed for the door.

"I'm so hungry I could eat a festering Wollimot," Tearan remarked as they sat down in the restaurant.

"The steam does that to you," Eishlo said. "Make sure you don't bolt your food. Eat healthily and chew properly."

Qen laughed. "Being healthy is a lot more work than not being healthy." All three laughed as they tucked in. Halfway through the meal, Hunter appeared at their table.

"Good evening, Gentlemen. Mind if I join you?"

Qen shook his head and shrugged. Eishlo indicated the empty chair beside him and Hunter sat down.

"Firstly, I want to thank you for volunteering to help us here at Dreamspinner. I know none of you remembers volunteering, and when the time is right for you to know about your original selves, you will be shown film footage of your interview for the project. This is done so that you can eventually be assured that you are indeed here willingly. It would be a waste of time for us to bring you here and do these experiments on you without your complete co-operation. If you did not want this, your mind would resist the process and it would not be a success. Failure would be guaranteed."

"Thanks, Doctor," Eishlo said.

"I also feel it prudent to remind you again that finding out about your original personalities before it is safe, is the best way to guarantee failure. Please try to be patient a little longer and believe that we will tell you what you want to know, when it is safe to do so."

Tearan blushed as he realised that the steam room was obviously not out of range of cameras and microphones. He felt as if he was seven years old again and being punished for stealing a freshly baked bun from the rack where his mother had left them to cool.

Hunter noticed and tried to put him at ease. "Don't worry, Tearan. It is natural for you to be suspicious. We understand that, believe me. See that man over there at the far table? The one eating that large red fruit? His name is Wesley Bayliss and he's one of our computer technicians. A year ago, he was John Lockerley, a man so crippled by social anxiety that he never left the confines of his parent's home. He had little education beyond that which his parents were able to provide and struggled to do much more than read and write. The problem was so severe that he tried to kill himself after a conversation in which his parents expressed their worry at how he would cope when they died."

The three men gaped wide eyed at Hunter. "He's been through the process?" Qen asked.

"Yes. He was our first great success and one we're very proud of. Why don't you talk to him sometime? He might be able to help assuage your worries."

"Thanks," Tearan said as he looked over at the man who was laughing with his colleagues.

"You're welcome. The reason we film you and listen in every moment is because we know what natural curiosity can drive a person to do. The moment we trust you will happily comply with our wishes without somehow trying to force our hand, we sentence you to fail. That automatically denies you the chance to live a brand new opportunity filled life."

"We get that, Doctor," Qen remarked. "It's just that knowing we used to be someone else but not being able to know about our old selves is so hard to cope with. Maybe you should never tell the volunteers that they've been through this at all. Let them go through their new lives thinking they've always been this new person."

Tearan and Eishlo nodded but Hunter shook his head. "We tried that when we started active trials on volunteers. Apart from the ethical questions, there is always the chance that something would happen to bring the person into contact with knowledge that they were once someone else. Being suddenly faced with such knowledge would inevitably result in a total mental breakdown. All it would need would be for someone to recognise them, a chance conversation, visiting a place they were once familiar with, seeing something on the media, the possibilities are endless. No, the only way to avoid such a calamity is to give the person that knowledge ourselves in a way that we can manage safely. Remember, the people such as yourselves who go through this process, do so because they need it. The new lives we are giving you are the only way you can hope to live normally and contribute positively to your societies. What each of you was before, whomever you were before, could not do that for whatever reason."

"That's a valid point," Tearan said. "I have to admit I never thought of that. I know you told me this process is for people who really need it, but I guess I never thought that I was one of them."

"We feel normal now, so we think we've always been normal," Eishlo said and everyone agreed.

"That kind of makes me scared to find out now," Qen said. "What will I find when you show me who I used to be? Was I mentally ill, a violent thug, a killer? Do I want to find out that's who I was?"

"That would be something," Tearan admitted. "To find out the person you were was any of those things would be heavy shit. Wow." He wondered how he might react in that situation. "But then I guess we all have to realise that's indeed what we were or we wouldn't be here in the first place would we? Fuck, I'm not so curious now. Thanks, Doctor."

"That's why we must wait until you're ready before letting you go there," Hunter said. "You will have to go there though, make no mistake about that. We can't let you out of here to live your new life if there's the slightest chance of suddenly finding out something you weren't prepared for. Everyone takes such an experience differently and that's why we can't give you an exact time frame for this whole process to be completed. It's up to you guys, it really is. This whole thing goes at your speed and no faster."

The three men fell silent, each lost in their own thoughts. The curiosity was still there within each, but now it was tempered with an awareness of the wider implications of this strange experience, and if they were honest, more than a little trepidation.

16

Life aboard the Novosentia was not the most exciting for Tearan and his new friends, but he found a kind of peace with the experience. Days became weeks, a month, two, and then one morning Eishlo stunned them at breakfast.

"I had a dream, from Eishlo's childhood. From my childhood."

Tearan and Qen exclaimed and congratulated him. This was something Doctor Hunter told them would happen when their new personalities had properly bedded in. It was something to look forward to, a momentous milestone to be celebrated.

"Wow," Qen said. "That's wonderful. How do you feel about it?"

Eishlo struggled to reply for several seconds. "I'm happy. It means I'm really Eishlo at last. I'm also scared."

"Scared?" Tearan asked. "Why?"

"Now that I have this confirmation that things are going well, I'm more scared of something going wrong."

"I suppose that's normal," Qen assured him. "Tell Doctor Hunter when you go for your session today." Eishlo nodded. "Do you want to tell us about the dream?"

It was as banal as dreams often are, but the three celebrated it anyway. It was the first of many, and as the days passed, Qen and Tearan noticed a change in Eishlo's demeanour. He was no longer the quiet one who smiled a lot but said little. The vacuous man they had come to like was gone, and in his place was a strong minded and self assured man neither had met before. This new Eishlo now often took the commanding position in their conversation and debate, pressing his views with a new voracity and passion. Gone were the "maybes, perhaps', and what ifs." Their places in Eishlo's conversation were now taken by new expressions of his confidence, the "you should's, you ought to's," and the one that annoyed Qen the most, the "one day you'll realise." Almost without them realising, a divide grew between the three, with Qen and Tearan on one side and Eishlo on the other. There was no animosity between the three friends; they continued to enjoy each other's company as they had done since their first meeting, but the dynamic of the group was permanently changed. By the time Doctor Hunter informed the three that in order for Eishlo to move forward with his rehabilitation, he would have to leave their group, Tearan's own dreams had begun.

The milestone was not greeted with celebration by Tearan. His dreams troubled him from the start and he felt instinctively that he should hold his tongue, at least for a while. From the very first dream, his experience of them was strange and unsettling. The woman who haunted his dreams was beautiful, but always the connection between them was tangible. Elestra; her name came the very first night she appeared within his dreams and he knew at once that he loved her deeply. In some of the dreams, he was passionately happy and in love one minute, then mad with rage at her the next. In other dreams she was almost a stranger, unrecognisable but always connected somehow. He dreamed dreams in which he was clearly Tearan Lindo, active serving member of the IGEC with an untarnished record, yet this strange woman would suddenly appear where she clearly did not belong. In other dreams, he did not feel like Tearan Lindo at all and in these experiences, his connection with the mysterious woman was the strongest.

The dreams had been happening nightly for a couple of weeks when they first became violent and this troubled him greatly. It always happened when he was dreaming in what he came to call his 'non Tearan state.' At first, it was feelings of annoyance, which grew into anger, which then evolved into rage that finally became physical violence. During such dreams, he would come upon her, dead and lifeless in the most incongruous of circumstances, as is the way of dreams. In one, he was planting a tree and the flowers at the ends of the branches changed into eyes. The eyes stared accusingly at him and he knew they were hers. In another, she turned from him and walked away after they argued about something stupid. As she walked, her left thumb fell from her hand and landed on the grass. She seemed not to notice and continued on her way as one by one, the other fingers disconnected themselves and fell away. He awoke sweating and gasping as her limbless body collapsed to the ground, the head rolling away down the slight incline into a puddle of water.

During his 'Tearan Lindo' dreams, he was happy and although still present, she was a stranger and their connection was easy to ignore. He would awaken from such dreams happy and sure beyond doubt that he was Tearan Lindo with a lifetime of memories that felt they truly belonged to him. Although his dreams had begun before Qen's, Tearan allowed his friend to proudly announce the onset of his own dreams without admitting his own had been apparent for over two weeks. He wanted to try to understand what was happening to him before sharing the experiences, even with Doctor Hunter and the other scientists. All he knew was that in one set of dreams he was clearly Tearan Lindo, but in the other set, he was not. What he did not know was why and his desire to reach his own conclusions about it kept him from sharing.

Knowing that he had been given a new personality that was still in the process of taking control from his original one, the fact that in his dreams he seemed to be two different people did not surprise Tearan. For a while, he worried that his original personality was resisting the takeover bid, but the continued presence of his 'Tearan Lindo' dreams and his waking memories and conviction of himself as Tearan, quelled those fears. Three weeks after the dreams began, he decided that knowing he had been given a new personality had caused this confusion within his mind.

"I guess my mind is a little sensitive to knowing there are two of me in there," he said to himself as he joined Qen for breakfast. His friend had been having dreams for almost a week and Tearan noticed changes in his demeanour. Before the dreams began, Qen had been a little on edge all the time, mistrustful of what he did not understand, a little defensive. The man that sat opposite him now was relaxed and calm; he smiled more and seemed to have lost several years off his face. Worry lines no longer creased his brow and his eyes met Tearan's with a new softness. The old Qen was fun and Tearan felt a great similarity between them. The new Qen was so relaxed he was almost boring.

The days were long and lonely since Qen left to continue with his rehabilitation. Tearan assumed he was finding out about his original personality and felt a rush of envy course through him. His own dreams continued in their strange format; some nights he was Tearan, others he was not and although his 'non Tearan' dreams were troubling, he was not unduly worried. During his waking hours, he never once felt unsure as to who he was. The personality of Tearan Lindo neither hesitated nor wavered whilst he was awake, so he did not worry that his old self, whatever that might have been, was returning to a position of control. On the third day after Qen left, Tearan told Doctor Hunter he had a dream in which he had most definitely been Tearan Lindo.

"That's wonderful, Tearan. Tell me about it."

"Well it was pretty ordinary really. My parents were there and we were walking round a large empty house with a view to buying it. Mother loved it but I was sure there was someone already living there and that if we moved in, we would always have this other person wandering around. Mother brushed off my concerns and said, "Oh well I can lay an extra place at the table." When she said that, it made everything all right and I said, "Oh okay then, he can share my room." Both men laughed at the incongruity of dreams and how we always accept the odd happenings within them. It is only when awake that we wonder at the strangeness of them.

And so it became a habit that Tearan would relate his dreams to Doctor Hunter, who would record things word for word, nodding from time to time, asking a question or two here and there. He chose not to pass on his 'non Tearan' dreams; he did not want anything to delay his forward momentum through the process. Although life was easy aboard the Novosentia, he was bored and longed to get out and on with his life. Coming clean about the other dreams would undoubtedly slow down his exit back into the real world and he wanted to avoid that if possible. He was happy the morning Doctor Hunter regarded him gravely, at the end of the daily routine testing session.

"How long have you been dreaming, Tearan?" Hunter asked. Tearan frowned and Hunter widened his gaze expectantly. "I mean, truthfully how long?"

The silence hung between them for long moments as Tearan struggled to find an answer. "I told you when they started," he said, attempting to continue his deceit.

Hunter was not easily fooled. "Tearan. I can only help you if you're honest with me. I know you were having dream sleep three weeks before you announced it to me. Your brain readouts told me that. I admit, you might not remember them for a few days, but three weeks? I'm sorry to say this so bluntly, but I know you're lying to me and that worries me."

Tearan blushed. "I'm sorry, Doctor. I wanted to get my head around it first."

"You've been dreaming from another personality's point of view haven't you?"

Tearan's eyes widened with astonishment. "How the fuck do you know that?"

"You've mentioned a woman by the name of Elestra a couple of times, and I know she does not belong with Tearan's personality. I put two and two together."

"Shit," Tearan cursed his stupid mistake. He had become so used to dreaming of himself as Tearan, that the woman's distant but constant presence within them had become normal. His mention of her name did not register as out of place in his consciousness. The ever vigilant doctor had noticed it though and now Tearan had to own up and explain.

"Don't worry and don't hold out on me. I'm not here to catch you out or halt your progress. I want this project to succeed you know and you're key to that. We're on the same side here, please remember that."

"Okay. I'm sorry. When I'm awake, nothing happens out of the ordinary. I'm Tearan Lindo without question. It's only at night when I'm dreaming. Sometimes I dream all the dreams I've told you about, exactly the way I've told you. I haven't lied to you about them. I just haven't told you about the other dreams, the dreams when I'm not Tearan."

"Tell me about them now, please."

For the next hour, Tearan unburdened himself about the troubling dreams, the anger, the violence, the woman whose body falls apart whenever he dreams of her. He told him about the strong feeling of love between them, how it's always tempered with anger, paranoia and a need to hurt her for something.

"That is most interesting. It is as if sometimes, something blocks Tearan Lindo when you're asleep and comes through into your dream consciousness. Tearan is dominant though, of that I have no doubt. The fact that these unsettling images never appear while you're awake proves that. You have no waking memories that don't feel they belong to Tearan?"

Tearan shook his head. "None."

"Good. Somehow, the personality of Tearan Lindo is not quite strong enough yet to fully take over your subconscious mind. This might rectify itself over time of course, but for now, it seems he is still fighting for dominance while you're sleeping. One thing that is strange though, even to me, is how the woman appears on both sets of dreams. Tearan Lindo never knew her, yet she infiltrates your dreams even when you are dreaming as him."

"Why should that happen?" Tearan asked.

"Well it shouldn't. It never has before. This is a first for me. My experience tells me not to worry just yet. Tearan Lindo is clearly the dominant personality, even if that dominance is not yet total. He's taken over control enough for us to be able to let things continue without interference for now. The mind, the personality, is still mostly unknown to us but is amazingly strong and adaptable when it needs to be. I can if you wish, terminate the experiment and delete Tearan Lindo from your mind altogether. It is up to you."

Tearan gaped in horror at this suggestion and it showed in his wide eyed, open mouthed gape as he stared at Hunter. "What? No way. It would be like killing me all over again. I'm Tearan Lindo and intend to remain so. Don't you dare."

"It's wonderful to hear you defend yourself so vehemently. It shows without a doubt how far the new personality has embedded itself within your mind. It is further proof that our best course of action is to wait and see. At the moment, Tearan Lindo is taking control as we expect him to. Over time, your 'non Tearan' dreams should lessen and we hope, disappear altogether. If you're happy to keep going as we are, then so am I."

Tearan agreed. "Even if nothing changes and I have to live with a few disturbing dreams now and then, it's an easy price to pay."

"Right. I want you to be completely honest with me from now on then. You must report all of your dreams, as fully as you can. I want to know if anything happens while you're awake that might indicate Tearan Lindo is losing his position of power. Any stray thoughts that don't belong, anything at all, no matter how trivial it seems, you tell me. Deal?"

"Deal. And you promise me you won't take me while I'm sleeping and wipe Tearan from my mind without my consent. I don't want you starting me over without asking me first."

"You have my word. This will be valuable research to add to the project's files. I won't want to lose this chance all the time that you're not suffering. This will teach us so much that will make the process easier for future volunteers." Hunter reached out a hand, which Tearan shook.

"Thanks, Doctor. Now I think I'll go and workout for a couple of hours."

The intercom crackled and Tearan reached for the button. "Lindo."

"Hey, Tearan, Doc Hunter wants to talk to you in his office after your shift."

"Okay thanks." Tearan had been working as a security guard aboard the Novosentia for four months, having been hired to work with the existing security team so he could contribute positively and to allay the boredom he had complained relentlessly about. Doctor Hunter suggested that it would be a way for him to live as normal a life as possible, whilst remaining available for testing and regular assessments. Most of his colleagues were polite but wary and he never quite felt he was in with the crowd when amongst them. This bothered him and he complained about it a couple of times to Doctor Hunter. Three of the other security guards became firm friends and they spent much of their off time together. Tearan gained a considerable amount of comfort from these friendships, which tempered his disappointment at the coldness of the others. The work was easy enough, even a little boring. The other volunteers seldom caused a problem that needed the security team's intervention. Consequently, when they did, it was big news.

Having several personalities uploaded at the same time often caused struggles as Tearan was well aware from his own experiences. One by one, the personalities battled it out, the weaker ones failing as those more dominant took control. The demise of those weaker personalities was sometimes a traumatic and violent experience, which necessitated Tearan and his team to remove them back to the lab for medical attention. He wondered how he had faired during his own time and asked Doctor Hunter about it one day.

"You had to be brought in each time one of the others lost out to Tearan Lindo. Your other personalities were strong; they fought valiantly. Be proud of them, Tearan, they wanted to be part of you so much they fought with everything they had to remain within you. This gives you a unique perspective when dealing with the other volunteers who are still where you once were. Your colleagues in security do not have that same perspective. They can learn from you, if you decide you wish to teach them."

There was only one occasion when Tearan clashed with his colleagues. One of the volunteers was having a crisis as one of his personalities was failing under the dominance of another and they were removing him back to the lab. The guard made a joke that was in bad taste and Tearan took offence. Once their shift was over, he waited for him in a little used corridor and beat him black and blue for his disrespect. Being a volunteer himself, his colleagues felt no compulsion to be protective and ratted him out to the supervisor, who called him in to explain himself. Doctor Hunter, Doctor Danvers, and Doctor Melissa Frost were also present.

After accepting a dressing down from his supervisor without retaliation, Tearan accepted the offer of time to explain his actions. "Officer Gannet was disrespectful to the patient's predicament, Sir. I've been in that situation myself and I know how much of a struggle this process is when you're new to it. The guy was in extreme distress as one of his personalities died within his mind and was convulsing as we conveyed him to medical. Officer Gannet remarked that he thought the patient was mad and should be locked up like a dog. I took offence to that remark, Sir and decided to teach him a lesson in a way someone like him would understand. It was wrong of me but I will not apologise for standing up for someone who can't do it for himself. It makes me wonder how I was treated when I was going through it."

After a break for the doctors and his supervisor to debate the matter, Tearan and Gannet were called in together to hear their fate. Gannet was given a written warning and told to apologise to Tearan for his remark. Tearan was given a verbal warning for his violent outburst and told to restrain himself in future. He assured everyone he would do so and apologised to the doctors later, away from the security team. Fully expecting them to have lost faith in him, he was surprised to find it seemed to bond them to him closer than ever. He had asked Hunter about it a day or so later, but he had skirted giving a precise answer and Tearan had not wished to press the matter. He put it down to the doctor's weird scientific brain and thought no more about it.

Doctor Hunter's familiar voice bade him enter when he knocked on his door after his shift. He entered to find Danvers and Melisa Frost there too.

"Hello, Tearan," Hunter said. "Come on in, sit."

"What's with the committee, have I done something wrong?"

Melissa looked him right in the eyes as she always did and allowed her genuine affection to crinkle the corners of her eyes. "No of course not. We are here to talk to you about your progress, that's all."

Her habit of holding his gaze never failed to make him trust her word and it always put him at ease. "Okay, no problem."

For over an hour, the four discussed Tearan and his experience in detail. His dreams, which still had not been totally dominated by the personality of Tearan Lindo, were the subject of much debate and he found himself describing the imagery over and over again. Yes, it was violent. Yes, it was unsettling. Yes, he felt connected to it whilst in the dream. No, he did not feel that connection once awake. No, he never felt anything other than totally Tearan Lindo. These and hundreds of other questions were fired at him and he answered them all truthfully. Five months had passed, during which he came to a peaceful acceptance of these troubling dreams. It was not as if they occurred every night; most of the time his dreams were those of Tearan Lindo. For the past month or so, the bad dreams had settled into a twice-weekly cycle that he felt relatively comfortable with. This last point was important, for he felt sure that these bad dreams were never going to go away and the three doctors worried about it constantly. He wanted them to be as sure as he was that he could cope with them and he stressed to them how talking them out helped him to cope.

"I'm happy to continue working here if you want to observe me for longer. Maybe you could give me a little more freedom bit by bit as time goes by and I'll admit that I'd find it reassuring to remain nearby for a while longer."

"I'm delighted to hear you suggest that," Danvers said. "We have something similar in mind and wanted to suggest it to you."

Melissa frost leaned forward slightly. "A group of doctors and technicians is going down to Earth for a week. It's partly for them to use some of their free time to catch up with family and relax and partly to attend a meeting about funding for the project. How would you like to tag along with them and get some fresh air? You can see the sights and do the tourist thing."

Tearan did not hesitate. "Wow, I'd love to."

"Good," Hunter said. "I was confident you would accept. There will be one or two constraints upon you I'm afraid. You are still under our care officially and we haven't yet signed you off as it were."

"That's okay I guess."

"You will be chaperoned at all times by one of the guys," Doctor Danvers said. "They are all trained in how to take care of you if something goes wrong suddenly, in which case they will sedate you and arrange for you to be returned here to our care. We will also install a locator chip under the skin on your wrist, in case you decide to take off on your own and give us all a headache worrying about you. You have to be okay with all of this by the way. This is non-negotiable."

"That's fine," Tearan said. "I understand. I'll be a good boy."

"Another thing you should be aware of," Hunter said. "We don't get to meet too many Arlenikans down there on Earth, so you will be a draw whenever you're out in public. You're going to get stared at, so be cool okay?"

"Thanks for the warning. I'll be polite, I promise."

Melissa Frost handed over a digital pad. "You're going to need an injection before you go. You need to sign your consent."

"An injection? What for?"

"Arlenikans have no immunity against a virus Earth people carry. It's a result of biological warfare from a few hundred years ago before we achieved inter-galactic travel. We're all immune but visitors aren't so for your own protection, it's a necessity. You can't go down there without it."

"I haven't caught it from any of you."

"We've all had gene treatment to eradicate it from our DNA. With all the different races we meet on the project, it made sense despite the huge cost. We can't pass it on to anyone now."

He gave a resigned shrug. Despite hating injections, he did not want to miss this chance so he agreed. After signing and handing Melissa back the pad, she got up and came around the table. Less than a minute later, Tearan was rubbing his arm and looking forward to getting away from the Novosentia for a few days.

Doctor Hunter smiled. "Enjoy the holiday, Tearan, you've earned it."

"Thanks."

"The shuttle leaves at nine in the morning," Doctor Danvers said. "Don't worry, we'll make sure you don't miss it."

Tearan found it cold on this planet called Earth, but he did not mind. That cold air was fresh rather than the over processed stuff he breathed on board the Novosentia and he breathed it in greedily. Being part of the Dreamspinner Project meant the group avoided all but the most basic of red tape. They were soon speeding away from the spaceport en-route to an ultra-secure military base where the meeting would take place. The soldiers were well trained, Tearan noticed and did not stare at him for more than a second before regaining their control. The civilians employed at the base did not possess such discipline and stared openly at this white haired stranger with death pale skin and eyes so blue they took your breath away. They stared as he passed, bent their heads to exchange astonished whispers with their colleagues and clutched hands to throats in automatic gestures of defence. Tearan realised they were scared and frowned at why this should be so. Making sure to smile and nod as he passed them by, he tried to appear friendly and non-threatening but this seemed to bemuse them even more.

Once settled within the team's accommodations, Tearan exclaimed in suprise.

"Hunter was right when he said I'd be stared at. Did you see them? They didn't even try to hide it."

"They don't get Arlenikans here that often," an enormous man nicknamed Brick replied. "Once they've seen you a couple of times, they'll quit staring. You won't be so new by this time tomorrow, trust me."

"Are we to stay the whole week here on the base?"

"Yeah."

"I thought I'd have the opportunity to see something of the area. Y'know, get out and about a little."

"You will, Tearan," A quiet natured man named Andy said. "We have a couple of days until the meeting, which will last for two days and then we have another three days afterwards. We're drawing up a list of things to do and places for you to visit. Do you have anything in mind? Any ideas?"

"Well umm, the IGEC doesn't really give us much time for hobbies or anything. I've spent the last few years in almost total operation mode."

"You like to work out don't you? They have state of the art facilities here and everyone has open access. Brick works out every day, so why not tag along with him?"

Tearan looked over at the huge man, who was nodding in his direction. "Okay, thanks. It would be nice to see something of the area outside the base, the city or whatever is out there. After spending so long aboard the Novosentia, it would be nice to walk down a real street, watch birds in a real sky, hear the sound of the wind in treetops, smell the ocean perhaps. Any chance of that?"

"That shouldn't be a problem," Andy said. "We're on the west coast here so the ocean is just a few miles away. Do you have water sports on Arlenika?"

The next two days sped by in a whirlwind of new experiences for Tearan. He rose early so as not to waste a moment of this limited time and after working out with Brick, he visited the market. He ate brightly coloured fruits fresh from the vendors' many baskets, walked barefoot on the beach and relished the feel of sand between his toes. In a single day, he learned to surf surprisingly well then listened to the night birds calling by the light of the full moon. On the third day, he boarded a passenger shuttle for a sightseeing flight of the city and the mountains that lay to the north. This was the first day of the meeting and Tearan had the company of Hank and Enrique, two security guards with whom he had always got on well.

"You enjoying your time here?" Hank asked.

"Yeah, very much. You don't realise what you're missing until the opportunity is taken away."

Hank and Enrique exchanged a glance.

Tearan noticed and frowned. "What? What was that look about?"

"I guess we take it for granted that we can come down here and enjoy ourselves whenever we want," Enrique replied. "You and the other volunteers have been stuck aboard the Novosentia for weeks and don't have the choices we have. I guess I feel bad about it."

He blushed and Tearan grinned. "Thanks, man."

During dinner that evening, Tearan learned that he had been invited to attend the meeting the next day, to speak about his experience of the Dreamspinner Project. He was nervous about it and it showed.

"They just want to ask a few questions about the project from a volunteer's point of view. It'll only be an hour or so at the most and it'll give you a chance to speak your mind and tell them what you think we can do to improve the experience for others like you. You don't have to do it; you can say no if you don't want to."

Their faces were stern, Tearan noticed and felt himself shrink inwardly from their imposing presence. The twenty-four men and women sat in a semi-circle before him and without knowing why, he began to tremble in fear. A hand on his shoulder almost had him leaping from his seat and running from the room. He felt sweat beading on his brow and he swallowed the proffered glass of cool water in one go.

"Good morning, Tearan," a solidly built man of middle years said as he stared into his eyes. Tearan smiled nervously in response. "We twenty-four before you are those who pay for what you've experienced over the past few weeks. We do this because we believe this will be of positive benefit in the not too distant future. We know what all the scientists are telling us, but we want to know what it's like from your point of view. You are the ones at the sharp end of this experience. It is you who will bring about any success or failure, so we need to ensure everything that can be done is being done. We're not here to interrogate you or anything sinister like that. We want you to tell us, in your own words, what life has been like for you since you woke up aboard the Novosentia."

Tearan swallowed hard. "Okay, I guess I can do that. What exactly do you want to know?"

The shuttle headed up into the light cloud and Tearan watched the military base shrink beneath him. He had enjoyed the week away from the Novosentia, even speaking at the meeting was a positive experience, he thought. The twenty-four quickly proved themselves benign and genuinely interested in his experience and he hoped his words would make a positive difference to future volunteers. Despite continuing to have disturbing and violent dreams alongside the pleasant 'Tearan Lindo' dreams, he had become used to their presence. Although frightening for them whilst in the midst of them, he found they faded quickly upon waking. The holiday had served to refresh him and he knew he had many happy memories that would stay with him for the rest of his life. The change of routine and environment also helped to clear his mind about how he would proceed with regard to the dreams and he decided to announce to Hunter that the disturbing ones had stopped. He wanted to know about his original personality and felt instinctively that it held the key to his dreams. If he was to continue as Tearan Lindo and leave any troubles from the past behind, he had to reconcile himself to that past, whatever it may contain. A little subterfuge would not hurt, he surmised.

17

Tearan returned to his duties a security guard aboard the Novosentia refreshed and with a new purpose. The daily tests continued; he answered the questions, put up with the brain scans and tried not to complain. As days became weeks, his dreams settled into a regular pattern, with one of the violent dreams every three or four nights. Although the pattern continued with reliable regularity, he slowly began to report a lessening of the violent dreams. He thought it best to pretend that they reduce slowly, rather than trying to convince Doctor Hunter that they had ceased completely all of a sudden. When he had not reported one of the violent dreams for two weeks, he risked asking Hunter about his prognosis.

"I haven't had any of the bad dreams for a couple of weeks now, Doctor. This has to be a good sign, yes?"

"Yes indeed it does. It's a very good sign."

"So does this mean I'm anywhere near being at the end of this procedure? When do I get to live a normal life, out there? When do I get to find out about the old me?" Tearan pointed out of the window into the void.

Hunter gazed out of the viewing window as he thought about the question. Tearan did not want to push the point for fear of appearing obsessive, so he waited patiently while the doctor pondered. "I'll level with you, Tearan. I'm worried about taking the next step."

"Why?"

"Because we've not had someone take the procedure in the way you've done."

"What do you mean?"

"The violent dreams."

"But they've stopped."

"So you say, but that's not the problem."

"Then what is? I'm sorry to push, but I want to know. How can I move forward unless I understand? This is me we're talking about remember. I'm a person and I did volunteer for this. It's not punishment that I have to submit to or anything, so I deserve the truth. I understood when you told me a few months ago that telling me about my old self might jeopardise the whole thing, but that was then and things have progressed since then. Cut me a little slack huh?"

"Please believe me when I tell you that we only hold out on you to avoid you regressing and getting into difficulty. It is precisely because this is you we're dealing with that we are being so careful. If we were using robots or cadavers, we would not need to be quite so careful. It is because we are aware that you volunteered for this, put your trust in us, that we are being cautious. Rushing it now and failing at this late juncture would not only be a damn shame after all this time and effort, but it might damage your mind and make further attempts difficult."

Tearan put both hands to his temples, closed his eyes and waited for the frustration he felt rising within, to dissipate. Hunter had a valid point and he found no adequate argument against him, so he had no choice but to resort to pleading.

"Please, Doctor. I've put my faith in you and your people since I woke up here and I've never gone against any of your demands."

"Requests, Tearan, we have never demanded anything of you. At least I hope we haven't."

"I'm sorry. I've gone along with every request. I've done the tests, answered the questions, slept with that uncomfortable hat on every night for weeks on end, and now I'm asking you to have a little trust in me. I'm Tearan Lindo, completely. I've told you my life history several times over, down to the finest detail and you've no doubt verified everything I've told you from my, umm his, records. I feel like Tearan Lindo. I can't imagine being anyone other than Tearan Lindo."

"Then why the stubborn curiosity about the old you?"

"Because he was who I was. I lived as him for thirty-three years until coming here. I'm alive and able to be here because of him. I have this new chance because of him and whatever the problems were that made this procedure necessary, he deserves some acknowledgement for his suffering. I feel like I killed someone. Maybe it was a mercy killing, but I can't walk away without acknowledging who I used to be. If I was a good person or bad, I have to know. To be able to leave him behind and move on whole. Please at least try to understand."

Hunter held Tearan's eyes for several seconds as something passed between them. finally, he nodded and slapped the table. "Okay. I will meet with the team and discuss the matter this evening. I will let you know at the earliest opportunity."

"Thank you. That's all I ask. At least stop putting it off and think about it."

Tearan entered and sat down. Having been aboard the Novosentia for many months, he knew everyone and was on first name terms with most. He regarded a couple of them as real friends, but despite this familiarity, he was nervous and it showed. Sweat beaded on his brow and heat flushed across the back of his neck and under his armpits. Gently caressing his top lip with a finger to stop the twitching, he took several deep breaths to calm himself.

"Are you sure you want to continue, Tearan?" Hunter asked. "We are here at your request and if you don't wish to go on, we can stop and leave it for another day."

Tearan thought about it. Since finding out the truth about the Dreamspinner Project, his every waking moment had been filled with the need to know who he used to be. Everything he told Doctor Hunter the previous evening was true; he was Tearan Lindo right through to the marrow and that would never change. There was this aching hole deep inside where his old self used to be, that Tearan Lindo could not fill, would never fill. That hole hurt. Sometimes it hurt gently, like a dark spot deep inside that gently tugged. At other times, it hurt so much it shredded his insides and tore at his mind. Those moments found him bent over the toilet puking up his dinner, after which he would cry himself to sleep and the inevitably violent imagery of his dream. Despite what he told Hunter, Tearan knew that living with that hole unplugged was impossible. He would go mad with the pain of it and lose his second chance of life as Tearan Lindo. He would die twice yet still be alive as some raging thing driven mad with grief and pain. No, he knew he had to know, but that did not stop him being nervous about what he was to find out.

"I want to continue. This is the only way I can move forward with one hundred percent of my focus."

Hunter looked at each of his colleagues in turn, then at Tearan. "Okay, what do you want to know?"

Tearan looked instinctively at Doctor Melissa Frost, whom he always felt to be the most open, honest, and compassionate. "Who was I? Y'know, before."

"Your name was Dosmik Lolien. Does that ring any bells?"

Tearan said the name over and over, but it felt foreign to him. He did not know whether to be pleased or disappointed. "No. It means nothing to me. I guess I was expecting some kind of feeling, but it's like you told me anyone's name."

"That's wonderful," Doctor Danvers said as he wrote furiously on a pad in front of him. "Believe me, Tearan, that is just what we wanted to happen."

"Can I see a picture of me, as I was back then?"

"Sure," Doctor Hunter said and opened a thick file. He slid a photograph across the table and Tearan found himself gazing into a photograph of himself.

He laughed. "But that's me."

"Of course it's you, Tearan," Melissa replied, the corners of her eyes crinkling. "It's your personality that has changed not your body."

Tearan blushed. "Sorry. That was stupid."

"No it wasn't," Danvers said. "Nothing you feel is ever stupid and don't you forget that. You are experiencing something only a handful of others have experienced, something we still know precious little about. You are teaching us something valuable each and every day and nothing you feel is ever stupid. You are struggling to understand something so incredible, so hugely out there that it's a wonder you cope with this whole amazing thing so well."

"Thanks. So I was Dosmik Lolien?" The question was aimed at Melissa Frost again.

"Yes."

"What did I do? What kind of man was I?"

Melissa hesitated for a split second and Tearan knew that meant he was not going to like what he was about to hear. Instantly, Melissa regained her composure. "You came to the Dreamspinner Project from Fila Dostil Penitentiary, Menaskil Island, Arlenika Prime. You were a prisoner there and volunteered for the Dreamspinner Project in return for a reduction in sentence."

Tearan's eyes misted over until a thick white fog enveloped him. His heart thudded in his chest as the aching empty hole inside, twisted painfully. The blood rushed in his ears as he gasped for breath and waited for the fog to clear. When it did, he found a hand clasping his and an arm around his shoulder. The hand belonged to Melissa; the arm was Danvers' and gripped him with surprising strength.

"Take your time, Tearan," Hunter said as he placed a mug of something hot in front of him. "Remember, we can stop anytime you want. Just say the word and this is over."

"I was a criminal?"

"Yes." Danvers said as he returned to his seat.

"What did I do? Was I inside for a long time? Did I hurt someone?"

"Tearan, I really think we should..."

"What did I do?" Tearan repeated, his voice raised significantly.

"You killed someone." Melissa's voice drew Tearan's gaze and everyone else faded from sight. For long moments, silence hung between them as their eyes held each other's gaze. "Dosmik Lolien killed someone and went to prison. He was sentenced to be executed for the crime and was offered the chance to avoid the death penalty by volunteering for the Dreamspinner project."

"You say that like it was someone else who did it."

"It was. You are Tearan Lindo, serving member of the IGEC with an exemplary record."

"But I was him. This Dosmik Lolien was me."

"And he has served his punishment for his crimes," Hunter said. "You said it yourself many times that it feels like your old self was killed and he has been. Besides, Tearan Lindo has killed. In the line of duty of course."

Tearan sniffed. "So you take one killer and turn me into a different kind of killer."

"Believe me, Tearan, there is a world of difference between Tearan's killing and Dosmik's."

"Who did he kill?" It was several seconds before Tearan realised he had referred to his old self in the third person. When he did, he was surprised. "I said he, not me."

"Of course you did," Hunter said. "Dosmik Lolien was another person. You are Tearan Lindo and as far as your mind is aware, you've always been Tearan Lindo."

"So who did he kill?"

"His wife and children," Danvers said.

"His wife, she was called Elestra?" Everyone nodded. "No wonder I dreamt of her and felt so connected. Why have I never dreamed of children though? Why kill a child? That is the sickest thing imaginable." Tears ran down Tearan's cheeks. "I'm sorry I did that, when I was him. I don't care what his excuse was, I'm sorry. He killed kids? What can anyone possibly say to make that right?"

"There is never anything right about murder," Hunter said. "That's why Dosmik was sent to prison and that's why he received such a severe penalty. No one will ever say we're trying to lessen the severity of his crimes by having you on this project. He was sentenced to die and he has died. His personality was wiped from his body, wiped from the universal consciousness if you want to be poetic about it. Either way, he has served his sentence."

"Why did he kill them?"

"He met her when she was dating his childhood friend. They were attracted to each other and she left the friend for Dosmik. A few months later, their daughter was born and they married when she was a few months old. When she was six years old, the child became ill and had to go into hospital, where it was discovered that her DNA did not match Dosmik. He confronted Elestra, who admitted that the child had been conceived before she had left Dosmik's friend. When she later admitted that she had known at the time she was pregnant, but chose to keep the fact from Dosmik, he became enraged. He had always been a little on the possessive side and this made him more paranoid than ever. He also chose to assume that their infant son was the product of secret liaisons between her and this childhood friend. His own mother had cheated on his father, and Dosmik knew the effect it had upon him. It drove him further over the edge and he murdered them all one night after hours of noisy rows that kept the entire street awake."

Tearan sobbed openly for the lives lost at the hands of the man he used to be, the monster of a man who was not fit to be alive in his opinion. Inside, the black and aching hole he believed would forever remain an open wound and which brought him such anguished dreams, melted away forever. The man who sat at the table with tears on his cheeks was now Tearan Lindo completely, wholly, fully.

"He cut her up didn't he?" he asked and Hunter nodded. "And that's why I never dreamed of the daughter, because she wasn't his. How did he kill her?"

"He drugged her and then suffocated her with his bare hands before cutting off her head. She was not aware of suffering, the level of drugs in her body made her totally unconscious. She just went to sleep and never woke up."

"And the infant? What happened to him? All that stuff Doctor Arma wrote on the walls of the medical bay. It wasn't crazy ramblings was it? It was Dosmik's memories."

"Yes," Hunter admitted. "The infant was also drugged first. He would not have been aware of anything happening."

Tearan was glad of that at least. "Of course, it makes sense he would do that."

"What do you mean?" Danvers asked.

"His anger was directed to Elestra, not the children. It was his wife who had betrayed him, not them. His killing of the children was not driven by rage, as it was with Elestra. No, they were simply in the way, a loose end he did not want to have to deal with. Single fathers don't bring up children on Arlenika; it simply isn't our custom. If a mother dies, the father puts the children with other female family members. He pays for them, visits them and has as much contact with them as he always did, but he never raises them alone. The daughter was not Dosmik's natural child and he believed the son wasn't either, so placing them with family members was out of the question; it would be a burden they did not deserve. He obviously felt the only possible option was kill them too. In his twisted mind, he probably felt he was being compassionate to everyone's place in the situation."

"You have amazing insight, Tearan," Hunter said.

"I guess I'm bound to have, seeing as I used to be him. Thank you for your honesty. I can fully understand why you were hesitant to do this and I apologise for my impatience."

"We forgive you, absolutely," Hunter said. "Now that you know the circumstances that brought you here, our advice is that you leave Dosmik Lolien alone now for good and move forward as Tearan Lindo. You can watch the vidicom of Dosmik giving his permission to be involved with the

Dreamspinner Project if you wish, but I will pray you decide against it. No good can come from holding onto that other person any longer. He had his life, now you have yours. We cannot change the mistakes of our past, but we can learn from them and endeavour to make the rest of our life positive."

Tearan nodded. "Yes, I agree. Thank you all. For giving me this chance to live a good life. I intend to make the most of every moment of it. What happens to me now?"

"You will remain here for a while longer so we can observe how you cope with things now you know about Dosmik Lolien and while we make arrangements for you to take up your life as Tearan Lindo. As Tearan, you are a serving member of the IGEC and have been on an extended leave of absence for health reasons. If you wish to, you can return to duty with your unit or we can give you a new life and career."

"It's what I feel is my life. One thing though, will the guys in my unit accept me? Will they take me for the Tearan Lindo they remember?"

Danvers leaned in. "Ahh, I'm glad you raised this point. The person who donated the personality of Tearan Lindo was not named Tearan Lindo. You know him as such, but his real name is kept secret. We only ever refer to him as Donor J771946-116R. He served with Unit 389C4 and died in action. You have been moved to a new unit, 831J2. This will save you from having to explain why your unit buddies don't remember you. When you're ready to go back to work, if you ever want to that is, you will also take possession of a new residence. This will prevent any awkward conversations with neighbours who knew your donor."

"That makes sense I guess. Can I ask another question?"

"Of course," several voices replied in unison.

"Dosmik's parents, his family. How are they coping?"

Melissa was still holding Tearan's hand and now gave it a little squeeze. "His mother passed away after a short illness when he was twenty five. His father was well into the initial stages of an advanced brain disease by the time he committed his crime, and has never shown any signs that he knows what happened. At the time of Dosmik's incarceration, he had difficulty remembering much more than his own name and when questioned, had no memories of his past family life. He is well cared for in an elderly person's care facility and apart from the steady progression of his brain disease, his physical health is reasonable for a man of his advanced years."

"I'm glad they were spared the knowledge of what happened, of the shame."

"It is probably for the best," Melissa agreed.

"You can if you wish, continue working here with us," Hunter said. "You will be paid the same as the other security guards and have the same health cover etcetera. Take however long you need to think about it. If you do decide to move out and return to the IGEC, we will require you to visit us for a week every few months to begin with, then once a year once we feel happy you are settled and not having any problems. At all times, we are just a call away. Any time you feel you are struggling or if things are happening that you can't understand, you call us, day or night. We're here for you always."

During the following two weeks, Tearan blossomed into himself so completely that the Dreamspinner Project staff were amazed and delighted. He did as Hunter said and thought about what to do with the rest of his life, but there was never any doubt in his mind. He was a soldier, a serving member of the most elite military unit in existence and he had no desire to give up the life he loved to be a security guard on a scientific research ship. This group of scientists had given him a new life and he would always be grateful, but his life was with the IGEC and he knew he needed to start his life properly.

Doctor Hunter said he would be sad to see him leave, but understood and wished him well for his future. Once the decision was made, Tearan helped the team to plan for his new life. A new apartment in a nice area of a large city on Arlenika's smallest landmass was purchased for him and furnished according to his taste. New identity documents were ordered for him and an account was opened in his name at Arlenika's largest bank. Since he had been away from active duty for some time, the IGEC required him to attend a two-week re-familiarisation course and Tearan readily agreed. It would give him an opportunity to get to know his new working colleagues and to bond with the team properly. He was looking forward to being able to be himself, to forget about the Dreamspinner Project and get on with life as Tearan Lindo. He was truly happy for the first time since he woke up, afraid and alone without knowing anything but his name and anticipation coursed through him as he waited for the day of his departure to arrive.

Doctor Hunter repeatedly reminded him that he was welcome to remain aboard the Novosentia if he wished, and Tearan always thanked him for the offer, but turned him down. He was truly grateful for what Dreamspinner had done for him and felt a little guilty at wanting to leave. Hunter shook his head.

"No, Tearan. Do not feel guilty at being the success that you are. You have given us a tremendous gift, the knowledge that what we do is helping people live better lives. There is no way for us to adequately explain what that means to us and every minute you are out there, living your life, being productive and happy, only compounds our success. Feel happy about that, not guilty."

The following morning, Tearan's modest belongings were packed and waiting for him in the shuttle bay, along with Hunter, Danvers, Melissa and his two security guard friends, Andy and Brick.

Tearan shook hands with Hunter, who reminded him to call them weekly and update them with his progress. He promised he would and thanked him for everything. Danvers man hugged him and wished him well, and Melissa kissed his cheek and made him blush. He thanked her for being so honest with him, for being someone he instinctively felt he could trust. It meant a lot to him when he was scared and trying to understand. Andy shook his hand, then punched him on the shoulder and laughed, his eyes welling with tears as he told him to take care of his stupid ass. Brick approached, his arms open wide and hugged him close. Tearan was about to tell his friend to look after Andy, when he realised his head felt funny. Confusion swept inside his mind as he watched all that he knew himself to be, fade and then disappear. For a moment, he was alone inside his empty mind and screamed silently inside the aching void of his own vacant soul. Just for a moment, then darkness claimed him.

"Congratulations, Doctor Hunter," Danvers said with a grin. "A very successful trial."

"The most successful yet by far," Melissa Frost said.

Hunter nodded as he put away the small device that was secreted in his palm. "Indeed. Such a shame we were never allowed to let it continue further."

Danvers shook his head. "The powers that be would never allow it, not until we can guarantee reliable results. There are still too many unknowns and variables to iron out."

"I know," Hunter replied. "I'm delighted at how this is progressing. I'm sure this one could have functioned quite successfully, led his own life and been productive."

"I agree with you," Melissa said, "but we must operate within the guidelines or we'll have our funding cut. We have to curb our enthusiasm. Better that than have to explain a tragedy. What would you do if this animal had regressed and murdered again? We can't forget what he is and what he's done."

"But we've proved we can not only tame the savage, we can change him," Hunter replied. "We can now make a leopard change his spots, permanently."

"Well I feel happier knowing this particular savage will never see the light of another day as a free man," Danvers remarked. "How you ever got permission for him to visit Earth like a normal person I'll never know. Whose ass did you kiss for that?"

"Quite a few," Hunter said. "It was worth it though. That visit was a roaring success and I happen to know that several of the committee members were seriously impressed with how he conducted himself at the meeting. He sowed seeds for us down there, Danvers, seeds of belief in Dreamspinner and what it will mean in the future. We deserve a drink. Let's go to my office and open a bottle eh?"

"We'll put this one back into storage, Doctor Hunter," Brick said as he and Andy carried the body from the shuttle bay.

"How many times can one person be uploaded do you think?" Melissa asked.

Hunter shrugged. "I've no idea but in theory there should be no limit to the number of times we can upload into a host. So long as the brain is kept functioning at optimum and no damage occurs, I don't see why we can't use each one multiple times. How many times as that crazy been used?"

"Tearan Lindo was his twenty-fourth time," Danvers said as he read from the file. "He first came to us aged twenty-one after butchering his wife and children. He stole her from his childhood friend, who killed himself directly after their funeral. That friend was the donor of the personality we call Mykus Romin."

"It was a gamble using someone connected to him as one of the implants," Hunter said. "The results were interesting though. They seemed to connect in a much stronger way than he did with any of the other personalities. Even though Tearan Lindo never knew the other man, they still connected with an instinctive friendship. That tells us so much about the way humanoids make connections with each other and how deep they go. It will help us fine tune our procedures."

"I'll write up my notes and make some recommendations for the next board meeting," Melissa said. "What do you want done with the crazy?"

"Let's leave him on ice for a day or two and then start over." He poured the drinks and handed them round before raising his glass for a toast. "To the crazies and murdering savages. Without them we'd all be out of a job."

His eyes flickered open and bright light burned into his awareness. Pain registered next, and he moved his body in response, only to discover his back was the source. As wakefulness overcame him, he frowned as he realised that he was lying down in a strange bed inside an equally strange room. Sitting up, groaning as his back complained, he swung his legs gingerly over the edge of the bed and swept his eyes around his immediate surroundings. He did not recognise the room and frowned as he tried to force his memory to explain how he got there. It was then he realised something that frightened him and he cried aloud.

"Who am I?"

THE END

www.ingramcontent.com/pod-product-compliance
Lightning Source LLC
Chambersburg PA
CBHW072226170626
46813CB00003B/1109

* 9 7 8 0 9 9 2 8 4 9 1 3 9 *